THE BAKER

NATHAN BURROWS

A NOTE FROM THE AUTHOR

Hi.

Nathan Burrows here. Thanks for buying *The Baker*.

This is the second book in the *Rub-a-Dub-Dub* trilogy. The first book is *The Butcher* — you don't have to have read it to enjoy *The Baker*, but I would recommend it. It's available direct from my website at nathanburrows.com or in all the usual outlets.

Speak soon, and I hope you enjoy *The Baker*.

Nathan B.

1

Jennifer Jones — known as Jenny to her friends, although she didn't have that many — stood on the low wall at the edge of the very top of Partridge Towers. In front of her and ten stories below her was the fine city of Norwich, although her concentration was fixed on the horizon. Jenny took a deep breath, and looked from right to left, taking in the skyline of the city with the sun setting behind it.

In the distance, the distinctive spire of Norwich Cathedral pierced the soon to be night sky. Between Jenny's vantage point and the spire was the squat rectangular outline of the castle, made spectacular only by the large mound of earth it had sat on since the Middle Ages. There was no other way to describe the sight — it was a fantastic view. Jenny didn't look down. She didn't need to. What was below her was only pavement and besides, she was fixated on what was in front of her and where she was going.

Today had started off like any other day. Jenny had got up, fed her elderly cat, and got ready for work. She was an administration assistant in the city library, and had been for the last ten years. Chances for promotion had come and gone. Jenny wasn't that interested anyway. She led a simple enough life, and her only regret was the fact that she was still single even though she was in her mid-forties. There had been one relationship in her past that she considered meaningful, and that had been a very long time ago. Nigel, his name had been, and despite promising her the world he'd delivered little of it. The last she had heard, Nigel was living in a caravan park in Great Yarmouth with a slapper called Betty who he'd met in 'Fallen Angels.' Great Yarmouth's Premier Lap Dancing and Gentlemen's Club, or at least it was according to their website. This was despite the fact that, in Nigel's opinion, the best thing to come out of Great Yarmouth was the A47 back to Norwich. Jenny had never bothered to find out how Betty had met Nigel, but if she was a dancer at Fallen Angels, Nigel was welcome to her.

Jenny's idea of a good night in these days was a few glasses of Pinot Grigio, a good book, and the company of her cat. She'd even listed 'reading' on her like of interests on the internet dating web site she'd signed up for. Jenny had only signed up on the site after meeting the young man that her friend Stacey had managed to find on it. He was young, fit, good looking, and way out of Stacey's league, at least in Jenny's opinion. After a few months of zero interest, even from the weirdos on the internet, she'd updated her interests to include 'Book Reviewing'. The truth was that Jenny wouldn't know a good book if the author himself ran up and slapped her round the head with it, but that didn't matter to Jenny. She looked again at the horizon and at the large red disc of the sun about to disappear behind the now closed furniture shop on St Stephen's street. None of what had happened before today mattered to Jenny. Not anymore.

Since around four o'clock that afternoon, Jenny had grown wings. Not the sort of wings that drinking Red Bull gave you, but proper wings with feathers and everything that wings were supposed to have. She raised them from her sides, and looked at the light of the setting sun glinting off the multi-coloured feathers. They were a fine set of wings indeed. She'd not had them this morning, she'd not had them at lunchtime. In fact, the first time she realised she had wings was about half an hour ago. Jenny had just been thinking about packing away her bag for the day when she was caught short by some vicious stomach cramps. She'd run to the toilet, thinking for a horrible moment that she was going to be sick, but apart from a load of saliva there was nothing untoward.

Earlier that day at lunchtime, Jenny had nipped out of the library to try something from the new sandwich van outside the Forum where the library was. Everyone, even her miserable sod of a manager, was raging about their artisan bread. Jenny had bought a halloumi and pickle sandwich, even though she wasn't sure what halloumi was, and had sat in the sun enjoying the sandwich. Halloumi, it turned out, was a type of foreign cheese. A few hours later, she was bent over the toilet, and a few minutes after that, she had emerged. With wings.

Jenny spread the wings now, allowing them to catch as much of the setting sun as possible, and marvelling at the multitude of colours reflecting from them. She looked again toward the cathedral spire. There was a pair of falcons breeding up on top of the spire, so she could swoop by and say hello to them. Then, she could bank to the right and buzz the castle. There were sure to be some Japanese tourists on the top who would jabber excitedly at the sight of a middle-aged, slightly frumpy librarian soaring past them.

She flapped her wings up and down, relishing the feel of the air filtering between her feathers. As she beat them faster, she felt her feet become lighter until she realised she was almost hovering above the low wall on top of the building. With a beatific smile, she stepped forward and prepared to escape the surly bonds of earth.

Whether Jenny was actually flying or not would depend on which definition of flying was being used. If it was moving through the air, flapping wings that didn't actually exist, then Jenny was in fact flying. If the definition included horizontal movement, as opposed to vertical, then she wasn't. She flapped her wings, a fixed smile on her face, as she waited for the air to get beneath them.

The wet thud as her head impacted the pavement ten stories below where she had started from confirmed the fact, at least to everyone that witnessed it, that Jenny couldn't actually fly. She was, however, quite good at falling.

2

'Where the hell is this place, anyway?' Rupert strummed his fingers on the steering wheel of his mother's car. He turned to look at Hannah, his girlfriend. 'Any ideas?'

'Not a clue,' she replied, looking up from the map that was balanced on her knee. 'It can't be that far away. Not according to this map, at least.' Rupert peered through the grimy windscreen of the battered Citroen. If the washer worked, he would have put the wipers on to clear the screen, but his mother had forgotten to fill the washer bottle up and he wasn't going to do it for her.

'Must be round here somewhere,' he muttered through gritted teeth as he swatted at his blonde dreadlocks which were threatening to block his line of sight.

'Well, if we had a sat-nav, that would help,' Hannah said. Rupert glanced across her with a frown.

'Well, we don't,' he said. 'I've told you, I don't like them. Why would you want something in the car that can track your every movement? You might as well put a chip in your head so the government can keep tabs on you.' Hannah folded her arms across her chest, creasing the map. This wasn't the first time they'd had this argument, but Rupert was insistent. According to him, sat-navs were a weapon of the establishment. She picked at a thread on her tie-dyed skirt before looking out of the window.

'Oh wow, look at that tree,' Hannah said, pointing at the side of the road. 'It looks just like a swastika.' Rupert looked in the direction she was pointing.

'It does, doesn't it?' He was just about to launch into a potted history of the swastika and how it had been misappropriated by Nazis when he noticed a small cluster of buildings a couple of hundred yards beyond the tree. 'Is that the farm, do you think?'

'I don't know,' Hannah replied. 'It might be. There's bugger all else out here, is there?'

Rupert slowed the car down and stopped by a turn off on the left-hand side of the road. A rutted track led toward the buildings. He got out of the car, careful to avoid the puddles so he didn't muddy his new red trousers, and stood on tiptoes to try to get a better view of the farm in the distance. Parked by what looked like a farmhouse was a silver car with a man in a suit standing next to it.

'I think that's the estate agent,' Rupert said, leaning down and speaking to Hannah through the car window. 'He looks like one from here. What do you think?'

'Well, if nothing else we can ask him for directions,' Hannah replied. 'Come on, let's get going.'

Rupert got back into the car and they drove up the track, the Citroen bouncing from side to side as they did so. More than once, Rupert swore as the bottom of the car scraped on the ground. It was a good job that Citroen made cars that could at least get down a farm track. Or at least, he thought as he looked at the tarnished blue bonnet of the 2CV, they used to make them. A few minutes later, Rupert pulled up next to the Mercedes in front of the farmhouse and he and Hannah got out. A young man in a nasty cheap suit walked over to them. Rupert's first thought when he saw the man up close was 'obsequious'. His second thought as the man extended a hand toward him was 'wanker'.

'Hey, you must be Rupert,' the man said, shaking Rupert's hand before turning to look at Hannah. 'And you must be the lovely Hannah. We spoke on the phone. I'm Marcus, from Nelson Estate Agents.' Rupert watched as Marcus shook Hannah's hand, holding on to it for far longer than Rupert thought was necessary. To Rupert's disgust, Hannah was smiling back at the smarmy estate agent, loving the attention from the looks of it.

'Yeah, right then Marcus,' Rupert snapped. 'Shall we get on with it?'

The first building that Marcus showed Rupert and Hannah round was the farmhouse. As he walked through the building, the estate agent kept muttering phrases like 'rustic charm' and 'so much potential'.

'It's a bit stark, isn't it Rupert?' Hannah whispered as they were shown into what was apparently a bedroom, but was only just larger than a cupboard. 'It doesn't look like anyone's ever lived here.'

'When do you think he's going to mention the history of the place?' Rupert whispered back. Hannah just shrugged.

'Now come through here, you must see this,' Marcus called to them from the kitchen. When Rupert and Hannah joined him, walking past the industrial sized oven, he threw open the back door with a flourish. 'Would you look at that view?'

Rupert looked out over the muddy field, the grey skies above it, and at the threadbare trees in the distance.

'Wow,' he said in a quiet voice. 'That's something else.'

Almost an hour later, Marcus had given them the grand tour of the whole farm. They'd looked around the pig sheds, and into a building that had at one point been an abattoir. The only positive thing that Marcus had said were some anaemic comments about how thick the stone walls of the buildings were. The three of them sat around the ancient kitchen table in the farmhouse, and Marcus had spread a pile of paperwork on the table. He pushed an A3 sized piece of paper over to Rupert and Hannah.

'This is an overhead aerial shot of the farm.' Marcus traced a red line that was drawn on the paper with a fat finger. 'This line here is the farm boundary. Just shy of twenty acres, so plenty of room for whatever you need it for?' It sounded as if the estate agent was fishing to try to find out what they were going to do with the property, but Rupert wasn't going to be fooled that easily. He looked across at Hannah, who to his irritation was staring at the estate agent. Rupert watched as Marcus glanced across at her and was rewarded with a smile. Rupert knew that smile well. It was the same one Hannah used when she saw something she wanted. It could be a cardigan, a new nose ring, or spontaneous middle of the afternoon sex. It didn't matter — the smile was the same.

'So, what can you tell us about the farm?' Rupert said, trying to stop Hannah's train of thought. The problem was that when she wanted something, she usually got it. Rupert was fine with that when it involved them both getting naked, but he didn't think that was the case here. 'Why is it so cheap?'

Rupert's last statement broke the moment for both

Hannah and the estate agent. Marcus's eyes widened, and he looked at Rupert.

'Well, er, now then,' Marcus stammered. 'It does have a bit of history, you see.'

'What do you mean, history?' Hannah said in a sweet voice, twirling a lock of hair around her finger. Rupert had to stifle a laugh.

'Oh, there was a couple of brothers living here until just recently.'

'So where are they now?' Rupert asked.

'In prison,' Marcus replied after a brief pause. 'They, er, they need some money for legal fees. That's why the farm's on the market for such a reasonable amount.' The estate agent glanced over his shoulder as if there was someone else in the room. Rupert was just thinking how much of a cock he was when Marcus continued in a stage whisper. 'I do know that they would be very amenable to sensible offers, given their circumstances.'

Rupert watched as Hannah leaned forward, placing her elbows on the table. He knew that Marcus would be able to see right down the front of her top, but to his credit, the estate agent never took his eyes off Hannah's. He went up in Rupert's estimation, but only slightly.

'So, Marcus,' Hannah breathed. 'What do you consider to be a sensible offer?' Rupert caught Marcus's eyes flicking down for a split second. The estate agent was human, after all.

'Well,' Marcus said, licking his lips. 'Perhaps an offer at about ten percent under the asking price would be reasonable?'

Rupert leaned back in his chair. Given the price that the farm was on the market for, ten percent under the asking price brought it well within his budget. He watched as Hannah arched her eyebrows in the estate agent's direction.

'And is there anything else that we can do to bring that price down a bit further?' she asked.

'Oh, gosh,' Marcus replied without even so much as a glance at Rupert. 'Possibly.'

3

Emily Underwood rapped hard again on the door of 'Perfect Pizza'. She knew full well there were people inside. A few seconds earlier, she'd seen a head pop up from behind the counter before disappearing again. Even though the sign on the door said 'CLOSED', she could see a drunk bloke slumped in the chair of the waiting area. Emily knocked on the door again before taking a step back and looking at her reflection in the glass of the door.

She ran her hand over her blonde bob, swearing as the hair she'd spent ages earlier trying to tame just leapt back up again, making her look like a school science experiment. Emily ran a critical eye over her reflection. Her flat mate, Catherine, had been on at her for ages about the fact that Emily had lost weight over the last few weeks. The trouser suit Emily was wearing was definitely looser than it had been, so much so that she thought she might have to drop to a size six and buy some more outfits. She leaned forward and angled her head at her reflection, trying to see if there was anything stuck in her teeth, when she saw a tousled head pop up again from behind the counter. It disappeared a few seconds later.

'Oi, I can see you!' Emily shouted, banging her fist on the door. 'Let me in, or I'll close you down from out here.'

The Perfect Pizza wasn't the most hygienic facility in Norwich by a long stretch of the imagination, which was why the Food Standards Agency had sent Emily round to inspect them. In her bag were copies of the many complaints the council had received about the place. Everything from allegations of food poisoning to foreign objects in the pizzas. Non-edible foreign objects. There had even been a complaint about a condom hidden under several layers of pepperoni, but the Food Standards Agency had to stop the investigation when the complainant had admitted to eating it. He said he thought it was a piece of squid, according to the coffee room gossip.

Emily drew herself up to her full height of five foot three inches as a man appeared from behind the counter and walked across the waiting area to open the door.

'We is closed,' the swarthy looking man said with a heavy foreign accent as he opened the door a crack. Emily pulled the inspection notice from her bag.

'No you're not,' she said, waving the sheet of paper at him. 'This says you're open.' With a sigh, the man opened the door.

'Okay miss, welcome,' he said as Emily walked past him into the shop, wrinkling her nose at the sour smell. 'Come on in.'

'Right then,' Emily said, trying to sound business-like. 'Where shall we start?' She glanced at the drunk slumped in the waiting room. He took a deep breath before letting it out through his cheeks, a low rattle coming from his chest. The sour smell got worse. 'Is he okay?' she asked the restaurant owner.

'He fine. Too much beer.'

'Right,' Emily replied. 'Let's crack on.' She glanced down at her paperwork. 'Can we start with the food preparation area?'

An hour later, Emily was almost done. Most visits she did were much shorter, but this one wasn't one that she wanted to take short cuts on. There'd been too many complaints for one thing, and from what she'd seen in the last sixty minutes, Perfect Pizza was about to be closed down. Emily knew that she would have to phone for assistance if she decided to shut the restaurant straight away — an incident a few months back with a small Chinaman wielding a machete had taught her that the hard way — but she wasn't about to let the owner know that. She glanced down at her list of offences, the first page of them at least. Credit where it was due, the restaurant owner had almost got a full house. Dodgy storage of food, poor cleaning practices, abysmal food preparation areas. It was all there. The only thing that was missing was contaminated meat, and that was always a hard one for the Food Standards Agency to prove anyway. If she'd found that, it would mean instant closure.

'Well?' the restaurant owner said as they stood behind the counter. 'What you think? We pass, yes?' He flashed a bright white smile at her.

'I need to check in with the office,' Emily replied. 'Let me speak to them, see what they say?' She returned his smile, but the way his face fell as she smiled at him told Emily that she'd not fooled him at all. She brushed past him into the waiting area. The drunk man was still there. Emily looked at him again, becoming concerned. Were unconscious drunks an offence? Emily didn't think so, but she'd need to check the rule book to be certain. He was definitely pretty out of it — Emily couldn't see him moving at all. She walked over to him to take a closer look. Emily stood there for a few seconds before reaching out her hand and placing it on his shoulder, grateful she still had latex gloves on.

'Hello?' she said, shaking him back and forth. No response. 'Are you okay?' Again, no response.

A few moments later, Emily was standing in the car park on the phone.

'Hello, which emergency service do you require?' the male voice on the other end of the phone said.

'Er, not sure to be honest,' Emily replied.

'What's your emergency?'

'I think I need an ambulance. Or maybe the police.' Emily glanced back at the drunk man in the waiting area of the restaurant. 'Actually, how about an undertaker. Have you got any of them?' There was a silence at the other end of the line.

'An undertaker?'

'Yeah,' Emily said, taking a deep breath. 'I just found a dead bloke.'

4

Hannah wriggled in the uncomfortable passenger seat of Rupert's mother's Citroen, trying to get as comfortable as she could as they bounced down the track toward the main road. Rupert sat next to her in the driver's seat. He'd not said a word to her since they'd left the farmhouse. For a 'progressive radical', as he liked to call himself, he could be incredibly stuck up sometimes.

'Well, I think that was a result, don't you?' Hannah said, breaking the silence. Rupert paused before replying.

'I guess,' he said. 'At least we managed to shave a bit more off the asking price.'

'We?'

'You.'

'Thank you,' Hannah smiled, running her fingers through her bright red hair. It was almost, but not quite, the same shade of red as Rupert's trousers. 'At the end of the day, we've got a good deal so we're happy. The brothers in the nick are happy as they've sold the place, and Marcus is happy as well.' Rupert thought back to the shit-eating grin Marcus had on his face when he and Hannah emerged from the spare bedroom.

'He certainly looked it,' Rupert said. Hannah looked at him, and realised he was trying to keep the anger out of his voice. In reality, the only person who wasn't that happy was Hannah. Marcus had turned out to be a bit self obsessed, and to be frank, quick off the mark.

'Oh, come on,' she said. 'You don't own me. I'm a free woman, a free spirit. That's what you've been telling me since we met.' Rupert didn't reply, so she slid her hand onto his thigh. 'I just got us another two grand off the asking price for a bit of…' she paused, wondering what to say next, '…handiwork in the spare bedroom.'

Rupert looked across at Hannah, taking his eyes off the road.

'Handiwork?' he said.

'Yep,' Hannah replied, settling back into her seat. 'That's all it took.'

'Well, I hope you washed them afterwards,' he replied. She watched as Rupert's face crinkled into a smile. He wasn't to know that she had Marcus's phone number written on her thigh in biro, and had every intention of getting a larger discount in return for more than just handiwork. 'Mind that tree.'

'Jesus Christ,' Rupert shouted as he jerked the steering wheel to the left, narrowly missing the swastika-shaped tree. 'Jesus Christ,' he repeated as he got the car back under control.

'That's what Marcus said back in the bedroom,' Hannah muttered under her breath.

By the time they got back to Norwich, Rupert seemed to have forgotten about Hannah's negotiating skills. He'd spent the thirty-minute drive droning on about the Sanskrit origins of the swastika, and how its true meaning was about being conducive to well-being. When Hannah mentioned that careering into a tree shaped like a swastika wouldn't have helped with their well-being, Rupert had ignored her.

'Right, this evening we need to get the whole group together,' Rupert said as he indicated to come off the A11. 'We'll meet in the Murderers.'

'Okay, I'll set it up,' Hannah replied. An evening at the Murderers was fine by her. It was a pub in the centre of Norwich that was one of her favourite drinking spots. It wasn't just hers though, people had been getting pissed there since the Middle Ages. Loads of nooks and crannies, a resident but long since unseen ghost, wooden beams all over the ceiling, and several dark booths hidden away in the corners that Hannah and a few of the local lads in Norwich had some happy memories of. 'You know it's not technically called the Murderers though?'

'What?' Rupert said.

'It's the Gardeners Arms. The pub bit. It's only the cafe next to it that's the Murderers.'

'No, Hannah,' Rupert replied, his irritation obvious. 'I was not aware of that.' He paused. 'Make sure the new lad comes as well.'

'What's his name again?'

'Adam, isn't it?'

'Not sure, let me look it up on my phone,' Hannah said, digging into her pocket for her phone. She ignored Rupert's dark glances as she looked at her mobile. He hated the things — they were nothing more than the eyes of the government — but there were some things that Hannah wasn't going to live without, and a mobile phone was one of them. 'Andy. He's called Andy.'

'Fuck, of course he is. Why can't I bloody well remember that?' Rupert replied, slapping his hand on the steering wheel for emphasis.

They sat in silence for a few moments, Hannah busy on her phone texting the rest of their group. It wasn't much of a group to be honest. There were only five of them altogether, including Rupert and Hannah, but what united them was their love for animals. At least, that's what Rupert told them all on a regular basis.

'Nearly home,' Rupert said as he steered his mother's Citroen down the slip road. Home, such as it was, was an abandoned office block in the centre of Norwich. It had been the headquarters of a supermarket chain which had since gone bust. The supermarket had moved out, and Rupert, Hannah, and the others had moved in. They had light, running water, even heating if they needed it. They also had the attention of the local police, who had been round a couple of times to ask them to move on. Rupert had been quite reasonable with them, asking them nicely to fuck off and come back with a warrant. The problem was, as the group had been discussing the previous evening, at some point they would.

Hannah looked across at Rupert, who glanced back at her with a quick smile. The first thing she had noticed about him — the first thing most people noticed about him — was his eyes. They were mesmerising. Pale blue in colour, but it was the way that he used them that was captivating. When Rupert was looking at someone, it was as if they were the only person in the world. Hannah grinned as she remembered the first night she'd gone to bed with him, a decision based almost exclusively on those eyes and the effect they had on her. She'd soon forgotten about his eyes, though.

When they walked into the Murderers, the other group

members had already requisitioned their usual table. It was tucked right at the back of the pub, almost hidden under the eaves of the roof, and far enough away from the stage that even if there was a band on they could still talk. Rupert peeled off to go the bar as Hannah approached the others. The new chap, Andy, was there. Hannah wasn't quite sure what to make of him yet, but Rupert seemed to rate him. Matthew, one of the original members of the group, was sitting next to the only other female member, Ruth. She was so thin she looked almost anorexic. She wasn't — she ate more than enough for two people — but Ruth never seemed to put an ounce of fat onto her bones. Hannah, who struggled through her teenage years with a variety of nicknames about her weight, thought that was most unfair.

'Everything okay?' Matthew said. Hannah regarded him, wondering if he'd told anyone about what the two of them had been up to in the old security office back at Partridge Towers. He was a good looking man — well built, chiselled jaw, and with a charming bedside manner — but easily led. Hannah guessed that they all were. If they weren't then they wouldn't be here.

'We'd better wait for Rupert,' Hannah replied with a sly smile. The way Matthew mirrored her smile told Hannah that the other night wasn't a one off. 'Shift up, Andy,' Hannah said as she sat down next to the new arrival. 'Plenty of room for all of us.' By the time Rupert came over to the table with a pint of lager for himself and a gin and tonic for Hannah, Hannah was sitting so close to Matthew that she could feel his body heat through their clothes. She let her hand drop below the table and brush against his muscular thigh. He didn't look at her, but she caught the flash of a smile on his face.

'Brothers, Sisters,' Rupert said when he had sat down.

He looked at each of the group in turn, spending longer gazing at Ruth than anyone else much to Hannah's annoyance. 'I have some good news.' Several sets of eyebrows went up around the table. 'We have a new home.'

5

Andy took a sip of his beer as he waited for the response to Rupert's announcement to die down. Matthew was full of questions about the farm. Even Ruth, normally as quiet as a mouse, chipped in with a question about how many toilets there were. Even though they were all effectively one, she still wanted a separate toilet for women.

It was now three weeks since Andy had become a full member of Rupert's group. Although it wasn't that long ago, it felt like a lifetime to him. The joining ceremony had been a bit on the strange side, and was Rupert's way of welcoming new members, apparently. Andy didn't mind the idea of it, even though he felt a bit stupid watching the others get absolutely hammered. Andy didn't mind a drink or two, but he'd never taken anything stronger than that apart from a couple of puffs on a joint when he was back at school. He'd watched the others get absolutely off their tits after the ceremony, but that wasn't his scene so he'd left them to it despite their pleas for him to join in.

He thought back for a few seconds to his life before he

joined the group, back in the 'Old World' as Rupert called it. Andy knew he wasn't supposed to think about it, that wasn't part of the way forward to his new life, but once in a while he did anyway. It hadn't been much of a life really, but Andy hadn't really realised that until he'd spent a few days and nights with the group. At the time, he'd thought he was quite happy, but Rupert had helped him see how unhappy he actually was. There were some things he missed though. Or more specifically, a particular person.

'Andy?' Rupert's voice cut through his thoughts. 'You with us, mate?' Andy looked over at Rupert, whose blue eyes were fixed on him.

'Yeah, sure,' Andy replied.

'What do you think about the collective?'

'Sorry, the what?'

'The collective,' Rupert repeated, a flash of irritation crossing his face.

'Cracking idea, Rupert,' Andy replied, not quite sure what he was talking about. Rupert stared at him for a few long seconds before he broke into a smile.

'Excellent,' Rupert said. 'I propose a toast.' They all raised their glasses and waited. 'To our new collective, which I have decided we will call…' he paused before continuing, '…Another Way.'

'Another Way,' they all mumbled in unison as they clinked their glasses together.

Several hours and several more drinks later they were making their way back to Partridge Towers in a loose group. Tired of the noise, Andy let the rest of them get ahead of him so that he could think for a bit.

'Are you okay?' Andy heard a female voice say. He realised that Ruth had also hung back from the group and was walking next to him.

'Sure, I'm fine,' he said. 'You?' He looked at the young

woman next to him. Ruth was a bit of an odd looking girl in Andy's opinion. Not unattractive, but unconventionally pretty. She was quite short, and slimmer than Hannah which made her very thin indeed. She was attractive, but in a timid sense, and had a perpetual look of anxiety on her face.

'I'm good,' Ruth said. 'They all seem happy enough with the farm, anyway.' She nodded toward the others twenty yards in front of them.

'Yeah, they do, don't they?' Andy replied. 'Hopefully it'll be more comfortable than where we are now, anyway.'

'We'll find out tomorrow.'

'Tomorrow? That soon?'

'Yes, tomorrow,' Ruth laughed, her eyes sparkling in the streetlights. 'You really weren't listening earlier, were you?'

'No, I guess not.'

'What were you thinking about? You looked really sad,' Ruth said. Andy wasn't quite sure what to say, so he said nothing. 'Were you thinking about the Old World?'

'Maybe just a little bit.'

'That's okay, you can think about it. It's only when you fully realise how wrong the Old World is that you can move forward.'

'That's what Rupert says.'

'But it's true,' Ruth said. Andy felt her hand slip into his. 'That's why you need to let it go.' She started humming the tune from the film *Frozen*.

'Thanks for that,' Andy said after a few seconds, laughing. 'That's going to be stuck in my head for the night now.'

They walked in silence for a few moments, hand in hand.

'You're different from them, you know that?' Ruth said,

breaking the silence and nodding at the group in front who were just approaching Partridge Towers.

'In what way?' Andy asked.

'I don't know. Just different.' She looked at him, and Andy saw that the frightened expression had returned to her face. 'In a good way, I mean.' Ruth stopped, pulling at Andy's hand to make him stop as well. He glanced toward the rest of the group, who were making their way into the building through the sheet of plywood they used as a front door. 'Do you like me?' Ruth asked.

'Of course I do,' he replied, realising they were on their own in the street.

'So how come you've never tried to sleep with me then?'

Andy's eyes widened. He'd not been expecting that question, and had no idea what to say.

'Er, well,' he mumbled. 'I mean, I do like you. You're an attractive woman.' He racked his brains for something else to say, but came up short.

'Are you gay?' Ruth asked.

'No,' Andy replied, realising a split second later that this might have given him a way out. Too late. 'Ruth, I do like you. But the whole "fuck whoever you want" thing doesn't do it for me,' he said.

'See,' Ruth said, a faint smile playing across her face. 'That's why you're different from them. They don't see it that way.' She took a few steps forward, tugging at Andy's hand. 'Could you do something for me, though?'

'Of course I can,' Andy replied, falling into step alongside her.

'Spend the night with me anyway. I know we're not supposed to have any secrets, but no-one needs to know we kept our clothes on.'

Andy looked at Ruth and put his arm around her

shoulder. Even though she had a thick jumper on, he could feel her angular shoulders. He pulled her closer.

'I can, but on one condition,' he said, almost in a whisper.

'What?' Ruth whispered in reply.

'You have to walk like you're a cowboy for the whole day tomorrow.'

6

Hannah opened her eyes, and shut them again straight away. The early morning sunlight was streaming in through the window of the office block. There used to be blinds in the windows, but they were long gone. There were a few things she was going to miss about Partridge Towers when they moved into the farm, but the early morning sunlight wasn't one of them.

She looked at Rupert lying next to her. He was snoring softly, oblivious to the world. He'd been just as oblivious in the middle of the night when Hannah had crept out of their bed and into Matthew's, but what Rupert didn't know wouldn't hurt him. Hannah knew that no matter how much he preached about togetherness and oneness, he didn't like it when she practised what he preached.

Today was going to be an important day in the history of their little group. They were about to leave their temporary home and move into a permanent one in the afternoon, and there was a focus group planned for the morning. That was their chance to spread the word and to try to get their message out to the 'great unwashed', as

Rupert called anyone outside the group. It was also a chance to recruit new members to the collective, but that was proving to be harder than they'd imagined.

While Hannah and Rupert had been at the farm the day before, the rest of the group had been handing out leaflets outside the Forum in the middle of Norwich. The huge glass fronted building housed many things. It was the control centre for Canary FM, the local propaganda radio station according to Rupert, and also the city library. What appealed to Rupert was the fact that there were several small conference rooms attached to the library which could be hired out, free of charge, by local interest groups. He'd spent a long time persuading a large woman who was apparently in charge of Events at the library that their group was a legitimate local interest group. Hannah thought that the woman had agreed just to get rid of Rupert — his blue eyes didn't work on everyone — but she would never admit that.

Hannah peeled herself out of bed and padded to what passed for the kitchen area. She flicked the switch on the kettle and thought about the oven at the farm while she waited for the water to boil. The oven was huge — more than big enough for what they had planned — and she couldn't wait to get started.

An hour later, the whole group were gathered in a windowless room on the top floor of Partridge Towers. When they'd first moved in the room had been full of over-filled beanbags, but Rupert had soon replaced them with yoga mats. They sat there now, having come down from the roof where they'd meditated as the sun rose over the city centre, and waited for Rupert to put in an appearance. They were supposed to be in the lotus position, but as Hannah looked around the room, she realised that she was the only one in the prescribed position. Even Andy, possibly the most pliable one in the room, was sitting there cross legged and deep in conversation with Ruth. As far as Hannah had gathered at breakfast, the two of them had spent the night together which might explain why Ruth looked as if she was walking a bit awkwardly this morning.

'Shalom, people,' Rupert said as he breezed into the room.

'Aleikhem shalom,' Hannah muttered in return as the rest of the room looked at Rupert with blank stares. They'd obviously not had that lecture yet.

'Right then, are we all set for today?' Rupert asked, his tone bright. There were a few nods, but the most enthusiastic person in the room by some distance was Rupert. 'Good,' he nodded with a bright smile. 'So, engagement event this morning. I want you all on your best behaviour. Smiles, happiness, love. If we're going to recruit some more members for the cause, they have to see us in the right light.'

Hannah looked around the room at the others. Only Andy seemed remotely interested in what Rupert was saying. She knew that Matthew and Ruth would brighten up though. They always did.

'Then, this afternoon, we're moving in to our new home. I know we've had some long discussions about land ownership, and how wrong it is.' Hannah remembered one or two of those discussions as well. 'But the only way we can move the cause forward is to consolidate into a business base. Which is why I've bought the farm. For the cause.' Rupert's intense gaze roamed around the room, daring anyone to disagree with him. As usual, no-one did.

Hannah had listened to Rupert time after time talking about moving forward. He wanted a proper group, a collective of hundreds of activists, as opposed to a small band of misfits and losers. For such a vocal anti-capitalist, he was doing a pretty good job of building a business. Investing the remainder of his parents Trust Fund into buying the farm was only the first step.

'We're going to create a nirvana for animals. A place where they, and we, can be free. A place where we can be who we want to be. Yes, Matthew?' Hannah turned to see Matthew with his hand raised like a schoolchild in class.

'What are we going to do about money?' he asked.

'Eventually, we'll be fully self sufficient. Until Hannah has expanded her bakery services enough, we'll rely on our benefits. God knows, we've worked hard enough to earn them.' Hannah had to suppress a smile. With the exception of Andy, none of them had worked a day in their lives. Both Rupert and Hannah had been to university, but neither of them had completed their course. Hannah had started off a psychology degree, but not even finished the first year before she'd quit. Rupert had managed to get through the first year of a chemistry degree before he'd left half way through the second year. Hannah had pressed him on his reasons for quitting several times, but the most she'd been able to get out of him was 'creative differences' between Rupert and the lecturers.

'The farm will give us the ability to raise some funds,' Rupert continued, breaking Hannah's train of thought. 'Once we've adapted it for our needs, it'll be perfect. Won't it, Hannah?'

'Yeah, it's going to be great,' Hannah said, stirring herself into life. 'We'll start off with artisan baking, organic bread that encapsulates what we stand for.' Rupert had made her practice this speech many times since he'd signed the paperwork to buy the farm. 'The kitchen's more than big enough for a reasonable production line.'

'And while we're building that product line,' Rupert added, 'we can continue with other aspects of the operation.' Hannah watched him switch his gaze between the other members of the group before he lowered his voice and whispered. 'Striking at the heart of the system.'

Hannah looked at the others. Andy, who was sitting next to Ruth, just looked blank. Matthew turned to Mark and raised his eyebrows.

'Why don't you go into a bit more detail, Rupert?' Hannah said, following the script they'd rehearsed. He looked at her and arched an eyebrow, also rehearsed.

'The only way we can get our message across is to take direct, positive action,' Rupert explained. 'I'm planning a series of activist events. High profile, daring raids to free trapped and doomed animals. Make no mistake,' he said, pausing to look each member of the group in the eyes, 'they will be dangerous. They will be risky. But - ' he prodded his finger hard onto the table, making some of the glasses wobble, ' - they will count.'

7

R upert looked at the small group of people sitting in the conference room at The Forum. There weren't as many people as he would have liked — maybe twenty or so — despite the fact they'd handed out hundreds of leaflets. Sitting in front of him was a pretty disparate bunch. There were a few small groups who obviously knew each other, but Rupert wasn't interested in them. He was only interested in the ones who had come on their own. They would be easier to target. As he looked around the room, he noticed a young woman sitting on her own near the back of the room. She was early twenties, waif thin, and was nibbling a fingernail. Rupert looked around for Hannah and when he managed to catch her eye, he nodded in the young woman's direction. A few moments later, he saw Hannah's red hair moving towards the back of the room.

'Thank you all for coming this morning,' Rupert said into the microphone on the table in front of him. He didn't have any notes, but he'd given the speech so many times, he didn't need any. 'Over the next thirty minutes or so, I'm going to tell you a story about a pig.' He paused, flicking his eyes around the room and making sure he looked at the woman at the back of the room for a few seconds longer than the others. 'By the time I'm finished, if you're not vegetarian or vegan already, you'll be considering it.' Rupert raised his eyebrows, daring anyone to challenge his statement, but as usual no-one did. The only noise in the room was the sound of knitting needles clicking in the front row. He frowned ever so slightly at the little old lady making the noise, but it had no effect. She just smiled back at him.

Rupert launched into his speech, telling the story of a piglet born on an intensive farm. It wasn't a true story, but a combination of stuff that he'd read about on the internet and worked into a narrative. A particularly nasty and brutal narrative, but one which was based on truth. By the time he got to the part where the piglet was ripped from its mother's teats so that the sow could be artificially insemi-nated again a few months after giving birth, he could see from the look of the faces in the audience that the words were hitting home. When he described the horrific death of the fictional piglet, there were several sobs around the room.

'That, ladies and gentlemen, is the story of one pig,' Rupert said in a whisper. 'A story that is repeated ten million times every year in this so called humane country of ours.' He paused for effect and to let the message sink in. 'But, there is another way.' Out of the corner of his eye, Rupert saw Hannah put a hand onto the arm of the woman in the back row, who was weeping silently. *Excellent*, Rupert thought. *She looks perfect*.

Rupert launched into the second phase of his speech, which was about how they could take action against the slaughter. As he approached the end, he got more and more animated.

'This is your responsibility,' he said, looking round the audience again and trying to make eye contact with all of them without losing any momentum. 'This is our responsibility.' He thumped his clenched fist against his sternum. 'I am doing something about this murder. The question that you all should ask yourselves, must ask yourselves, is what are you doing about it?' He sat back in his chair with a deep breath, as if the effort of his fervour had drained him. It hadn't, but none of the audience knew that. There was a stunned silence around the room, which was interrupted by the old lady in the front row putting her knitting needles down and clapping her arthritic hands together.

Twenty minutes later, the crowd had thinned out to just Rupert, Hannah, and the woman from the back row. Rupert said goodbye to an earnest middle-aged man who wanted to do whatever he could to help. From the way that he was speaking though, Rupert didn't think he'd able to contribute much either in terms of talent or money. He'd taken the man's phone number and had promised to get in touch. As the middle-aged man sloped off toward the entrance, Rupert turned his attention to Hannah and the young woman. He walked across to talk to them.

'Rupert,' Hannah said as he approached. 'This is Amy.' Hannah had her arm draped across the woman's shoulders.

'Amy,' Rupert said in a soft voice as he crouched down and knelt in front of her. Amy was sniffling into a well-used tissue, so well-used it had almost disintegrated. 'Amy, I'm Rupert.' She raised her head and looked at him through red-rimmed eyes. Rupert made sure that he widened his own eyes by a fraction and avoided blinking to give Amy the full blue-eyed treatment.

'Hi,' Amy said in a quiet voice. Rupert didn't reply, but just stared at her. When she looked away from him, returning her attention to the sodden tissue, Rupert glanced up at Hannah who gave him an almost imperceptible nod.

'Amy, why don't you come for a drink with me and Hannah. There's some of friends going to be there as well, and I know they'd love to meet you.' Amy's face brightened.

'Really?' she asked. 'That would be nice.'

Rupert leaned forward and took her hand — the one without the tissue in it — in his. He pressed their hands together down onto her thigh. If Amy objected to the contact, she didn't show it. 'Can I just nip to the toilet first though? I must look a right mess.'

Both Hannah and Rupert shook their heads in unison. Hannah opened her mouth to say something but Rupert cut her off.

'Not at all, Amy,' he said, squeezing her hand. 'You look perfect as you are, but if you need to freshen up we'll wait right here for you.'

The minute that Amy was out of reach of their voices, Rupert turned to Hannah.

'Well? What do you think?' he asked.

'Perfect, Rupert. Absolutely perfect. Look at her.' The both turned to watch Amy as she walked out of the room. Rupert didn't say anything to Hannah, but he knew she wouldn't be thinking what he was thinking. 'She went to Norwich Independent School, then Cambridge.' Rupert whistled through his teeth.

'Blimey,' he said. 'That's got to be twenty-five grand a year, that school. What did she do at Cambridge?'

'Something useless. Puppetry management, I think she said.'

'There's a degree in puppetry management?'

'Think so.'

'For fuck's sake, that's where my tax is going is it?' Rupert saw Hannah suppress a grin. His actual contribution to the taxation system was zero, a fact he was very proud of.

'Anyway, she's now left Cambridge and can't get a job so is just floating round living off her inheritance.'

'Inheritance?' Rupert said. 'What, no parents?' This time, Hannah didn't try to suppress her smile.

'Nope. Daddy died of a heart attack in a brothel, and her mother died in a freak yachting accident.'

'Oh my Lord,' Rupert said, 'That is priceless.' He nodded toward the door. 'Here she comes now.'

'Turn it up, Rupert. She's perfect,' Hannah dropped her voice to a whisper as Amy walked back across the room. 'Absolutely fucking perfect.'

8

E mily Underwood sighed as she slipped her shoes off
and wriggled her toes on the cool slate floor of her
bathroom. What a day that had been. By the time the
police had worked out that she wasn't a crank caller and
actually sent someone round to the pizza restaurant, it was
an hour after she was supposed to have finished. The first
policeman who turned up looked about fifteen — barely
old enough to shave — and in the alleyway next to the
restaurant, he'd confessed that he'd never seen a real-life
dead body before. Emily had just rubbed his back and
made soothing noises, hoping that his stomach was
now empty.

When the grown-up police arrived, things got a lot
more serious. Emily recognised the policewoman in charge
from the television. She was a fierce looking woman called
Chief Superintendent Antonio, and the minute she arrived
all the other coppers started scurrying around with scared
faces. The Superintendent had barked orders at her
minions, streams of blue and white police tape had
appeared to seal the restaurant off, and a small crowd had

gathered the other side of the tape. When a black van with the words 'Private Ambulance' stencilled on the side appeared, most of the onlookers had raised their phones to film the body being wheeled out of the restaurant but the most entertaining thing that had happened was a minor scuffle between a local reporter from the local radio station, Canary FM, and the policewoman in charge. Emily recognised the reporter — he was a jovial looking chap called Bob Rutler, who sported an impressive beard. It turned out he was no match for the Superintendent, though. Emily couldn't be one hundred percent sure as she was being interviewed at the time, but she was fairly sure that the policewoman had given the reporter a nasty rabbit punch to the kidneys at one point.

Emily leaned forward and twiddled with the taps on the bath before pouring a generous amount of her flat mate's stupidly expensive bubble bath into it. Catherine would never notice. As Emily slipped out of her business suit and hung it up to drop the creases in the steam, she wondered where Catherine was this evening. Or more probably, whose bed she was in. Emily loved Catherine to bits, but her flat mate was a complete slapper. Emily turned the taps down to a trickle, and nipped into the kitchen to pour herself a generous glass of wine.

'Fuck me, that's hot,' Emily gasped as she dipped her toes into the water a few moments later. There were already beads of perspiration on both her brow and the wine glass, but she pushed on and after several gasps and sharp expirations of breath, she was submerged. 'Oh, that's bliss,' she said, loving the warmth and comfort of the hot water, as she picked up her book and found her page.

Emily was reading the latest chick-lit bestseller, *Girl on a Bike*, which was a poorly disguised attempt to cash in on some earlier success another author had with a similar title.

It was entertaining enough, though. Ten minutes later, Emily was just topping up the bath with some more hot water when she heard Catherine banging around in the flat. A few seconds later, there was a knock at the bathroom door.

'Emily? Are you in there?' Catherine's voice came through the door.

'No, I'm in the garden,' Emily replied.

'Very funny,' Catherine replied. They didn't have a garden, just a small balcony where they shared the occasional joint as they watched the world go by. 'What are you doing?'

'I'm having a monkey bath,' Emily replied with a sigh. What did Catherine think she was doing in the bathroom?

'A what?'

'A monkey bath.'

'What's that?' Catherine asked.

'It's a bath that's so hot when you get in it, you go "ooh ooh, aah aah" like a monkey.'

'Oh,' Catherine replied after a brief pause. 'Well, you'd better not be using my bubble bath. That cost a sodding fortune.'

'I'm not, don't worry,' Emily said, looking at the almost empty bottle. She would have to remember to fill it up from the bottle of Lidl bubble bath before she left the bathroom. Emily heard Catherine's footsteps receding from the bathroom door. A few seconds later, Catherine called out again.

'Have you got the wine?' Emily looked at the half-empty bottle that was balanced on the toilet lid.

'Yeah, sorry.' Emily heard Catherine shout 'Bitch' from somewhere further away in the flat.

Twenty minutes later, Emily, dressed in a baggy t-shirt and her most comfortable track suit trousers, was curled up on the sofa sipping a mug of hot chocolate. Catherine had nipped to the shop around the corner to restock the wine and was sitting opposite Emily in their lounge.

'So, you not heading out tonight, then?' Catherine asked.

'What do you think?' Emily replied with a smile.

'Well, you've got your fat pants on, so I'm guessing not.'

'Got that right.'

'Emily, listen babes,' Catherine said, leaning forward on her chair. Emily groaned. *Not again*, she thought. 'You need to get out there. Play the field. Forget him.' Emily put her hot chocolate down and considered going to the kitchen to get another glass of cheap wine instead.

'Catherine, please,' Emily said. 'I don't want to forget him.'

A few months earlier, Emily and Catherine had gone on holiday to Ibiza. At the time, Emily was in the early stages of a relationship with a young man who she'd met in rather unusual circumstances that she'd tried very hard to block from her mind. Emily had thought that things were going well with her new suitor, but when she'd got back from Ibiza, he'd done one. Just disappeared without a trace. Story of her life.

'He's a bastard, Emily,' Catherine said, echoing Emily's thoughts. 'They all are.'

'Hmm,' Emily replied, 'If you say so.' Catherine got to her feet with a sigh and made her way to the kitchen.

'Well he is, isn't he? Or at least, he was,' she called back through the open door. 'Left you without so much as a goodbye. That makes him a bastard in my eyes.' Catherine walked back into the lounge and, to Emily's relief, she was carrying two large glasses of white wine. 'There you go, babe. Get that down you,' she said, handing a glass to Emily.

'Thanks,' Emily said. She'd not said anything to Catherine, but Emily's ex-boyfriend hadn't left without a goodbye. He'd sent her a letter — a proper letter with a stamp and everything — to try to explain why he'd left. He was going on a journey, according to the letter, and apparently it wasn't a journey that Emily was ready for. The writing was a scrawl, not like his normal careful writing, and Emily figured that he was probably off his face on something when he wrote it. According to the note, he had found another way to live his life, and that didn't include Emily.

She took a large sip of the wine, grimacing at the sour taste. Catherine must have chosen the cheapest wine in the entire shop.

'Ew, that's rank,' Emily said.

'Well, there's gratitude,' Catherine replied with a smirk. 'Anyway, let me tell you about a bloke I met the other night down on Riverside. His name's Roba, and he's from Japan. We ended up going back to his hotel room. In the Holiday Inn by the football stadium as well. So, you know, a bit more upmarket.'

'Right, good,' Emily said. 'God forbid that you should have to slum it in a Travel Lodge.' The last time Emily and Catherine had been in the Travel Lodge near the bus station, all the staff had greeted Catherine like an old friend — much to Emily's amusement. 'What was his name again?'

'Roba. He's now half way back to Japan I think. Hopefully with a smile still on his face. Do you know what the funniest thing is?'

'Oh God,' Emily replied. 'Go on then.'

'Roba's not his real name. It's a nickname.'

'Okay,' Emily said after a pause, 'and the nickname means what?'

'It's Japanese.'

'Obviously. But what does it mean?' Emily asked. Catherine looked at her with a mischievous smile before replying.

'It's Japanese for donkey.'

'Really?'

'Yes, really. An entirely appropriate nickname, if you get my drift,' Catherine replied with a wry smile.

'Oh, for fuck's sake.'

9

Andy took a large sip of his lager, relishing the taste of the cold liquid. One thing the Murderers pub did very well was a decent pint. No better than any other pub in Norwich, but the quirky interior of the pub and the fact that any minute now he might see a real-life ghost made the experience just a bit more special. At least, that was Andy's opinion. Matthew — who was sitting next to him — nudged his leg and Andy looked up to see the door to the pub swinging open.

'Here they come,' Matthew said. 'Looks like they got one, too.' Andy saw Rupert and Hannah walk in, either side of a very pretty blonde girl. They both had an arm laced through hers, and they led her over to the table that Andy, Matthew, and Ruth were sitting at. Andy glanced across at Ruth, who was regarding the new arrival with a suspicious look.

'Hey everyone,' Rupert said as they arrived at the table. 'Meet Amy.'

'Hi, Amy,' the three of them replied in unison. Ruth, her face now angelic, raised a hand in greeting.

'So, left to right, this is Andy, Matthew, and Ruth,' Rupert said. They all smiled in turn.

'Hi,' Amy said with a broad smile. 'Pleased to meet you all.'

'Shuffle round, Ruth,' Hannah said. 'Make some room for Amy.' As Ruth moved round the bench, Rupert looked at Andy.

'Mate,' Rupert said. 'Give me a hand with the drinks, would you?' Matthew had only just got a round in, alerted by a text from Hannah that they were on their way, but Andy got to his feet anyway. If Rupert needed a hand carrying one drink over, then so be it. 'Amy, what would you like to drink?'

'Oh, thank you Rupert. Could I have a lime and soda?'

Andy watched Rupert's face as she said this, knowing that in Rupert's opinion at least, lime and soda was not a drink.

'Sure.'

Andy followed Rupert toward the bar, but at the last minute, Rupert peeled off and headed for the toilet. Andy followed him into the Gents, and after Rupert had checked the cubicles for other visitors, the two men faced each other.

'That woman out there is going to be the latest member of the group. She's half way there already,' Rupert said. 'We'll get into the farm, once it's ready, and work on her until then. You know the way, so you take the lead.' Andy did indeed know the way — he was the last person to go through it — but at the same time he realised the need to increase the size of the group. He was surprised that Rupert seemed to be giving him a level of responsibility in the woman's induction.

'But I get first dibs,' Rupert said, folding his arms

across his chest. 'Just putting that out there, so let the others know.'

'Okay, you're the boss,' Andy replied. 'I'll tell them.'

'See if you can get Ruth to have a go as well. You seem to be pretty tight with her.'

'Sorry,' Andy said. 'Have a go?'

'Yeah, you know. Bit of sister on sister. I mean, I know Hannah's not up for that sort of thing, but I reckon it would help the women bond more if they were, well, into that.'

Andy kept his own counsel, wondering what Rupert would say if Matthew suggested a bit of brother on brother with Rupert on the same basis. When he'd first met Matthew, Andy was pretty convinced that the other man was fairly laissez-faire about who he slept with from a gender point of view. It was only a suspicion based on a few comments Matthew had made about Rupert, but Andy was pretty sure Rupert wouldn't see them as compliments so he kept his thoughts to himself.

'Okay,' Andy said, 'you're the boss.'

'Good lad,' Rupert said, clapping Andy on the shoulder. 'I'll let you know when Amy's up for sloppy seconds.' He swung the door to the toilets open, and Andy followed him back into the bar. For the leader of the group, Andy thought, Rupert was a prize wanker at times. A few minutes later, Andy was sitting back at the table having watched Rupert carefully with Amy's drink. He wouldn't put it past the man to slip a loosener of some sort into her drink, but Rupert didn't add anything as far as Andy could see.

Amy was sitting almost directly opposite Andy, Hannah on one side and Rupert now on the other. Andy had seen Amy's face brighten as soon as Rupert shuffled in next to her. His blue eyes were working their magic, that much was obvious. Andy leaned across to Matthew and whispered in his ear.

'Lovebomb.' Matthew nodded in reply.

'So Amy,' Rupert said. 'Tell us about yourself.'

'Er, okay,' Amy giggled. 'But what do you want to know?'

'I've got a question for you, Amy,' Ruth said. She reached out and ran her fingers through the ends of Amy's hair. 'Where did you get your hair done? It's gorgeous.' Amy laughed, running her own fingers through her hair and tucking an errant strand behind her ear.

The questions went on for about half an hour. They all took turns asking Amy things, questions designed to compliment her. Andy asked a couple of questions about her degree in puppet mastery, at least that's what he thought it was in. They all gasped and sighed as Amy told them about how she had been captivated by a world-famous puppeteer from Norwich.

'I remember the first time I saw him, on Gentleman's Walk in the city. He had this puppet, a snake made from a worn sock, that he'd called 'Roy Waller'. When he made Roy come to life, I was just, just so…' Her voice trailed off.

'Just what, Amy?' Rupert said, and they all leaned forward. Andy saw Rupert move his arm and knew from the look on Amy's face that he had just put his hand on her thigh. Andy also knew from the look on Hannah's face that he wasn't the only one who'd noticed this.

'He made Roy Waller dance like, I don't know, like Rudolf Nureyev or Wayne Sleep. It was as if it wasn't a puppet, it was if it was a real man. Dave — that's the puppeteer's name — brought him to life with such elegance that…' Her voice trailed off again for a few seconds before she looked at Rupert, her eyes wide and teary. 'I cried for Roy. I cried for a puppet.'

Rupert leaned forward, as did Hannah, and they both put their arms around Amy. Ruth reached across the table and took Amy's hand in hers.

'That's beautiful,' Ruth murmured, rubbing her thumb across the back of Amy's hand. 'So beautiful.' Andy risked a look at Matthew, but looked away again when he saw the corners of Matthew's mouth twitching.

10

T he next day, Rupert woke up with a start. He looked at his watch, groaning when he realised that it was only just after six o'clock in the morning. Bright sunlight streamed in through the windows of the boardroom and he knew that any chance of a lie in was gone.

He rolled over on the stained mattress but Hannah wasn't there. She must have got up even earlier than him — she was much more of a morning person than he was — and with any luck was on her way back with a cup of tea. Rupert stretched and yawned, pleased that they'd all left the pub at a reasonable time the night before. Today was going to be a busy day for all of them. They'd hired a small lorry that he would be picking up later on, even though it was a bit too big for his driving licence. The hire firm hadn't seemed to care whether or not he could legally drive it, so he wasn't that fussed either. The basic plan was to park the lorry in the car park of the tower, throw all their worldly goods into it along with anything else that might be useful, and decamp en-masse to the farm. Except for him and Hannah, the others hadn't seen it yet and he was looking forward to showing them round.

The door to the boardroom opened, and Hannah tiptoed into the room holding her shoes between her hands. Rupert saw she had a broad grin on her face which he thought faltered for a split second when she saw him looking at her.

'Morning, Rupert,' she said, her smile as bright as it normally was. He must have been mistaken about it slipping.

'Morning,' Rupert replied. 'You okay?'

'Yeah, all good,' she said. 'Just nipped to the toilet. Do you want a cup of tea?' Rupert looked at the door that she'd just come through.

'The toilets aren't that way though.'

'I went downstairs.'

'Why?' Rupert said with a frown.

'They flush better,' Hannah pressed her hand to her abdomen, 'and I've got women's problems, you know? I didn't think that the first thing you'd want to see in the morning was a —'

'Yeah, yeah,' Rupert cut her off with a wave of his hand. 'I get it, don't worry. I'll have a cup of tea though.' As Hannah walked over to the area of the boardroom they called the kitchen — in reality, a kettle, a microwave, and a beer fridge with a cracked glass door — Rupert rolled himself off the mattress and pulled his jeans on. At some point over the next few days he needed to lose the others and sneak back to his parents' house to do his laundry. They took it in turns to do the laundry, but after the last time Matthew had done it, Rupert's best pair of Calvin Klein underpants had come back too small for a ten-year-old to wear. Not only that, but they were also a subtle shade of pink. Rupert had inherited from the same wash a pair of yellowed Y-fronts with a horrifying stain in the gusset, despite the fact they'd been washed. At least his mother used fabric conditioner, he thought as he pulled a t-shirt over his head and walked over to the kitchen area.

'Thanks, babe,' Rupert said as Hannah handed him a cup of tea.

'You're welcome,' she replied. They sat at what used to be the boardroom table of the firm that had inhabited Partridge Towers, and watched the sun rise across the skyline of Norwich. Rupert wasn't going to miss much about squatting in a disused tower block, but he would miss the view from the boardroom. 'What time are you picking up this lorry?' Hannah interrupted his thoughts.

'Oh, ten o'clock.'

'Where from?'

'Some dodgy place over in Thorpe Saint Andrew. I should be back by eleven, so if you could make sure the others are ready to move out as soon as I get back, that'd be magic.'

'Sure,' Hannah nodded. 'No worries, I'll make sure they're all ready.'

They sat in companionable silence for a few moments. Rupert sipped his tea, grimacing when he realised there was no sugar in it.

'Jesus, Hannah,' he exclaimed. 'How long have we been together for?'

'What?'

'Nearly three years, and you still forget my sugar.'

'Get your own fucking sugar.'

Rupert got to his feet, suppressing a smile. The two of them went through a variation of the same routine almost every morning. A couple of times, Rupert had even laced Hannah's tea with sugar even though she didn't take any. To his dismay, she hadn't batted an eyelid. Maybe he should try lacing it with acid instead? That might be interesting. He was in the middle of considering how soluble LSD would be in tea when he realised Hannah had said something.

'Sorry, what?' he said. Hannah mumbled something under her breath. It sounded suspiciously like 'oh, for fuck's sake'.

'I said, I can't wait to move into the farm.'

'Me neither,' Rupert said, returning to join Hannah at the table. 'Did you find someone to buy the bread?'

'Not exactly,' Hannah replied. 'I've found an outlet for it though. They want to try a sample batch, see how it goes down.'

'Right,' Rupert said. That wasn't exactly what he'd briefed her. She was supposed to be selling it, not giving it away, but he could see the point of a free sample. 'So, is that one of the local supermarkets?'

'Not exactly,' Hannah replied. 'It's a sandwich van.'

'A sandwich van? A fucking sandwich van?'

'Yes, Rupert,' Hannah said with a warning look that he knew well. 'It's a fucking sandwich van. Is that okay with you?'

'Yeah,' Rupert said. 'Of course it is, babes. Great idea.' He sipped at his tea, thinking hard. If he dosed her tea with acid, the chlorine in the water would probably neutralise it. If he dissolved it in alcohol though, it would stay very potent. 'We'll get the move done, get your bread to the sandwich van, and then…' He paused for a second. 'I think I'll buy you a bottle of your favourite gin to celebrate.

'Ooh,' Hannah said. 'That sounds like a great idea.'

11

Hannah flicked an errant strand of red hair behind her ear and regarded the interior of the kitchen at the farmhouse. She'd spent the previous few hours with a paintbrush, trying her best to tidy up the room. It hadn't been touched for years from the looks of it. At least now, with a fresh coat of bright yellow paint, it looked a lot brighter and more homely. If Rupert's plan came to fruition, she would be spending a lot of time in here. Not in a barefoot and pregnant in the kitchen sense, but as the main breadwinner on the farm. At least to begin with.

'Hey, Hannah.' She turned at the voice from the door to see Ruth standing there. 'Wow, look what you've done with this place. It's amazing.'

'Thanks, Ruth,' Hannah said. 'It looks a bit better, doesn't it?' Ruth nodded her head, looking around the room.

'All it needed was a woman's touch really,' she said, pointing at the counter near the sink. 'A few flowers there, it'll be perfect. I can't believe it's ours.'

'Well, it is. This is what Rupert has provided for us. To

move us forward.' On one level, Hannah felt bad about trotting out the party line that Rupert had provided, but it was a lot better than squatting in a tower block. She glanced at her watch, wondering how the boys were getting on with what Rupert had planned for the afternoon. It should be happening any time now.

'Yeah,' Ruth said, trailing her fingers across the scarred kitchen table before she took a seat. 'Could I talk to you about Rupert for a minute?'

'Of course you can,' Hannah replied, sitting on a chair opposite Ruth. 'Something wrong?' Knowing Rupert, which Hannah did, there was almost certainly something wrong.

'Well, this new girl, Amy,' Ruth said, twirling her hair in her fingers. 'He's suggested that if I'm really committed to the cause, and recruiting into it, I should, er, I should…'

'Be more sapphist?'

'Oh, yeah. He did use that phrase. I had to look it up on my phone. Rupert really doesn't like phones, does he?'

'No. We've had that discussion too many times already. What did you say to him then?'

'Well,' Ruth said. 'I wasn't sure what he was talking about. Like I said, I had to look the word up. But when I realised what it meant, well, I mean, it's just not my thing. Amy's lovely, but not in that way. You know?'

'Yeah, I know,' Hannah sighed. 'It's a bit of a thing with him. Do you know what the best thing to do is?' Hannah watched as Ruth's eyes widened in anticipation.

'What?'

'Tell him to fuck off, and that he's a dirty pervert. Chances are he'll want to film it for his wank bank and put it on the internet for everyone else's.'

'Oh.'

'I'm not kidding,' Hannah continued with a sharp

laugh. 'Rupert's a dirty little man. He's been going on for years about how I need to release my inner lesbian.' She put her hand on Ruth's shoulder. 'So, just ignore him, okay?' Ruth smiled.

'Okay, thanks.'

'Cool.' Hannah looked at her watch. It was almost two o'clock, and there was a delivery due at the farm between three and four. 'Do you want to come with me to Cost-Co? We need to get some flour.'

Hannah led the way to the barn outside the farmhouse. It was the same as all the buildings on the farm — solid stone walls with a grey slate roof. She pushed the door open to reveal a battered old Land Rover inside.

'Oh, wow,' Ruth said. 'We've got a car?'

'We have now,' Hannah replied with a smile. 'It came with the farm. It's seen better days, but Matthew managed to get it going last night. We'll have to stay on the back roads, though. No road tax or insurance.' She fished in her pocket for the keys. 'Rupert reckons that paying for either would be a betrayal of our principles.'

'But what if we get caught?' Ruth said. Hannah looked at her and realised that the poor girl was nervous. Rupert had been right to leave her out of their plans. *I don't think she's got it in her*, he'd said. *Not yet, anyway.* It looked to Hannah like he'd been spot on.

'If we do, it'll be me who gets in trouble,' Hannah said with a reassuring smile. 'Come on, hop in.'

Hannah managed to get the Land Rover started on the third or fourth try. When the engine did eventually catch, clouds of black smoke billowed out of the exhaust. She put the car in gear and they moved off down the track. Hannah glanced at her watch again.

'Could you get something on the radio, Ruth?'

'Yeah, sure.' Ruth fiddled with the radio, turning the dial to try to find a station. The only station that she was able to find was Canary FM, which was just in the middle of a breaking news story.

'Good afternoon Norfolk,' an excited female voice said. 'We're going to go straight back to the scene of this afternoon's breaking story. Live at Pets 4 You, just near the big Asda in Tuckswood, is our correspondent, Bob Rutler. Bob, what's going on?'

'Thanks Amelia,' the reporter said. 'I'm live at Pets 4 You where there's an ongoing situation developing.' In the background, Hannah could hear raised voices and the occasional scream. She turned to Ruth and smiled.

'Is that the boys?' Ruth asked.

'Yep,' Hannah replied. 'That's the boys. Striking a blow to the heart of the system for animal freedom.' They both turned their attention back to the radio, where Bob was describing the 'scenes of horror' at the pet shop. He had managed to find an eye witness, a teenage girl, who was breathlessly explaining what had happened.

'Well, me and Mum was in there buying some food for Bertie. He's our dog. A dachshund. He's only a puppy, so we have to get him special food and my Dad always complains about how expensive it is.' The girl took a deep breath.

'Jesus, get on with it,' Hannah muttered.

'Then these two blokes ran into the shop. They had like big hankies or something over their faces, and they ran to where the reptiles and that are. One of them tried to get the door off the spiders cages, but they're locked, so they picked up all the cartons of crickets and locusts and stuff, opened them up, and threw them into the air.'

'Oh my goodness,' Bob said. 'Then what happened?'

'Well, everyone started screaming like.' Just as the girl said this, Hannah heard a woman screaming in the background about a cricket in her fucking hair. 'Running around and trying to get away from them. Then the men went to the hamster cages but there was a security guard coming, so they ran away.'

'Bob, Bob, I'm going to have to interrupt you. We're getting reports in of a similar incident at the Pets 4 You up by Longwater Business Park, so it looks like this is a coordinated attack.'

Hannah started laughing. Ruth looked at her uncertainly before joining in.

'What's so funny?' Ruth asked a moment later. 'Why are we laughing?'

'Well, when Rupert told me he was going to strike a blow to the heart of the establishment,' she started chuckling again, 'I was imagining something a bit more dramatic than liberating a load of reptile food.'

12

Andy ran as fast as he could with Matthew only a few feet behind him. When they reached the edge of the business park, they both piled into some bushes and turned to look back at Pets 4 you.

'Well, that went well,' Andy said as he pulled the bandana down from his face. He looked at Matthew excited expression, realising that it matched his own. They were both flushed and breathing hard from the run.

'It was awesome,' Matthew replied before putting out a hand with his fist clenched. Andy looked at it for a second before he realised that, for the first time in his life, he was about to fist bump someone. 'Boom' Matthew said as they touched fists. 'Bloody awesome.' In the distance, Andy could hear sirens.

'We should put a bit more distance between us and the pigs,' Andy said. 'Someone might have seen us hiding in here.'

The two of them pushed their way through the bushes and onto the main road behind the business park.

'It was a shame we couldn't free the other animals, though,' Matthew said as they walked down the road.

'Yeah, but it was a start,' Andy replied. 'Rupert might have got on a bit better, but what we did do was enough to send a message.'

'That was a message, alright,' Matthew said with a laugh. 'Did you see the look on that woman's face when I threw the mealworms at her?'

'She wasn't happy, was she?' Andy laughed as the sound of sirens in the distance grew louder. He looked over his shoulder to see where they were coming from, but couldn't see anything. 'Why don't we cut through the estate to the bus stop on the other side? We can get the number 28 from there and walk back across the field to the farm.'

'Sounds like a plan to me,' Matthew replied.

The two men walked in silence for a few minutes before Matthew continued. 'So Andy, what do you think of that new girl then? Amy, is it?'

'Yeah, that's her name,' Andy said. 'Seems nice enough. Bit posh, but that's not her fault.'

'Rupert seems to like her,' Matthew replied. 'Mind you, that's no surprise. I was talking to Hannah the other night, and she was saying that apparently this new one's minted.' Andy frowned for a few seconds, trying to work out when Matthew had been able to speak to Hannah. They'd been all over the place for the last few days, what with moving into the farmhouse, but Andy couldn't think of a time when Hannah and Matthew had been together.

'When did you speak to her?'

'Er, the other night.'

'Yeah, you said. But when?' Andy asked.

'Oh, I can't remember exactly when. It was just, in passing, like.' Matthew replied. Andy stopped walking and looked at him.

'When you say 'night',' Andy asked, 'do you mean the middle of the night?' Matthew didn't reply, but just looked at Andy with a blank face. 'It's just I got woken up the other night in the tower by someone clumping around. Was that you?'

'No,' Matthew said, looking relieved. 'Wasn't me.' Andy looked at him and although he could tell Matthew was telling the truth, there was something else.

'Was it Hannah?' Andy pressed. From Matthew's expression, Andy knew he'd hit the right spot. 'It was, wasn't it? You dirty bugger.'

'It's not dirty,' Matthew replied. 'It's natural. Rupert says so. Our seed is designed to be sown in as many furrows as possible. That's what he told us in the last Brothers' Group, wasn't it?'

'I'm not convinced that Rupert would be that impressed if he knew you were sowing it in that particular furrow, though,' Andy said, the ghost of a smile on his face as he set off down the footpath.

'You won't say anything, will you?' Matthew said, following him. 'Please? I mean I know Rupert said it's okay, but like you said, he'd be a bit pissed off. Don't you think?'

'Of course I won't say anything. You're only doing what he says. If he doesn't like it, then he shouldn't say it.'

'Besides,' Matthew said, 'you're balls deep in Ruth.'

'Oh, please,' Andy replied, 'that's just crude.'

'Sorry. I meant you're planting the fruit of your loin into the freshly tilled…oh bollocks, there's the bus.' The two of them broke into a run to try to get to the bus stop before the Number 28 did. Andy got to the bus stop first and waved his hand frantically at the bus driver. For a second, he was convinced that the driver was going to carry on and leave them behind, but the miserable looking old bugger behind the wheel stopped the bus with a squeal of air brakes and opened the doors to let them on.

Half an hour later, Andy and Matthew were standing on a deserted country road some miles outside Norwich. Not for the first time, Andy wondered why there was a bus stop here. It was in the middle of nowhere. The farm was probably the closest building to the stop, and even then, it was a good twenty-minute hike away across the fields. The two of them had barely spoken on the bus journey, both of them making the most of the free wi-fi on the bus. The Pets 4 You attacks were listed as 'Breaking News' on the Eastern Daily News website, and they both had a good laugh at an eyewitness account of the carnage that Rupert had caused. According to the website, Rupert had managed to liberate three rabbits and a couple of guinea pigs, but the exact details were still sketchy. They'd had a brief conversation about trying to persuade Rupert to get broadband installed at the farm before agreeing that it was very unlikely, and then returned to their phones to read about the anonymous press release that Hannah had sent in to the paper.

By the time they got to the farmhouse, both men were sweating from the effort of trudging across freshly ploughed fields. Leaving their mud-caked shoes at the door, they walked into the kitchen. The first thing that Andy noticed when he walked in was the mouth-watering smell of freshly baked bread.

'Oh my God,' he said. 'That smells amazing.' Hannah, who had been standing with her back to the door, turned and smiled.

'Thank you,' she said, brushing her hands on the flour-stained apron she was wearing. Andy looked at the trays of fresh loaves that were on top of the cooker.

'Can I have some?' Matthew asked. 'I'm bloody starving after traipsing across those fields.'

'Not yet, no,' Hannah laughed. 'It's still warm. You'll get stomach ache.' She untied the apron, hanging it up on a hook, and sat down next to Ruth at the kitchen table. 'So, it went well then?'

'It was brilliant,' Andy said with a grin. 'Did you see the news coverage?'

'What, in here?' Ruth nodded at the thick stone walls. 'No chance of getting a signal through them.'

'Here, look,' Andy said, sliding his phone across the table. 'I've still got the Eastern Daily News website up.' Ruth picked up Andy's mobile just as the land line on the wall rang, making them all jump. Hannah leapt to her feet and rushed across to pick it up.

'Hello?' she gasped into the receiver. 'Yes, that's me. Who is this?' Hannah asked a few seconds later. Her eyes widened and she looked over at Andy and the others around the table. 'It's the hospital,' she mouthed at them, her hand over the phone. 'What's going on?' she said into the phone, removing her hand. Andy could just hear a woman talking on the other end of the line but he couldn't make out any of the words, so he watched Hannah's expression carefully. At first, she was frowning with her lips pressed together, occasionally barking questions. 'What do you mean, head injury? Is Rupert okay?' As she said the words 'head injury', Andy saw her face darken before it gradually became much lighter as she listened to whatever the other woman was telling her on the phone. By the time she hung up, Hannah was still frowning

'What's going on?' Andy asked. Ruth reached her hand across the table to take his before she asked the same thing. He squeezed her hand in what he hoped was a reassuring gesture.

'Small problem,' Hannah said. 'Rupert's been arrested, and is in hospital.'

'Oh my God,' Ruth said. She let go of Andy's hand and moved her own to cover her mouth. 'Is he okay?'

'Was it the pigs?' Matthew asked. 'Did they do him over?'

'Bloody fascists,' Ruth chimed in. 'That's what's wrong with this country. Police brutality, in a pet shop full of kids.' She slammed her fist down on the table. 'Bastards!'

'No, it wasn't that,' Hannah replied with a mischievous glance at them all, a barely concealed smile on her face. 'There was some sort of incident during the liberation. That's how Rupert got hurt, but the woman from the hospital wouldn't say exactly what had happened. Patient confidentiality, apparently.'

'How come you're laughing if he's been injured?' Matthew asked. 'That's not really funny, is it Hannah?'

'No, you're right,' she replied, not concealing her smile any more. 'But the woman on the phone did say that it was only a minor injury. It was just the way she was talking.' Hannah paused for a second, looking at them all before continuing. 'She couldn't stop laughing.'

13

Emily smoothed out the creases on the trousers of her business suit as she climbed out of her Mini. It was a new suit, one that she'd had had altered and taken in to make her look, in Catherine's words, 'slightly less of a vagetarian'. Emily had never heard the term vagetarian before, so had tried to look it up on her computer at work. The automatic web filtering software had blocked every site with the word, and when she used her phone to look it up instead, Emily could see why. Catherine was getting more creative with ways to tell her that she looked like a lesbian in her business suit. Emily reached back into the car to grab her clipboard and paperwork and made her way over to the pub across the road from where she'd parked. The pub was called The Fat Canary and was a popular watering hole for Norwich City home fans on their way to the ground. Emily drove past the pub all the time, but the only time she ever saw people inside was when there was a home game on, as there would be later that afternoon.

In the concrete slab of a beer garden outside the pub

was a grotty looking trailer with a window cut in the side. Rickety looking piles of bricks at either end of the trailer kept it almost level. Across the top of the window were the words 'Toast With The Most' and as she approached the trailer the smell of toasted sandwiches made her mouth water. Despite the shabby looking trailer, in Emily's opinion, this was the best sandwich van in the county by some distance.

As she approached the trailer, the sweaty, obese man inside it saw her coming and flicked a cigarette into the beer garden. It landed with a shower of sparks before rolling under a table. Emily smirked,

'Emily,' the man called out. 'Emily, is that you?' She raised a hand to greet Sam, the owner of the trailer and the magic recipe behind the sandwiches. He was grey haired, pudgy fingered, and dressed in chequered blue trousers with a substantial gap between them and his white chef's tunic. There was a pale roll of his stomach poking out from the gap, just as there had been for as long as Emily had known him.

'Hey Sam,' Emily said. 'How are you doing?' The trailer wobbled on its bricks as the owner opened the door and climbed down onto the concrete of the beer garden. Emily walked up to him and he grabbed her in a hug, just like he always did. Emily tried to hug him back, but her arms wouldn't reach all the way round so she made do with a couple of pats on his substantial flanks.

Sam let her go and took a step back. 'My God, Emily,' he said. 'You look more beautiful every time I see you.' She looked at Sam, who had to have fifty years on her, and smiled.

'Sure I do, Sam,' Emily said. Sam lifted his head back and laughed, a cackle that rippled through him. Even under the stained apron he was wearing, Emily could see his folds wobbling.

'Emily, Emily, how many times do I have to tell you,' he said, a wide grin on his face. 'All you need to do is say the word, and I will take you away from all this.' He waved an arm round in the general direction of the pub and the beer garden. 'We can run away together, and make a new life for ourselves in Hemsby.' Every time she inspected his trailer, it was the same thing but a different dump that they could run away to.

Almost an hour later, Emily had finished her inspection of the trailer. It normally would have taken half that time, but Sam was one of her favourite customers — if he could be called a customer. He sat on a stool that shouldn't have been able to take his weight and chatted away as she made her way down the checklist. Despite the van's shabby exterior, the inside was spotless and Emily couldn't find a single thing to comment on. Apart from the cigarette that he'd been smoking as she approached that was, but Emily wasn't about to mention that in her report.

'All done, Sam,' Emily said. 'Ten out of ten, as usual.' He put a look of mock disappointment on his face.

'Really?' Sam said. 'There's no need for me to try to bribe you with sexual favours?' Emily laughed, and grabbed the counter to keep her balance as Sam got to his feet.

'Not this time, Sam,' she said as the trailer stopped lurching from side to side. 'Maybe next time, hey?'

'I will hold you to that, young lady,' Sam said. He put his hand on Emily's shoulder and gently pushed her away from the counter. 'Now, watch as I prepare you my latest masterpiece.'

Emily spent the next ten minutes watching Sam put together a toasted sandwich with white granary bread, mozzarella cheese, ham, dijon mustard and at the very last minute, a sprinkling of spring onions. Her stomach grumbled as he put the sandwich under the hot press.

'Why is it that whenever I try to make one of those, they never taste anything like yours?' she asked. 'I use the same ingredients, make them the same way, but they're completely different. No-where near as nice.'

'It's because you don't have the magic touch, Emily,' Sam replied with a smile, 'and that's why you're only a Food Standards Agency inspector and I'm a toasted sandwich God.' He lifted the hot plate and slid the sandwich out, wrapping it in a napkin before handing it to Emily. 'Sit, eat before you fade away to nothing.'

Emily sat on the stool that Sam had been sitting on and tucked into the toasted sandwich while he served a couple of enthusiastic football fans who were way too early for the match that afternoon. The only reason Sam was here was because of the football crowd that would soon be streaming past him to Carrow Road, and Emily had made sure she came down early before he got too busy. It was going to be an important game for Norwich City, as they continued their unlikely journey towards the Champions League, not that Emily was that bothered.

The sandwich was, as Emily knew it would be, amazing. The mozzarella was just the right consistency, the flavour of the mustard and spring onion perfect. Even the bread had exactly the right amount of 'bite'. Emily knew that she would try to make Sam's latest recipe herself at some point, and like all the other times she'd tried to replicate his sandwiches, her version would be a pale imitation.

Sandwich finished, and hunger sated, Emily said goodbye to Sam as she left the trailer. She gave him a peck on the cheek before leaving, promising him his five-star rating from the Agency. His broad smile would stay with her for the rest of the day.

'If I could give you an extra star for that sandwich,' Emily said, 'you know I would.' She was walking back to her car, wondering why all her visits couldn't be like Sam's sandwich trailer, when she felt her phone buzzing in her pocket.

'Hello?' Emily said as she unlocked her car, climbing into the front seat.

'Hi Emily,' the male voice on the end of the line said. 'It's Mr Clayton.' Her boss.

'Hey Mr Clayton. Everything okay?'

'Kind of,' he replied. 'Where are you?'

'Near the football ground. I've just done Toast With The Most.'

'How was it?'

'Oh my God, amazing. Sam's got a new recipe. It's to die for.' Emily said. There was a pause at the other end of the phone.

'The inspection, Emily,' Mr Clayton said. 'Not the food, the inspection.'

'Of course, sorry. Nothing at all to report.'

'Good, good. Is he still parking up outside the Fat Canary?'

'Yep.' Emily ran her tongue over her teeth, searching for any leftovers. She was stuffed, but if Sam gave her another one of those sandwiches, Emily was sure she'd make a fairly big dent in it.

'Excellent. I've got tickets for the match so will try the new recipe out.' There was another pause, this one longer.

'So, er, was there anything else, Mr Clayton?'

'Yes, sorry. Just checking the website to see if the team sheet is out. Could you make your way to Pets 4 You up at

Longwater? There's been some sort of animal liberation protest. Crickets all over the place, apparently.'

'Crickets?'

'Yes.'

'Oh.' Emily said. 'Why do they need us? They should be used to dealing with them, surely?'

'It's not them, it's the Police. They won't let the shop re-open until someone from the Food Standards Agency has given them the all clear.'

'That's a bit strange.'

'Isn't it,' Mr Clayton said. 'But according to the press release the activists sent to the local media, it's the start of some sort of campaign by the bloody idiots. Let me know how you get on.'

'Will do,' Emily said, ending the call and starting the car. She turned on the radio and listened as the excited journalists thrashed whatever mileage they could out of the incident.

'Crickets?' Emily mumbled to herself. 'Whatever next?'

14

Rupert lay back on the hospital trolley in the Accident and Emergency Department. He was at the Norfolk and Norwich Hospital, a large complex on the outskirts of Norwich built as a private finance initiative a few years ago. In Rupert's eyes, this made the entire establishment one step away from a corporate gulag, an opinion that hadn't gone down too well with the doctor who'd been treating him earlier. They'd even made him wear a ridiculous pink hospital gown that wouldn't tie up properly at the back. It was, in Rupert's opinion, just one more way of taking away his individuality and trying to turn him into a faceless drone.

He reached for the call button and pressed the red disc in the centre. In the distance, he could hear a soft but insistent beep, but no-one came rushing to his aid. He pressed the button a few more times, but it didn't make any different to the beeping in the distance. After a few minutes, the curtain that shielded him from the rest of the emergency department swished open a couple of inches and a hard-faced nurse looked in. Her green scrubs were as wrinkled as her skin, and Rupert wouldn't have been surprised if it said 'Benson and Hedges' on her name badge.

'What?' she barked.

'Could I have some pain relief?'

'No.' The curtain was almost closed before Rupert had a chance to respond.

'But I'm in pain,' he said. 'I need something. Just a fentanyl lollipop or some morphine. Please? Something?'

The curtain opened back up and the nurse stepped through. Rupert tried to look as uncomfortable as he could. He even managed a slight moan as she approached his trolley.

'Really?' she said. 'You're in pain?' She didn't look the slightest bit like the nurses on the television. Rupert had caught an episode of *Holby City* on the television the other night while he'd been waiting for his mother to do his washing. At least the ones on the telly looked as if they gave a shit, even if they were only acting.

'I've got a significant head injury.'

'No, you haven't. You fainted when a bunny rabbit bit you, and we put three stitches in your head.'

'I didn't faint, I collapsed from the trauma.'

'That's called a faint.'

'Whatever, but I need some pain relief. Like, now.' He flicked his fingers. 'Come on, chop chop.'

The nurse crossed her arms over a non-existent chest. Rupert realised that even her arms were wrinkled. She smiled, or at least that was what he thought she was doing.

'Okay, we'll sort you out with something. It'll be one of my colleagues though, I'm about to go off shift.'

Fifteen minutes later, Rupert was just about to press the red button again when the curtains were pulled back. The nurse that walked in was quite different to the previous one. For a start, it was a man, and his green scrubs weren't wrinkled in the slightest. Quite the opposite — he looked as if he was about to burst out of them like a health care related version of the Incredible Hulk.

'I hear you need some pain relief?' the male nurse said, pulling the curtain shut behind him. In his other hand, he held a small paper tray. Rupert couldn't see what was on it, as the nurse's enormous hands were covering the contents.

'Yes please,' Rupert said. The nurse put the tray down on the trolley and pulled on a pair of latex gloves. He wiggled his oversized fingers in the air, and to Rupert's surprise, winked at him.

'Sure, no problem,' the nurse replied. 'Now, because you've had a significant head injury, we're a bit limited in terms of pain relief. Oh, and we've run out of needles.' Rupert stared with horror at the white bullet shaped suppository on the paper tray, next to a well-used tube of lubricant with a suspicious brown stain on the side.

'Er,' Rupert said. 'Er, actually, I'm feeling a bit better.' He glanced at the nurse's hands. They were like shovels.

'Roll you over,' the nurse replied with a grin as he flipped the lid off the tube of lubricant. 'This might sting a bit, even with the lube.'

'No, honestly, I'm feeling much better now. Thanks, all the same.' Rupert shuffled down the trolley to the end and hopped off it onto the floor. 'Wow, I feel great.' He pulled the curtain back to make his escape.

'Where do you think you're going, sunshine?' the uniformed policeman on the other side of the curtain said. 'As soon as you've had your medicine and been discharged, we need to have a little chat.'

Rupert looked back at the nurse, who grinned and waved a latex clad hand at him, and then back at the policeman.

'Okay, we can have that chat now. I'm good to be discharged, no need for any medicine really. Waste of taxpayers' money anyway.' Rupert flashed a smile at the male nurse. 'Thanks for the offer, though. I'll just get dressed.' Rupert's backside, exposed through the gap in the hospital gown, clenched involuntarily as a cold breeze blew across his buttocks. He clenched them even tighter as the nurse picked up his tray and took a menacing step toward him.

'Are you sure you don't want to take your medicine?' the nurse looked down at the suppository. Rupert swallowed as the nurse and the policeman exchanged wry smiles.

'Honestly, I'm fine,' he replied.

Almost an hour later, Rupert was at the reception desk in the Accident and Emergency Department. Screwed up in his pocket was a penalty notice for criminal damage that the policeman had issued after a few phone calls to Pets 4 You. Rupert was also eighty-five pounds worse off, thanks to the on the spot fine. One area that the policeman and Rupert had agreed on was that Rupert had got off quite lightly, all things being considered. The manager of Pets 4 You had been advised by his head office not to press charges. They didn't need the bad publicity, and the shop had emptied so quickly after Rupert and Mark had liberated the crickets that by the time the police turned up there were no witnesses. One thing Rupert did learn was that Pets 4 You didn't have working CCTV cameras, which he tucked away for future reference.

'Sorry, excuse me?' Rupert said to the woman behind the reception desk. She turned and fixed him with a hard stare.

'Yes?'

'I need a lift home.'

'Why?'

'Well how else am I going to get home?' Rupert asked with a sigh. The receptionist obviously wasn't going to make this easy for him.

'We don't do transport home I'm afraid. You'll have to get a taxi or a bus.'

'But I haven't got any money. That bastard copper cleaned me out.' The receptionist put her hands on her ample hips and leaned forward. She looked at Rupert over the top of her glasses, and for a few seconds Rupert was back at school, about to be told off by his witch of an English teacher.

'No,' the receptionist said. 'You got yourself here, you'll have to get yourself home.'

'I didn't bring myself here,' Rupert complained. 'I was rushed in by ambulance.'

'Rushed in?' the receptionist laughed. 'I don't think so. Not for a bunny bite you weren't. Now go on, off you trot. I've got work to do.' She turned her back on him, still laughing.

'This is fucking ridiculous,' Rupert said. 'I pay your bloody wages I do. I want transport home, and I want it now.' He emphasised the word 'now' by thumping his fist on her reception desk. She turned to face him, any laughter long gone, and looked at him with a face like thunder.

'What did you just say?' she whispered. The change in her tone made Rupert pause, but it was too late to back down now.

'I know my rights. I'm entitled to a lift home.' Rupert saw her look behind him, and turned to see the policeman was still hanging around the hospital.

'The only thing you're entitled to, sunshine,' the policeman said, 'is a lift to the police station where we can re-negotiate that fixed penalty notice and nick you for criminal damage. I'm more than happy to oblige if you don't fuck off in the next five seconds.' Rupert looked at his expression and realised that he wasn't joking. A range of insults ran through Rupert's head, but he decided to save them for another day. Better to cut his losses.

As he walked toward the door, he could hear the two of them chatting behind him.

'Thanks for that, Donald,' the receptionist said.

'No problem. Do you know what he's got in common with a rabbit?'

'What?'

'Little shit.'

15

Andy got to his feet, wincing as one of his knees popped. He'd been crouched down trying to decipher the instructions to the flat-pack beds that had been delivered to the farmhouse that afternoon. The plan, according to Rupert, was for each of the bedrooms to have bunk beds in, four in each room. That was apart from Rupert's bedroom of course. That would only have one bed in it, a double for him and Hannah.

The bed delivery had been later than expected as the driver had some trouble finding the farm. It wasn't in his sat-nav, he'd tried to explain as Andy and Matthew unloaded the beds. It had taken two of them to carry Rupert and Hannah's bed into their bedroom, but the bunk beds could be carried by a single person. That said a lot about the relative quality of the furniture, but Andy had said nothing at the time. If Rupert wanted a more comfortable bed, that was up to him. After all, he had paid for them.

'What do you think, mate?' Andy turned to see Matthew leaning in the open door of the bedroom.

'Looks bloody complicated to me,' Andy replied. 'Can't make head nor tail of these instructions. Can you?'

'Nope. The fact they're in Chinese doesn't help.'

'Can I have a look?' Andy realised that the new girl, Amy, was standing behind Matthew.

'Hey, Amy,' Andy said. 'I didn't know you were here.' He walked across to her and gave her a hug, as per Rupert's instructions. Always a hug for a new recruit, never just a wave, never just a greeting. Always a hug. 'How are you?'

'Not too bad, thanks,' she replied, tucking a strand of wispy blonde hair behind her ear. 'Rupert suggested I come by to have a look round, maybe have dinner with you all.'

'Fantastic,' Andy replied. 'It's great to see you again.' She gave him a shy smile.

'You too.' Amy walked over to the pile of random looking planks of wood strewn on the floor and picked up the instructions. The minute Andy had tipped the components out of the box, he realised that it was a mistake. Several important looking parts had rolled across the floor. Andy thought he'd found most of them, but there was a nagging doubt at the back of his head that they'd finish putting the beds together only to find a vital component had gone missing. 'There's no such language as Chinese, you know?' Amy said to Matthew.

'Er, okay,' Matthew replied. 'I didn't know that.'

'Mandarin or Cantonese, and a load of different dialects, of course,' Amy said, examining the single sheet of paper that had come with the bunk beds. Andy looked at Matthew, who just shrugged his shoulders in reply.

'Cool,' Andy said, not quite sure what else to say.

'We used to live in Hong Kong,' Amy explained.

'Can you speak Chinese then?' Matthew asked. 'Any of them?'

'Oh God no,' Amy replied with a grin. 'But look,' she pointed at the diagrams on the paper, 'you can just follow the pictures.' Fifteen minutes later, the three of them were looking at a completed bunk bed. In the end, the two men had stood back and let Amy crack on. It was much quicker. By the time she had finished, the room looked a lot more like a proper bedroom even though the only furniture other than the bunk bed was a large full-length mirror on the wall.

'Right, I think I've got that,' Matthew said. 'I'll crack on with the rest in the other room, leave you two to these ones.' He disappeared into the next bedroom and a few seconds later, Andy heard one of the boxes being upended.

'So, how long have you lived with Rupert and the others?' Amy asked as they picked up the next box.

'Only a few months,' Andy replied. 'But I love it here. It's just so, I don't know how to describe it, so important. What we're doing.' There was no reply from Amy at first, so Andy started to open the box.

'I was listening to the radio on the way here from Norwich,' Amy said a few seconds later. 'About the incidents at Pets 4 You.' She paused, and looked at him, biting her bottom lip. It was, Andy thought, a curiously attractive gesture. Amy dropped her voice to a whisper. 'Was that you guys?'

'I'm not supposed to say anything,' Andy said, looking over his shoulder as if he was checking for someone behind him. It didn't matter if there was, this was all part of Rupert's plan. 'But it was us, yes.'

'My God,' Amy gasped. 'I knew it was you lot. Rupert told me he had something planned, and that I should listen to the local news. But I had no idea it was something as exciting as that.' She clapped her hands together. 'What was it like? Were you scared?'

'No more scared than the animals we freed,' Andy said with what he hoped was a grim face. He slowly relaxed it into a smile. 'But that's what I mean about it being important. What we did today, it might have been small scale but it made a difference.' He saw Amy's eyes widen and knew that Rupert's script had hit the mark. 'We've got much bigger things planned as well, as soon as we get the farm off the ground and get some more cash together.' Andy looked down at his lap. 'Look, Amy, I think I've said too much. Please, could you do me a favour and not say anything?' He gave her his best hangdog expression. 'It's just that I think you'd fit in really well here, but it's not up to me.'

Amy didn't reply, but turned her attention back to the planks of wood they were supposed to be turning into a bed. They worked in silence for a few minutes, Amy giving Andy the occasional reassuring smile. Before long they had another bunk bed in front of them, and they started on the next one. Andy made sure that he kept touching Amy, like Rupert had told him to. The occasional brush of a hand against hers, nothing overt, and certainly nothing that could be construed as sexual. Rupert had been quite clear on that.

When the beds were complete, Andy and Amy lifted one of the bunks on top of another one. They wriggled the upper bunk back and forth until the grooves in the wood matched up.

'So how is this one supposed to be secured then?' Andy asked. 'Shouldn't it be latched on somehow?' Amy picked up the instructions and examined them.

'Not sure. Is there a bit missing?' she said, peering at the join between the upper bunk and the lower one. 'It looks like there should be something here to secure the top bed.' Andy stood next to her and peered at the instructions over her shoulder. The smell of her shampoo was familiar, and it reminded him of the other world just for an instant.

'Possibly,' he said. It was time to move to the next stage of Rupert's plan, the 'acquiescence test' as he called it. Andy plucked the instructions out of Amy's hand and let the paper flutter to the floor. 'Amy, can I trust you?' He took her hands in his and moved until he was standing directly in front of her. 'Please don't say anything about what I told you. It's not my place, but I could see you here with us.'

'Of course you can trust me, Andy,' Amy replied in a whisper. She squeezed his hands, looking directly into his eyes. If Rupert was right, then this would be when Amy kissed him. If she didn't, then he was supposed to kiss her. Amy reached up on tip-toes and leaned her face toward Andy. He resisted the temptation to lick his lips and closed his eyes, looking forward to the next bit, only to be disappointed when he felt her lips brush his cheek. It wasn't quite the kiss that Andy had been hoping for, but he supposed in a sense Rupert had got it right.

16

Hannah swore under her breath as she turned the ignition key for the fourth time. The engine of the Land Rover they'd inherited rattled, coughed, blew some acrid smoke out of the exhaust, and then died.

'Oh, for fuck's sake,' she said, this time out loud. Hannah pumped the accelerator pedal a couple of times like Matthew had told her to do, and tried again. This time, the engine caught and burst into life. The smell of thick exhaust fumes overpowered the aroma of freshly baked bread inside the car, so she put the Land Rover into gear and pulled out of the barn. The last thing she wanted was to turn up at the customer's house with a bunch of loaves that stunk of diesel. He wasn't really a customer, at least not yet, but he could become one. Hannah had been given strict instructions to do everything within her power to turn him into a paying customer, which in Rupert-speak meant pretty much anything.

In the back of the Land Rover were twenty-five loaves of bread, baked earlier this morning. Rupert had gone on about the significance of five loaves, times five, but it had been lost on Hannah. As far as she was concerned, it was bread. Her plans for the morning were to deliver the order to the customer, and then head to a farmer's market near Diss. On the passenger seat next to her was a shopping list that Rupert had put together, but she was going to take the list with a pinch of salt. She was the baker, not Rupert.

Last night had been the group's first full night in the farm. Andy and Matthew had put the bunk beds together, and Rupert and Hannah had assembled their own bed. Hannah had to admit that it was luxurious to say the least, and they had tested it out quite extensively before deciding that it met their needs. Hannah wasn't quite sure how the layout of the farm would fit with her extra-curricular activities when Rupert was asleep, but there was plenty of time to work that one out. What didn't help was that the door to Hannah and Rupert's bedroom had hinges from a horror film. There was no chance of her being able to sneak out at night until she'd managed to get her hands on some WD40.

Hannah hummed to herself as she followed the sat-nav on her phone to the customer's house. She got lost a couple of times in the warren of streets in the estate he lived in, but she found it in the end. After parking on the street outside his house, she walked down the path and knocked on the door. She was just about to knock again when the door opened, and a large grey-haired man peered out at her.

'Hi,' Hannah said, injecting a bright note into her voice. 'I've got some bread for you.'

'Well, hello,' the man said. 'You must be Hannah, then. Come on in.' He turned and walked back into the house. Hannah looked at the size of him and decided that this customer wouldn't be getting any special treatment. It wasn't just his age — it was the size of the man as well.

She shuddered at the thought of offering him any sort of inducement to become a customer, no matter what Rupert said. If Rupert was that desperate, he could come round and give Sam a cheeky tug himself.

'I'm Sam, by the way,' the grey-haired man called over his shoulder. 'I think we spoke on the phone. Can I interest you in a toasted sandwich? I'm trying out a new recipe and could do with a second opinion.'

'That sounds great, thank you.'

'In fact,' Sam said, turning around. 'Why don't we use one of your loaves? You could be the first to try the new recipe with some of your own bread.'

'Okay,' Hannah replied. 'What's in it?'

'Well, there's the usual ingredients for a toastie,' Sam said with a smile. Hannah looked at his enthusiastic expression and warmed to the man. 'Bread and butter, for example.' His smile widened. 'Plus some cheese, onion, a few secret ingredients. Are you one of those vegetarian types? I mean, don't take this the wrong way, but you look like you might be. Because I can leave the breaded ham out' Hannah wondered exactly what a vegetarian was supposed to look like, and from the look on his face, Sam realised he might have offended her. 'Sorry, that sounded wrong. I hope I've not said the wrong thing?'

'Not at all,' Hannah replied. She paused for a few seconds, wondering what to say next. Technically, she was a vegan. At least, that's what Rupert thought. What he didn't know was that Hannah wasn't quite as strict as he wanted her to be. It had started off with the odd Baby Bell cheese here and there, just as a special treat, and then gradually become a regular thing. Meat she could do without, but dairy products were something else altogether. No animals died producing milk, after all. 'I am vegetarian, yes,' she said, 'but anything else is fine by me.'

Sam smiled, his grin lighting up his whole face, and Hannah couldn't help but smile as well.

'Excellent,' Sam said. 'I've got some ridiculously tasty mature cheddar from one of the local farms. It really is to die for. Do you want a hand with the bread?'

After they had carried the bread into the kitchen, Hannah sat nursing a cup of tea and watched him bustle around his kitchen as he prepared a couple of toasted sandwiches. They'd put the loaves onto his kitchen table, and he'd carefully selected a loaf from the batch after prodding and squeezing several of them.

'This one,' he'd said as he chose a loaf, 'will be ideal for what I have in mind. A perfect loaf for a perfect woman.' Sam had winked at Hannah as he'd said this, but there was nothing untoward in it at all. He'd given her a running commentary as he'd prepared the sandwiches and a few moments later, Hannah was looking at the most amazing sandwich on a plate in front of her. The bread — her bread — was lightly browned, and melted cheese was bubbling onto the plate. Hannah's mouth started watering as she picked it up. She took a large bite of the sandwich, and then squealed as a molten blob of cheese fell onto her chin.

'Oh, my goodness,' Sam said as he rushed over to her with a tea towel. He dabbed at the cheese, wiping it off. 'I'm so sorry,' he exclaimed as Hannah tried to eat the scalding hot mouthful of sandwich as quickly as she could. Partly because it was so hot, but mostly because it tasted amazing.

'No, no, my fault entirely,' she said when she'd swallowed the last piece. It burned her throat on its way down, but that didn't detract from the taste. 'That is an amazing sandwich, Sam.'

'You're a sweetie, you are,' Sam replied, a broad grin

on his face. 'I could really fall for someone like you.' Hannah returned the smile as she took another bite.

The two of them sat in silence for a few moments, both concentrating on their sandwiches. Hannah noticed Sam frown a couple of times as he was eating, and when he had finished, he jotted down a couple of notes in a dog-eared notebook.

'Just slightly too much mayo, I think,' he said, closing the notebook with a flourish and brushing crumbs from the folds of his stomach.

'Not at all,' Hannah replied. She'd not even noticed there was mayonnaise in the sandwich. 'I think it was perfect. So, er, what did you think about the bread?'

'Oh my goodness, I never even noticed the bread,' Sam replied. Hannah's face fell. Was it that bad? 'If you don't even notice the bread, then it's superb. You only pick up on it if there's something wrong.' He laughed, sending a shower of crumbs that he'd missed to the floor. 'So, to answer your question, the bread is ideal. How much can you supply?'

Hannah's face broke into a broad smile. That wasn't what she'd been expecting him to say at all.

'How much do you need?'

17

The harsh ringing of her mobile phone woke Emily up with a start. At first, she thought she'd forgotten to turn her alarm off — although it was only Thursday she'd taken the day off — but when she realised it was someone ringing her, she slapped her hand on her bedside table to find the phone.

'For God's sake,' she muttered as she squinted at the screen, prodding at the phone to answer the call. 'What?' she barked, wincing as the effort sent a sharp jolt of pain through her head. Bit too much wine last night, then.

'Hey Emily,' a familiar voice came down the line. 'How're you doing?'

'Well, up until about twenty seconds ago, I was doing absolutely fine and sleeping like a baby.' She manoeuvred herself up onto one elbow and reached out for a glass of water from the bedside table with her spare hand. 'Then some wanker phoned me up.' Emily took a large gulp from the glass. At least she hadn't been that pissed when she'd gone to bed that she'd forgotten her water.

'Oooh, someone's tired.'

'Er yeah, that's kind of my whole point, Gary. What do you want, anyway?'

Gary worked in the laboratory at the Food Standards Agency, and when Emily had first met him, she'd been convinced for a while that he was the one for her. The only problem with that scenario was that Emily wasn't a man.

'That's nice, Emily,' Gary said. 'I only phoned up to make sure you'd not topped yourself in a fit of sexual frustration.'

'Oh God, don't you start.' Despite her headache, Emily smiled. 'Have you been talking to Catherine?'

'I don't need to,' Gary said. From the sound of his voice, he was smiling as well. 'Listen, what are you up to today? There's someone I want you to meet.'

'Sorry Gary, I've taken a day's leave because I'm meeting Benedict Cumberbatch for lunch, and he's taking me to a new sadomasochism dungeon on Yarmouth seafront. It's quite the place to be seen, apparently.'

'Cool. I'll be round in half an hour. Put the kettle on.' Emily groaned as she heard the dial tone. She shuffled to the edge of the bed and got to her feet, stretching her arms above her head before walking over to the mirror in the corner of the room.

'God, you look like shit,' she said to her reflection. There was no reply.

Emily made her way into the kitchen, ignoring the two empty bottles of white wine in the sink. She'd tried to binge watch the latest season of *Game of Thrones* last night, but ended up getting pissed off at the amount of sex that everyone was having and settled for back to back episodes of *Police Interceptors* instead, before finally wandering off to bed when all the wine was finished. Even two bottles hadn't stopped a filthy dream about Constable Tom Dickens, who'd been an interceptor for three years and, according to her dream, knew his way round a set of handcuffs in a way they hadn't shown on the programme.

She flicked the switch on the kettle and went for a pee while it boiled. Her flatmate's bedroom door was half open. The bed wasn't slept in so Catherine hadn't come home yet again. Emily yawned as she gathered a couple of mugs together. At least Catherine paid her share of the rent, regardless of how many nights she actually spent in the flat.

Half an hour later, almost to the minute, the doorbell rang. Emily had thrown some clothes on, but not bothered with doing anything with her hair and face. She opened the door to Gary who, as usual, looked as if he'd just walked in from a fashion shoot.

'Emily,' he said as he air kissed her cheek. 'You look, er,' he took a step back and regarded her, 'tired.'

'Yeah, thanks Gary,' Emily replied. 'Come on in. Nice to see you, too.' She waved in the general direction of the kitchen, even though Gary knew where it was. 'Kettle's just boiled.'

The two of them sat either side of the kitchen table. Emily cupped her hands around the mug of tea and looked at Gary.

'Catherine not in, then?' he asked.

'Nope.'

'She went out last night I take it.'

'Yep.'

"Christ, you're hard work this morning.' Gary smiled, and Emily looked at his straight white teeth. He didn't even have the decency to have one slightly crooked tooth.

'Sorry, I'm tired. I was planning a lie in, but some

bastard woke me up.' Gary's teeth got even whiter as his smile broadened.

'Yeah, but come on,' he said. 'We've both got the day off and the sun's shining. The whole day is ahead of us like an uncharted sea of sexual mystery.'

'Oh, for God's sake, Gary,' Emily sighed. 'You have been talking to Catherine, haven't you?'

'Might have been,' he replied. 'I bumped into her in the Loft last weekend, and we had a bit of a chat.' Emily frowned. The Loft was one of Norwich's livelier gay clubs. Not Catherine's normal hunting grounds by a long stretch of the imagination. 'Anyway, that doesn't matter. There's a bloke I want you to meet.'

'Gary, I don't want to meet anyone. How many times do we have to go over this?'

'How long has it been, Emily? Since he dumped you?'

'Few months. Since Ibiza.'

'So you need to get out and about a bit. This guy I know, Robin. He's a really nice bloke. Good looking, funny, decent job.'

'No, Gary.'

'Just come for lunch with me and a few of the boys. He'll be there.' Gary fixed Emily with his baby blue eyes. Emily was just about to make a comment about running out of dog biscuits, when Gary reached across the table and took her hand. 'Emily, it's just lunch. That's all. You can meet the man, see if there's anything there. Can't you?' His eyes bored into her, and Emily felt her resolve weaken. Since she'd found out Gary was gay, they'd become best friends of sorts, but the truth was that she still fancied him a tiny bit. Emily knew that Gary knew this, courtesy of an evening when she'd had far more wine than she'd had last night and been far more honest than she would have been if she was sober. Not that the conversation had led to what her wine-fuddled brain had hoped it might have done. Emily sighed, knowing she was cornered.

'Alright then. What time?'

'Might as well head out when you're ready,' Gary replied. 'I'm guessing it'll take you a while to sort yourself out and get changed. I'll make us another cup of tea while you get ready, and we'll head into the city then.'

Emily left him fussing at the sink, and went back into her bedroom to get changed. She had been planning on wearing the clothes she had on for the day, but she supposed she'd better make a bit of an effort. She changed quickly, throwing on something slightly more feminine, and spent twenty minutes or so putting her make-up on.

'He'd better be bloody worth it,' Emily muttered to herself as she widened her eyes to put some mascara on.

'How do you know this Robin bloke, anyway?' Emily asked Gary as they sat in his car half an hour later, stuck in a traffic jam that was mostly full of families heading for an exciting day out at the Castle Mall.

'Just from around, that's all. He's a good guy.'

'So you keep saying.' Emily regarded Gary, whose attention was fixed on the brake lights of the car in front of them. 'Is he gay?'

'What?' Gary glanced across at her. 'No. Why would you ask that?'

'Would you sleep with him? If he was gay?'

'Well he's not, so that's a stupid question.' Emily saw Gary's knuckles whiten ever so slightly on the steering wheel.

'Is he a bit gay?' Emily pressed.

'He's not gay.'

'Not even a little bit?'

'He might be a little bit, er,' Gary flashed a quick look at Emily, 'ambidextrous?' She examined one of her cuticles with a critical eye while they sat in an awkward silence.

'You've slept with him, haven't you?' Emily asked, her eyes fixed on the traffic jam in front of them. They'd not moved for at least five minutes, and from the look of it, wouldn't be any time soon.

'Er…'

'I'm getting out here.' Emily unclipped her seatbelt and opened the passenger door. She turned to look at Gary, fixing him with a fierce stare. 'I love you to bits Gary, but you can be an utter bastard sometimes.'

Emily tried to slam the car door behind her, but the only damage she managed to do was to break a fingernail.

'For fuck's sake,' she muttered as she sucked her finger and walked in the opposite direction to the traffic jam.

18

By the time Rupert got off the bus at the stop closest to the farm, it was almost dark. He had a blinding headache, not helped by the stitches in his head which were starting to itch like mad. As he walked across the fields toward the faint light of the farmhouse, he muttered to himself and practised what he planned to say to the others about what had happened today. Come what may, he was going to come out of it as a hero. A war hero with the battle scars to prove it.

His priorities when he got to the farm were to revel in the glory of his achievements, have a stiff drink, and skin up a rather fat joint with some of the Lebanese cannabis resin he'd managed to get his hands on earlier in the week. It tasted of diesel, but did the job nicely. As he swore under his breath at the amount of mud that was sticking to his shoes, his thoughts drifted to Amy, the new girl. He was hoping that she'd spent the afternoon at the farm while he and the others had been wreaking havoc in Norwich, and was still there now. Rupert's plan was to walk into the farmhouse like a wounded but battle-hardened veteran coming in from the fields of Agincourt or Waterloo, admired by the men and lusted after by the women. The men would want to be him, and the women would want to be with him. Especially Amy. That was the plan, at least.

By the time he got to the farm, his priorities had changed a bit. Number one on his list was to get the hell out of his mud-caked, soaking wet shoes. Number two was a hot bath to warm up, perhaps combined with the drink and joint. Rupert kicked as much of the mud from his shoes as he could at the front door, and pushed it open. The heat from the inside was like a wall, and the smell of cannabis and baked bread intoxicating.

'Hey, how are you all doing?' Rupert said as he walked into the kitchen. He glanced around to see who was there. Hannah was at the far end of the table. Andy was there, a can of beer half raised to his mouth, and Matthew was puffing away at a roll up. The only people Rupert couldn't see were Ruth or the new girl, Amy.

'Rupert, are you okay?' Hannah got to her feet and walked across to him. 'The woman from the hospital said that you'd been hurt? I would have come and got you but the bloody Land Rover wouldn't start.'

'No worries, it's nothing really,' Rupert replied, putting his bandaged hand to his head to make sure everyone saw the injuries. 'Just a few scratches.' The look on Hannah's face was pure concern.

'What happened?' she asked.

'Fucking pigs. Got right into it with them, I did,' Rupert said. 'Fascist bastards, the lot of them. I managed to take a few down before they piled in though.' Just as Rupert said this, he saw Amy appear in the door to the kitchen. Her mouth was half open in an 'oh' shape, and her eyes widened as he carried on. 'Ended up being rushed to hospital with a nasty head injury. Bloody truncheon. I was squaring up to three of the bastards when another one got behind me and clubbed me down. Not exactly a fair fight.' Rupert saw Amy's eyes widen even more. 'But at the end of the day, there's a bunch of animals in Norfolk tonight who are now free. That's what counts.' He fixed Amy with his trademark stare. 'Not my injuries. They're inconsequential, and they're scars I'll gladly bear for their freedom.'

'Oh my goodness,' Amy gasped. She walked into the kitchen and across to Rupert. 'That looks really nasty.' She raised a hand to Rupert's head and touched the bandage covering his stitches. 'Does it hurt?'

'It's nothing,' Rupert replied with what he hoped was a winning smile. He turned his attention to Andy and Matthew, looking at each of them in turn. 'How did you boys get on?'

'Yep, all good,' Andy replied. 'Got in there, got the job done, and got out. We were lucky though. How come the police got to you so quickly?'

'There's a new doughnut shop that's opened up on the business park. I didn't know but there were two police cars sitting outside it,' Rupert explained. He paused, waiting for Andy or Matthew to ask the obvious question about why he'd not seen the police cars, but they read his expression the way Rupert wanted them to and kept silent. 'Right, I'm going to jump in the bath and then we can all have a catch up.'

Rupert was laying in the bath a few minutes later, covered in foam bubbles up to his chin, when there was a delicate knock at the bathroom door.

'It's open,' he called out. The door opened, and Amy's head appeared. Perfect. 'Come on in, Amy,' Rupert said. 'Don't stand on ceremony.' She walked in and looked around for a few seconds before closing the lid to the toilet and sitting down.

'Hannah asked me to bring you in this,' she said, holding out a joint. It wasn't as fat as it would have been if Rupert had rolled it himself, but one thing Hannah was very good at was skinning up.

'Excellent,' Rupert said. 'Would you mind lighting it up? I think we should share it.' Amy smiled.

'It's been a long time since I've had one of these,' she said as she fished in her jean pockets for a lighter, 'but I was hoping you might say that.' She lit the joint and inhaled deeply, brushing a few sparks that fell from the end off her jeans. Careful not to disturb the glass of single malt that was balanced on the edge of the bath, Rupert manoeuvred himself into a sitting position and watched her take in another deep lungful of smoke before coughing and passing the joint over to him.

They sat in silence for a few moments, enjoying the spliff. When it was finished, Amy stood and flicked the butt out of the half open bathroom window. She had to kneel on the toilet seat to reach the window, and the view of her backside this gave Rupert was, in his opinion, rather nice.

'Oh gosh, I feel a bit dizzy now,' Amy said, sitting back down with a deep breath. 'Can I stay here for a moment?'

'It's only a head rush,' Rupert replied, 'and you can stay as long as you want.' He looked at her, widening his blue eyes to give her the full effect of them. Amy's eyes were dark, the pale green irises almost hidden completely by her dilated pupils. She returned his gaze, not looking away, not even blinking. 'You like it here, don't you?'

'I love it here,' she whispered. 'It just feels so comfortable.'

'You can be whoever you really are here, Amy,' Rupert said, keeping his voice low and in a monotone. 'You can do whatever you want, be with whoever you want to be with. Without guilt, without consequence. That's how we live here.' The ghost of a smile played across Amy's lips.

'Really?' she said, closing her eyes. 'That sounds nice.'

'Why don't you stay here tonight, Amy? Relax with us for the evening.'

'I've not slept in a bunk bed since I was a child,' Amy replied with a smile.

'You wouldn't have to sleep in a bunk bed,' Rupert said. If it was up to him, and his headache stayed away, she wouldn't be sleeping much at all.

'But Hannah…?' Amy said, her voice so faint Rupert hardly heard her. 'What about Hannah?' For a second, Rupert thought about suggesting that Hannah joined in with them, but he knew he would have to at least discuss it with her first. Just because she'd said no in the past didn't mean that tonight, with Amy's lithe body on offer, Hannah would say no this evening. Although, Rupert reflected, she almost certainly would.

'Hannah will be fine,' he replied. 'It's what she wants for you, Amy. She thinks it's what you need to be able to start letting go and becoming yourself.' Rupert knew he was stretching the truth a fair bit with that last statement, but Hannah wasn't in the bathroom with them. He looked at Amy, and saw her smile return. It was a different smile now though, an impish one that changed her whole face. She kept her eyes closed as she spoke.

'Maybe.' Amy opened her eyes and glanced across at Rupert before getting to her feet. 'I'd better go and join the others, anyway. I'll see you later.' She held his eyes for a few seconds longer than necessary, and Rupert knew that there was no 'maybe' about it.

As Amy closed the door behind her, Rupert reached for his flannel and shower gel. He squirted a large dollop of the gel onto the flannel and muttered to himself.

'Better give my bits an extra scrub then.'

19

Andy nudged Matthew's foot under the table as Amy came back into the room. She'd been gone for about ten minutes — not enough time for her and Rupert to get up to much in the bathroom — but she had a smile on her face like a cat that had got the cream.

'Look at her,' Andy whispered, his hand half covering his mouth. 'She's off her tits.' Matthew started laughing but stopped when he saw Hannah glaring at him. Amy walked past them all without a word, opened the front door, and stepped outside. She closed it behind her as if she was doing it in slow motion. The three of them waited for what felt to Andy like ages until they heard the latch click.

'Bloody hell, did you see the state of her?' Hannah said, starting to laugh herself. 'I didn't think I'd put that much dope into the joint.'

'Maybe she's just sensitive?' Matthew said.

'She'll be sensitive later on if Rupert has his way. I guess that's me in a bunk bed tonight, then.' Hannah walked over to the other side of the kitchen and started messing about with saucepans. The effort she put into banging them into each other spoke volumes.

'Listen, mate,' Matthew said in a low voice. 'You're boning Ruth, right?'

'I don't know if I'd use the word 'boning', Matthew,' Andy replied. 'I certainly wouldn't if she was here.'

'Alright, princess,' Matthew said. 'But you are, aren't you? I was just thinking, how about if you and Ruth stay in one bedroom tonight, and me and Hannah can stay in the other one. Assuming Rupert is going to show Amy a shortcut to heaven, that is.'

'Right,' Andy said after a long pause. 'Could do, I guess. Do you think Rupert will be alright with that?'

'I don't really think he's in a position to say anything, is he?' Matthew replied. 'Can you imagine it. "Hannah, I'm going to shag Amy tonight in our bed so you can bugger off. By the way, don't shag anyone else while I'm busy." Besides, if he thinks we're swapping rooms so you can do likewise to Ruth, he might not even realise.' Andy started laughing, partly at the earnest expression on Matthew's face and partly at the thought of the conversation.

'I don't think he's that stupid, Matthew.'

'I think he probably is,' Hannah called from the other side of the kitchen. 'Sounds like a good plan to me, though. I'm fed up with sneaking about, and if he wants to have his cake and eat it, then so do I.' She turned and winked at Matthew, whose cheeks started colouring.

'Bloody hell, you've got good hearing, Hannah,' Andy said. He got to his feet. 'Where is Ruth, anyway?'

'She's down in the sheds,' Hannah replied. 'I bought a load of rye seed at the Farmer's Market earlier. She's transferring it into tubs for me to keep it dry.'

'I'm going to go and give her a hand, then,' Andy said,

crossing to the front door. 'I'll make sure Amy's okay
as well.'

He walked through the door, hearing Hannah and
Matthew laughing as he did so. As he inched it shut, he
looked around for Amy. At first he couldn't see her in the
dark, but as his eyes adjusted he could see her standing by
the barn with her arms folded, staring up at the sky.

'Are you okay, Amy?' he called out. She didn't reply,
but raised a hand and gave him a brief wave, still staring
up at the sky. Andy left her to it and set off toward
the sheds.

It was a clear night, not a cloud to be seen. Andy
looked up at the sky a couple of times as he made his way
down the track, careful not to fall into any potholes as he
did so. He couldn't blame Amy for staring at the stars,
whether she'd been smoking something or not. There must
have been millions of them twinkling away up there. When
he got to the sheds a few moments later, he'd managed to
find the plough and the pole star. It was the extent of his
astronomical knowledge, but he was pleased with himself
anyway. Andy pushed open the door of the only shed with
a light on.

'Ruth? You in here?' There was no reply. Andy looked
around the inside of the shed. He'd had an unpleasant
experience in one of these sheds before, but he was determined not to let it get to him. Andy was just about to leave,
figuring that Ruth must be somewhere else, when he saw
her in the corner of the room. She was hunched over and
using a trowel to shovel seed from an industrial size bag
into large white tubs. White trailing wires from her ears
explained why she'd not heard him, so he walked across
and put a hand on her shoulder.

Ruth screamed, turning and slashing out at Andy with

the trowel. It whistled in front of his face, and he took a step backward and put his hands out in front of him.

'Jesus Christ, you scared the shit out of me,' Ruth gasped, pulling the headphones from her ears. 'I didn't get you, did I?'

'No, almost but not quite,' Andy laughed. 'Do you want a hand?'

'There's only one trowel, and I'm pretty much done anyway, Cheers, though. So, what's going on?'

'Looks like tonight's the night for Amy and Rupert. She's shit-faced, and Hannah and Matthew have commandeered one of the bedrooms to give them some space. So it's you and me in the other one. I'm bagging the top bunk though.'

'Fine by me,' Ruth laughed, her thin face angular in the fluorescent light. 'Do you want me to walk like I've had two hip replacements in the morning?'

'No, you're good,' Andy replied. 'Just smile at me a lot over breakfast.' Ruth giggled and turned back to the rye seed. A few moments later, she was done shovelling and the two of them started walking back down the track toward the farmhouse.

'The stars are amazing, aren't they?' Andy said as he steered Ruth around what he thought was a particularly deep pothole. He pointed up at the sky. 'Look, there's the plough. That way's north.'

'Wow,' Ruth replied. 'You're quite the Bear Grylls, aren't you?' She paused for a few seconds before continuing. 'So, who is she then?'

'Sorry, who is who?'

'Whoever you're carrying a candle for,' Ruth said. A statement, not a question. 'The one in the photo you keep at the bottom of your underwear drawer.'

'Why were you in my underwear drawer?' Andy replied, not able to think of anything else to say.

'I needed socks and yours are nicer than mine anyway. She's very pretty.' Ruth was right, Andy thought with an unexpected pang of sadness. He said nothing in reply. A moment later, Ruth continued. 'If you don't want to talk about her, that's fine.'

'I don't,' Andy replied with what he hoped was an air of finality. He didn't want to talk about the girl in the photo, at least not with Ruth.

They walked on in silence for a few moments before Andy continued. 'Can I ask you a question?'

'Fire away.'

'What's your take on uncomplicated sex?'

'How do you mean?' Ruth stopped walking and turned to look at Andy. 'Is that an offer?'

'No,' Andy replied. 'You know it's not. I was just wondering what your take on it was. I mean, all the others are well into it, so how come we don't seem to be?' Andy watched as Ruth chewed her bottom lip.

'It's what separates us from the animals.'

'You might have to explain that to me,' Andy replied. Ruth glanced up at the stars.

'Well sex is only fun if it's complicated. Don't you think?' Andy didn't have an answer to that one.

Hannah banged the last saucepan a bit harder on the counter than she'd intended to, breaking the handle and putting a dent in the side. She swore under her breath before shoving it in the cupboard. As well as the one with the broken handle, a fair few of the other pans had new dents in them.

'Hey, you okay?' Matthew said in her ear. Hannah jumped. She'd not heard him coming up behind her.

'Yeah, I'm cool,' she replied. 'Just a bit pissed off with Rupert, that's all.'

'But he's only doing what you're doing. And you're only doing what he's doing because he says it's okay.' Hannah paused for a few seconds to process what Matthew meant.

'It's not that, Matthew,' she replied, turning to look at him. 'It's just a bit, I don't know, predatory? I'm sleeping with you because I want to sleep with you. Amy will be sleeping with Rupert because Rupert wants her to. There's a difference.' From the look on Matthew's face, he couldn't see that there was. She flapped her hand at him. 'Never mind. Rupert's all about the conquest. He enjoys climbing the mountain, not the view when you get to the top.'

'Hannah, I haven't got a clue what you're talking about,' Matthew said with a frown. 'What mountain?'

'I know you haven't got a clue, Matthew,' Hannah said, taking a step forward so that she was only inches away from him. 'That's why I like you,' she whispered in his ear, her hand drifting to his crotch. 'I'm not interested in your mind, I'm interested in your —'

Matthew took a rapid step back as the kitchen door opened and Rupert, dressed in a pair of baggy shorts and wife-beater vest, walked in. He had a sheen of perspiration on his forehead, and beads of water dripped from the end of his blonde dreadlocks onto the stone floor.

'Put him down, Hannah,' Rupert said. 'You don't know where he's been.' Hannah fought the urge to laugh at the look on Matthew's face. Even though he'd been with the group for a few months now, he still clung onto some of his old ways.

'I know exactly where he's been,' Hannah retorted.

Rupert walked over to the table, grabbing a tobacco tin from the kitchen counter as he did so. He scraped one of the heavy wooden chairs from under the table and perched on it.

'Where're the others?' he asked, popping the lid of the tobacco tin and picking out some roll-up papers and a cigarette. With the tip of his tongue, he moistened the seam on the paper of the cigarette and unzipped it, emptying the tobacco onto the kitchen table.

'Andy and Ruth are in one of the sheds,' Hannah said, 'and Amy's outside somewhere.'

'Is she okay?'

'She's off her face.'

'Excellent,' Rupert said. He turned to Matthew. 'Mate,

could you see if you can round them up? We've got a lot to discuss.' Matthew didn't reply, but just walked to the kitchen door. When he'd gone, Hannah sat opposite Rupert at the table.

'Pass the tin over,' she said. 'I'll give you a hand. Might as well put a few together. It could be a long night.' Rupert grinned at her as he slid the tobacco tin across the table.

'I hope so.'

Twenty minutes later, all five of them were sitting around the kitchen table passing a joint between them. The only one who didn't actually smoke any of it was Andy. Hannah watched him regard the spliff with curiosity as he passed it from her fingers to Amy's. He'd told the group not long after he'd joined that it just wasn't his thing, which was fine with everyone except Rupert. Andy's mind wouldn't be opened enough, according to Rupert, if he didn't get off his head on a regular basis. Hannah had spoken to Andy about it later, and it turned out he didn't give a shit what Rupert thought so that was that.

'Right then,' Rupert said, worrying at the stitches in his head with a freshly bandaged hand. 'Today went well, I thought. We struck a blow, just not as hard as we needed to have done.'

'It was a pet shop though,' Hannah replied. 'Limited opportunities, don't you think?'

'Yes, Hannah,' Rupert said through a cloud of grey-blue smoke. 'But it was a start. It put us on the map.'

'You got off lightly though, mate,' Matthew said, handing the spliff over to Ruth who took it with wide eyes.

'What do you mean? You call these injuries getting off lightly?' Rupert replied with a snarl, gesturing at his head.

'No, not the injuries. I mean getting off with a fixed penalty after fighting with all those policemen.'

'Maybe they knew that they were in the wrong?' Amy piped up. The others all turned to look at her. They were the first words she'd said since walking out of the kitchen earlier. 'And that they'd beaten up an innocent man.'

'See, she gets it,' Rupert said, smiling and pointing the remains of the joint toward Amy. 'Thank you.' Hannah looked at the way they smiled at each other, and spent the next few seconds wondering what it would be like to punch Amy hard in the face. Her thoughts were interrupted by Andy saying something.

'Er, sorry, Rupert?' Andy said.

'What?'

'You've got your foot between my legs.'

'Oh,' Rupert said, adjusting his position on the chair. 'Sorry.' A few seconds later, Amy's smile broadened and Hannah was back to imagining punching her. Her daydream was just extending to putting some more dents in the saucepans — Amy shaped dents — when she realised Rupert was talking to her.

'Miles away. What?' she said, shelving the daydream for later.

'We need some new targets. Any ideas?'

They spent the next thirty minutes or so swapping ideas for what Rupert had termed 'freedom activities'. The only common goal was that by the end of the activity, some animals had to be freed. Andy had been dispatched to fetch a notepad, on the basis that the rest of them had been chain smoking joints, and take some notes. Ruth had padded off after him, but the two of them weren't gone for long. That meant one of two things in Hannah's mind. Either Andy was very quick off the mark, or there wasn't actually anything going on between the two of them, no matter how much they pretended there was.

'What've we got, handy Andy?' Rupert said when Andy and Ruth had settled back into their chairs. Hannah knew from experience that Rupert was making a concerted effort not to slur his words. She glanced across at Amy, who looked just as stoned. Wild night ahead, then.

'Top of the list is the vivisection laboratory at the University,' Andy read from his notebook. 'Then we've got battery hen farms. Plenty of them in Norfolk.' He sucked at the end of his pen. 'The stud farm at Newmarket, then the fish shop at Taverham garden centre. I can't see those last two working though.'

'Why not?' Rupert said, any attempt at hiding how far gone he was abandoned.

'Well, I'm not sure how freeing a bunch of race horses would work. It's not as if they would just go feral in Thetford forest. The fish shop is just a stupid idea.' Matthew stirred at Andy's last comment.

'What do you mean? That was my idea,' he said. 'We could release them into the Norfolk Broads. They'd be free, completely free.'

'Not for long, they wouldn't,' Andy replied. Hannah looked between the two of them. She was enjoying this.

'Why not?'

'They're marine fish.'

'So?'

'The Norfolk Broads isn't very salty,' Andy said, 'or very warm.' There was an uncomfortable silence for a few seconds, and Hannah returned to imagining smacking Amy with some kitchen implements. She looked at the other woman, and to Hannah's delight, it looked as if Amy had passed out.

'Right then, vivisection lab is top of the list, then a

battery farm or two. Agreed?' Rupert asked. 'Round the table? Andy?' Rupert went around them all, including Amy. She regained consciousness enough to say 'oh yes' before closing her eyes again. She wasn't as out of it as Hannah had hoped, but maybe Rupert was. Hannah decided that she didn't care and got to her feet.

'I'm going to bed,' she said, staring at Matthew. At least he was still awake, and as she looked at him, he looked as if he was in pretty good shape considering how much cannabis they'd got through between them. 'Anyone else ready for bed?'

'Blimey, I'm tired,' Matthew got to his feet and did a good impression of yawning and stretching his arms above his head. 'Think I'll turn in.' Hannah saw Ruth glance across at Andy before they both stood up as well.

'Yep,' Andy said. 'Me too. Been a long day.'

As Hannah was leaving the kitchen after the others, she heard Rupert's voice behind her. She turned to see him leaning over Amy, patting her cheek with his hand.

'Amy. Amy? Wake up, would you?'

21

Emily opened the door to her flat and threw her bag down in the hall. As she closed the door behind her, she heard the television in the front room. She eased her shoes off and walked into the lounge to find Catherine curled up on the sofa watching a soap opera.

'You alright, Catherine?' Emily asked. 'Not out tonight?'

'No, can't be arsed,' Catherine said, looking at Emily over the rim of a very full glass of wine. 'Besides, we've not had a girly night for bloody ages. Fancy a film or something?'

'Yeah, could do.' Emily's original plan for that evening had been a film anyway. She'd just not been expecting company. 'Are you sure you're okay? You've not stayed in on a Thursday night, since, I don't know when. Probably the Eighties.'

'Ha bloody ha,' Catherine said, settling back into the sofa. 'Go on, get yourself sorted out with a shower and glass of vino and I'll find us something on Netflix.'

'Have we got enough wine if we're both staying in? Or have you drunk most of it already?'

'We've got loads. I went to Sainsbury's on the way back from work. Twenty-five percent off for six bottles or more. So I got twelve.'

As Emily showered, she tried to remember the last time Catherine hadn't gone out on a Thursday evening. Or a Friday, Saturday or even Sunday night when she thought about it. It must have been at least a couple of years ago. Thinking back, it was about the time she got all loved up with the lad from the Fish and Chip shop around the corner.

'What was his name?' Emily muttered to herself as she rinsed her hair. He'd been a weird looking thing if she remembered correctly, not Catherine's normal type at all. He was thin, lanky, had permanently greasy hair and the smell of fish and chips stayed for a long time after he did. Emily remembered Catherine saying something about 'hidden talents' at the time, which in Catherine's world was code for well hung. Her flatmate had been monogamous for at least a month before finally splitting up with him. Emily thought maybe Catherine had met someone else who was special, and that was why she was suddenly not bothered about going out.

Emily finished showering and put on a pair of fleecy pyjamas that she would only ever be seen wearing by Catherine. Grabbing a fresh bottle of wine from the fridge and a glass, she made her way into the lounge.

'Shift your fat arse up the sofa, Catherine,' Emily said. 'I don't want to lean on one of your folds by accident.'

'Yeah, and I don't want one of your bony little stick elbows in my toned abdomen,' Catherine retorted as she shuffled to make more room for Emily to sit down. They both started laughing, and Emily splashed some more wine into Catherine's glass.

'What've you found then?'

'Hang on,' Catherine pointed the remote control at the television. 'I've got an oldie, a horror, and a documentary to choose from. Right then.' An image of a pig appeared on the screen. 'There's the oldie. *Delicatessen*. Here's the horror,' she stabbed at a button until a face half hidden in darkness came up. 'That's *Hannibal*, with that Anthony Hopkins bloke, and finally, this one.' There was more button pushing. 'A documentary about a plane crash. *Alive*. What do you think?' Emily paused for a few seconds before replying.

'I think you're a twisted, sick individual with no compassion or respect for other people's dignity.'

'You knew that already.'

'Yep, you're right. Is there nothing with Benedict Cumberbatch or someone like that in?' Emily said.

The two women ended up watching what was supposed to be a romantic comedy that turned out to be not in the slightest bit romantic or funny. Its only saving grace was that it had Benedict himself in it. By the time the film had finished, they were on their third bottle of wine between them. Emily was feeling just the right side of pissed, but knew she'd have to slow down to avoid a thick head in the morning. Then again, she thought as she topped up Catherine's glass and her own, she was on leave tomorrow as well and she had absolutely nothing planned.

'Come on, slowcoach,' Emily said to Catherine. 'You're falling behind.'

'Yeah, yeah, whatever,' Catherine replied, picking up her glass from the coffee table and taking a hefty slug.

'So, who is he then?' Emily asked. Catherine paused,

her hand poised over the remote control, and gave Emily a sharp look.

'Sorry, who is who?'

'Whoever you're not out with tonight?'

'I don't know what you're talking about.'

'Bollocks,' Emily said. 'When was the last time you stayed in on a Thursday night?' Catherine just stared at her.

'Am I not allowed a night in with my BFF?' Emily snorted at Catherine's reply, almost spilling her wine.

'BFF? Really? Have we suddenly become teenagers again?'

'Maybe you're the reason I wanted to stay in, Emily,' Catherine leaned toward Emily and put her hand on her knee. 'Maybe I look at you in your fluffy over-washed grey pyjamas and think "hmmm, I wonder what it would be like to…"'

'Ew, shut up,' Emily laughed. She slapped Catherine's hand away from her leg. 'You're just changing the subject.'

'Is that a no, then?' Catherine said, a look of mock disappointment on her face.

'It's a definite no.'

'You shouldn't knock it until you've tried it, Emily.'

'Still a no.'

'You're just cold inside.'

'Whatever. If you don't want to tell me, then don't tell me. But I know you too well,' Emily said.

'No you don't,' Catherine replied. Just for a second, Emily caught a serious expression cross her flatmate's face before Catherine continued. 'What'll we watch then?'

'I don't mind, you choose. Is the news on? I fancy a laugh.'

Catherine prodded at the remote control until the familiar theme music of the local news came on. On the screen, a thin-faced blonde woman talked earnestly at the camera. She was caked in makeup, but it didn't do anything to hide her extensive laughter lines.

'Can you turn it up a bit?' Emily asked Catherine.

'We're now going to our special correspondent, Bob Rutler, with an exclusive report about the recent anarchist attacks on our local pet shops,' the woman on the television said.

'Ooh, I was there,' Emily said. 'I had to go in after and make sure there were no mealworms being mistreated.'

'Thank you Amelia,' the picture changed to a bearded man sweating heavily in a suit that looked several sizes too small for him. 'We've obtained, exclusively, some CCTV footage of one of the attacks. As you can see, it doesn't quite go to plan.'

On the screen, a black and white image appeared showing the inside of the pet shop. It flicked forward, one frame every few seconds. A male figure appeared, heading toward a small animal enclosure in staccato jumps. The figure leaned into the enclosure, dreadlocks falling over his shoulders, and he stood back up with a rabbit in his hands. The next freeze frame showed the rabbit sinking its teeth into the figure's hand, the one after that had an image of his screaming face and the rabbit in mid air making a bid for freedom, and the one after that just had the attacker standing upright with the rabbit disappearing into the distance. Emily and Catherine watched as the footage continued, showing the man swaying and eventually collapsing. He caught his head on the enclosure on the way down and ended up in a heap on the floor.

'Ooh, that looked nasty,' Emily said as a policeman stuttered into view, giving the prone figure on the floor a gentle prod with his foot.

'Blimey,' Catherine replied. 'That's going to smart

when he wakes up.' The view changed back to the male reporter.

'The man who we just saw fainting at the sight of his own blood,' the reporter said, 'was taken to hospital and released later with a police caution. This is Bob Rutler, reporting live for —'

'Yep, thanks Bob,' the woman in the studio cut him off. 'Now, in other news, widespread allegations of fraud are threatening to derail the annual 'I've Got Crabs' festival in Sheringham.

'Bloody hell, that's local news at its finest,' Emily said, getting to her feet to fetch another bottle of wine from the kitchen.

'Believe me, Emily,' Catherine said with a yawn, 'you've not lived until you've caught crabs in Sheringham.'

'I think I probably have,' Emily muttered as she made her way into the kitchen.

22

A ndy lay on the top bunk, wide awake but determined not to wake Ruth up. He could hear her snoring gently on the bottom bunk, and he really didn't want to disturb her. The problem was he was busting to go to the toilet, and knew he couldn't hang on for that much longer. He turned to look at the window, seeing the first glows of the sunrise behind the curtains, when a rhythmic noise started coming through the walls of the bedroom.

'Oh for fuck's sake, not again,' Andy heard Ruth mutter from below him a few seconds later. 'That's got to be what, the fourth time?'

'Fifth, I think,' Andy replied. 'I think you slept through the last one. He's got a fair bit of endurance, has Matthew.'

'What I don't get,' Ruth said, 'is how when the walls are about a foot thick we can still hear Matthew and Hannah shagging through them.'

'You're right, I don't understand that either. But it's what we can't hear that's interesting,'

'How'd you mean?' Ruth asked.

'Well, Rupert and Amy are in the room on the other side of us.'

'So?'

'Not a squeak,' he said. Ruth giggled, and Andy swivelled his legs over the side of the bunk bed. 'I need a pee, sorry,' he said. He was just about to jump down from the top bunk when there was a horrendous crash from the room next door. Andy looked between his feet and saw Ruth staring back up at him. They stared at each other wide-eyed for a few seconds before the muffled sound of screaming came through the thick stone walls of the farmhouse.

'Jesus Christ, what was that?' Ruth said, throwing her duvet off and swinging her feet out of the side of the bed.

'No idea,' Andy replied, jumping to the floor. 'Come on, we'd better go and find out.'

The two of them rushed into the bedroom that Hannah and Matthew were in. The bunk beds that had been there last night now looked like a single bed, and Andy watched as it shook from side to side.

'Fuck's sake, get us out would you?' Matthew's voice came out from underneath the collapsed bunk bed. Andy thought back to when they'd put the beds together and remembered something rolling across the floor.

'Ruth, get the other end,' Andy said. 'Grab the headboard bit, and we'll go on three.' Ruth grabbed the struts at the bottom of what used to be the top bunk and nodded at Andy.

'One, two, three,' Andy counted. On the word three, they both heaved the bunk up in the air before side stepping it to one side. Underneath it, on the bottom bunk, Hannah was splayed on top of Matthew, arms and legs either side of him, and naked as the day she was born.

'Ooh, I didn't know you had a tramp stamp, Hannah,' Andy said, looking at the ornate whorls of a tattoo on the small of Hannah's back. 'That's a lovely pair of slag's antlers, that is.'

'Not the time,' Andy heard Hannah reply through gritted teeth. 'My fucking back's knackered. Can you lift me off him?'

'Er, okay,' Andy replied. 'Ruth, do you want to get the other side? Same drills as before? We'll take an arm and a leg each, and go on three.' He looked at Ruth and could see that she was struggling not to laugh. They both manoeuvred themselves into position, and Andy counted to three again.

When they got to three and tried to lift Hannah off the bed, Matthew started squealing.

'Ow, ow. For fuck's sake, stop!'

'What is it, mate?' Andy asked.

'That fucking hurts, that's what it is.'

'Just zip it, Matthew,' Hannah said. 'Get me off him.' Andy and Ruth managed to lift Hannah off Matthew, and as they did so he whimpered loudly.

'For fuck's sake, rip my cock off why don't you?' Matthew said. Andy could see Ruth out of the corner of his eye, and knew that he wouldn't be able to look at her and keep a straight face.

Twenty minutes later, the four of them were sitting in the kitchen nursing cups of tea that Ruth had made. Andy looked at Hannah, who was sitting bolt upright on one of the kitchen chairs. Every time she moved, even if it was just to take a sip of her tea, she winced. Ruth and Hannah had spent some time in the bathroom, and according to Ruth, Hannah had some nasty abrasions on her back that

Ruth had cleaned and applied salve to. While they were doing that, Andy had a conversation with Matthew where the state of his friend's penis was briefly discussed. No matter how macerated Matthew claimed it was, there was no way Andy was going to apply salve to it. Matthew was on his own there.

'Bloody hell, what a start to the day,' Ruth said, blowing at her tea.

'You're telling me,' Matthew replied. 'I was just on the vinegar strokes when the bloody bed collapsed.'

'Shut up, you twat,' Hannah barked, 'the bloody bed landed on me, not you.' There was a noise from the bedroom that Amy and Rupert were in. 'Not a word, right?' Hannah shot sharp looks at the others before limping over to the kettle. A few seconds later, Rupert appeared at the door of the kitchen.

'Morning all,' he said, sounding a lot brighter than he looked.

'Morning,' Andy and Matthew mumbled in reply. Ruth raised a hand in greeting, but didn't say anything.

'Everyone sleep okay?' Rupert asked.

'Like a sodding baby,' Hannah replied, staring at the kettle. 'Where's Amy?'

'In the bathroom. She's woken up with that conjunctivitis thing in her eyes. All stuck together they are. She reckons it's the polyester in the pillows.'

'Oh, okay,' Hannah said. Andy looked at the two of them, realising that they were having a conversation without looking at each other.

'Are you still okay to give me a lift into Norwich later, Hannah?' Rupert asked.

'Sure,' Hannah replied, finally looking at him. 'No problem.'

Andy considered offering to drive Rupert to wherever

he needed to go so that Hannah wouldn't have to, but he didn't really want to chance it in the knackered Land Rover. One thing Andy had managed to hang onto was a clean driving license, and he didn't fancy his chances in an untaxed, uninsured, and barely legal Land Rover.

'Is there any chance of a lift into the city as well, Hannah?' Andy asked. It was a spur of the moment decision, but he'd just remembered that his parents would be at their caravan in Hemsby all weekend so he could nip back home without having to face their endless questions.

'Yeah, no worries,' Hannah said, pouring boiling water into mugs. 'We'll go after breakfast.'

'Perfect,' Rupert said. 'Sounds like a plan to me. What are you going into the city for, Andy?'

'Er,' Andy replied before pausing to think. He couldn't exactly tell Rupert he was going back to his parents to get pissed on his own in front of his Dad's fifty-inch plasma television before getting a decent night's sleep in a real bed. 'I've just got some stuff I need to get done, that's all.' It was the best he could come up with on such short notice.

'Fine,' Rupert said, his eyes hardening. 'Just don't forget that's your old life now. You belong here, not in the other world.

'Yes, thank you for reminding me, Rupert,' Andy said, thinking on his feet and wondering how to get Rupert off his back. 'I was actually going to have a closer look at the horse sanctuary in Lakenham.'

'Why?' Rupert asked. 'They rescue animals. They're our people, they are.'

'Are they?' Andy replied. 'There's a constant stream of horses being rescued there, but they never seem to have that many in the fields. We go past the place on the bus back here. Have you not noticed that?'

'My God, you're right,' Rupert said, a look of surprise

on his face. 'What are you thinking?' Andy pressed his lips together as he looked at Rupert, a random thought popping into his head.

'Glue factory, Rupert. I think it's a glue factory.'

23

Rupert thanked Hannah for giving him a lift to the university, said goodbye to Andy, and watched as the Land Rover disappeared in a cloud of thick grey smoke. Hannah had said almost nothing during the drive and looked as if she was in pain. When Rupert asked her if she was okay, she'd just dismissed him with a wave of her hand. Rupert turned to look at his target, or at least the buildings where his target was located.

When it was built in the Sixties, the University of Eastern England was ground-breaking. Although it was a polytechnic at the time, the soaring angular concrete construction won several architectural awards. By the time it became a university in the late Seventies, according to the website that Rupert had used for his research, it was one of the leading academic institutes in the country. Rupert looked at it, remembering his brief time here as a student, and thought the place looked like a big, ugly, concrete slab.

Rupert's eyes were diverted by a couple of young

female Asian students hurrying past. He nodded at the one nearest him and received a shy smile from her in return. They scurried off and the one who had smiled at him turned to look back, still grinning. Maybe he should spend a bit more time here, Rupert thought. It could be a very fertile recruiting ground for the cause.

The map that he'd printed out in the Internet cafe clutched in his hand, Rupert walked around for ten minutes or so until he found what he was looking for — the Animal Studies Department. He stood in front of it, looking carefully for any signs of extra security such as cameras or alarms. The building looked much like the rest of the campus — squat, ugly, and built of concrete. He glanced at his watch. It was almost nine o'clock in the morning, so the place should be open. He walked over to the front door.

'Good morning,' a female voice greeted him as he walked into the foyer. Rupert saw a young woman with shoulder length ginger hair sitting behind a reception desk in the far corner of the room. There was no strawberry blonde about her. She was ginger and proud of it, that much was for certain. 'Can I help you?'

'Morning,' he replied, crossing the foyer to the desk. The woman was younger than he'd initially thought. She was also very pretty, although the white lab coat she was wearing over her normal clothes didn't really do it for Rupert. 'I wonder if you can?' He gave her an intense look, hoping that his eyes would work their magic.

'I'll certainly try,' she said with a broad smile that showed off some expensive dentistry at some point in the past. The woman twirled a finger round and round in her hair. Bingo. 'What can I do for you?' Rupert's eyes flicked to her name badge.

'So, Lauren. I'm thinking of becoming a student here,' he said, 'and was wondering if I could have a look round?'

'Well, we run open days every couple of months for people to have a proper tour,' she replied, looking back at the computer in front of her. He tried to look disappointed.

'Oh, okay,' Rupert said. 'It's just I've come quite a long way, and hoped I might be able to see the place I've read so many fantastic things about.' He was lying through his teeth, but Lauren didn't seem to have noticed. She looked back up at Rupert and smiled, tilting her head a fraction to one side as he gave her the eyes again.

'But classes don't start for another hour, so I could give you a quick one now if you want?' Rupert felt the corners of his mouth twitch. She certainly could, he thought. Right here, right now, bent over that desk she was sitting behind.

Lauren got to her feet as Rupert tried to push the image from his mind, and she pulled out a white starched lab coat from a cupboard behind the desk.

'You'll need to wear this, I'm afraid.' As Rupert shrugged his way into the coat, some nasty memories of wearing one in the chemistry laboratory came back to him.

They spent the next forty minutes walking around the building. Rupert tried to memorise the internal layout of the building, but it was such a rabbit warren that he gave up after a while and just grabbed a map showing the location of the first aid kit from a noticeboard. There were several small classrooms, each of them with no more than six desks in them. It all looked depressingly familiar to Rupert. The only things that were missing were the bunsen burners. At one point, they walked past a grey steel door with a sign on it warning against unauthorised access.

'What's in there?' he asked as Lauren walked down the

corridor and straight past the door without pausing at it as she had done at the others they'd passed. She glanced over her shoulder at him.

'Oh, that's the research laboratory,' she explained. 'We can't go in there.' No surprise there, Rupert thought. They wouldn't want random people poking around the room where they kept the animals, now would they? The problem was that was the one room that Rupert really wanted to have a look inside.

'How come?' he asked.

'Director's orders,' Lauren said. 'He won't allow anyone else in there apart from him and his senior researchers. It's all tightly controlled by these things.' She waved one of the cards that hung off a lanyard around her neck. Rupert glanced at the card for a few seconds and wondered how he could press the issue, but decided against it. The last thing he wanted was to make it obvious that he had a keen interest in the laboratory, so he followed Lauren down the corridor to where she was already extolling the virtues of the crew room.

Lauren turned out to be a very good tour guide. She also turned out to be twenty-four and very recently single. In Rupert's mind, that made her almost certainly on the rebound. Most important of all, she was also free on Sunday evening. By the time he left, he had her phone number scribbled on a compliments slip but as he didn't possess a mobile phone, it wasn't much use to him. He also had arranged to meet her outside the Murderers pub in the middle of Norwich at eight o'clock sharp on Sunday.

Rupert made his way to the bus stop on the road outside the university, daydreaming about finding out whether or not Lauren was a genuine redhead, or one of the growing band of women who seemed to think that being ginger was cool. He stood at the bus stop, thinking about asking one of the students already waiting there what time the next bus was. Looking at them, they probably didn't speak a word of English, so he didn't bother.

There were two more things Rupert wanted to do before he headed back to the farm. There was a burger restaurant he needed to do some more reconnaissance on, and he had a meeting planned with an old friend. Danny, the purveyor of wild herbs and proscribed chemicals, was back. He'd been unavailable for a while due to a short stint in Norwich prison for trying to sell some industrial grade Rohypnol to an undercover policeman, but according to Rupert's sources, Danny was once again open for business. He had a very fine shop indeed, or at least he did have before he got busted, and Rupert had a shopping list to get ready for Amy's graduation evening, whenever that was going to be. What she was given would have to be carefully titrated though, after last night when she'd passed out after a few joints. By the time the bus arrived, Rupert had it all worked out in his head. He'd start her off with a touch of coke to get her going, then a mild hallucinogen of some sort — he'd have to see what Danny recommended — and then something later on to calm her back down and help with any memory issues. Rupert thought about even popping into a chemist to pick something up for himself, now that those little blue pills were available over the counter. He wouldn't want to let the side down, not after the other night anyway. At least Amy hadn't woken up when he'd sorted himself out, although she had complained of sticky eyes when she'd woken up in the morning.

'Can I hop off near the Burger Queen at the Thickthorn roundabout, mate?' Rupert said to the bus driver once he'd bought a ticket. The driver answered him with a grunt at first before replying.

'Depends if I stop or not. If I don't, I'll open the doors anyway.' He regarded Rupert with rheumy eyes that looked as if they'd seen a lot of whisky over the years. 'You can rag doll out if you're brave enough.'

24

'My bloody back is killing me,' Hannah complained as she climbed out of the Land Rover. She had spent the morning in Norwich, trying to line up some more customers for their business venture without much success at all. There was a stall on Norwich Market run by a greasy-haired little man who said he'd be interested in some free samples and 'anything else he could get his hands on'. He'd said this last comment with his eyes fixed on Hannah's chest, so it was most unlikely he'd be getting his hands on anything at all.

Amy and Ruth, who were sitting on a bench outside the farmhouse, got to their feet and walked over to greet her. Hannah had managed to avoid Amy for the previous day, not wanting to get into a discussion about how she had got hurt, but she couldn't hide from the woman for ever. As she'd left, Hannah had given Ruth instructions to tell Amy that she'd been in a minor accident, but leaving the details for Ruth to come up with.

'Are you okay, Hannah?' Ruth asked, a look of genuine concern on her face.

'Ruth told me what happened,' Amy said. 'It sounds awful.' Hannah narrowed her eyes in Ruth's direction. 'I mean, I can't imagine turning over in bed and the whole thing just collapsing like that. You're lucky you weren't more seriously hurt.'

'Aw, that's really sweet of you, Amy.' Hannah walked over and gave her a hug. As she did so, she looked at Ruth and mouthed the words 'thank you' at her. Ruth just smiled in response.

'So, what are we doing today then?' Amy asked as she disentangled herself from Hannah. 'I think it's just us girls. Matthew's gone back to bed.'

'Is he okay?' Ruth said.

'I think so,' Amy replied. 'I did see him crying when he came out of the toilet earlier, though. He was walking a bit funny as well, but I didn't say anything.'

'I'm sure he's fine,' Hannah said sharply. 'Just needs to man up a small bit, that's all.' She looked at Amy, whose mouth was half open as if she was about to say something else, but it closed again. 'Where's Rupert gone?'

'He got the bus into the city. Said he was going back to look at a burger place, do an assessment of it.'

'I thought he did that yesterday though,' Hannah said, more to herself than the others.

'It was closed yesterday, apparently,' Amy explained.

'Yeah, right,' Hannah said. 'More like he got so out of it round at his drug dealer's flat that he couldn't go do anything.' She clapped her hands together, dismissing Rupert and whatever he was doing. 'We've got some baking to do later on, that's what we're doing today.'

'Ooh, cool,' Amy clapped her hands together. 'I've never baked anything before. The closest I've come to it is watching that *British Bake Up* thing on the television.' Hannah and Ruth exchanged a quick glance.

'Need to get some more flour first though,' Hannah said. 'I've only got a bit left. Amy, would you like to come to the farming wholesale place with me?'

'Oh yes,' Amy replied. 'Can I?'

'Of course you can,' Hannah said with a smile. 'Is that alright with you, Ruth?'

'Fine by me,' Ruth said. 'I'll stay here and look after Matthew.'

'Well if you are looking after him,' Hannah arched an eyebrow, 'don't forget he's a bit tender in places.'

Twenty minutes later, Hannah and Amy were bouncing their way down the farm track toward the main road. The Land Rover was coughing smoke out behind them, but it was still going.

'So, Amy,' Hannah said as they pulled out of the track onto the road. 'How was the other night?'

'How'd you mean?'

'With Rupert?'

'Oh, nothing happened, Hannah,' Amy put a hand on Hannah's arm, and looked at her.

'Nothing?' Hannah said, glancing across at the other woman. 'Nothing at all?'

'No, nothing. He was the perfect gentleman.'

'Well that's not like Rupert,' Hannah mumbled.

'I mean, I know he's your boyfriend and all that, but it's not really my thing.'

'I'm not his girlfriend, Amy,' Hannah replied, emphasising the work 'his'. 'That's not the way our relationship works. It's much more about freedom, not ownership.'

'Okay,' Amy said, 'but like I said, that's not really my thing.'

'Well, that's fine. It doesn't have to be. Not everyone is into sex in the same way, are they?'

'I didn't say I wasn't into sex,' Amy replied, examining her fingernails. 'I'm just not into sex with men that much, that's all.'

'Oh,' Hannah replied. She'd not been expecting that response, and kept her eyes fixed on the road in front of them while she tried to work out the best way to respond. In the end, Hannah decided that saying nothing was probably the best option.

They spent the rest of the journey to the farming wholesale shop in silence. When they pulled up to the low-slung grey warehouse ten minutes later, Amy finally looked up from her fingernails.

'Blimey, that's a bit industrial looking,' she said.

'Yeah, it's pretty functional,' Hannah replied as she parked the Land Rover. 'Not really designed for the general public. Come on,' she said as she turned the engine off and undid her seatbelt. 'Let's see what we can get.'

They walked into the warehouse, and spent a while browsing the aisles. Amy seemed delighted with the whole experience, constantly asking Hannah what various products were for. Hannah was no expert in farming, but she had a rough idea and as it turned out, in comparison to Amy she was a veritable expert. Hannah paused in front of a large pile of industrial sized bags of flour.

'Blimey, they aren't cheap,' she muttered, looking at the handwritten price. Just because it was written in a jaunty manner on a bright pink cardboard star didn't mean it was any cheaper.

'It doesn't matter' Amy said. 'I've got loads of cash.'

'Can I help you?' a male voice behind them said. They turned round to see a shop assistant behind them. Hannah looked at him with a critical eye. He was early twenties, about five foot ten, broad shouldered, and had a slightly crooked smile. 'Are you looking for anything in particular?'

'We need some rye flour,' Hannah said. 'Organic preferably.'

'That's not organic, that lot,' the shop assistant nodded at the bags of flour Hannah and Amy had been looking at. He had a broad Norfolk accent, and ran the words together so that they were almost one word. 'Posh stuff's over there.'

Hannah looked in the direction that the assistant had nodded. There was another pile of flour bags, which were even more expensive. Amy was trying to whisper something in Hannah's ear about paying for the flour, but Hannah brushed her away.

'It's okay, Amy. I've got this,' she said before turning to the assistant. 'They're all a bit expensive though. Is there any room for negotiating?'

'Well, we might have something out the back I could show you?'

'Sounds interesting,' Hannah replied, looking at the lazy smile that was playing across the assistant's face. 'Will I meet you at the Land Rover, Amy?'

'No, I'm good,' Amy replied. 'I'll come as well.'

'Amy,' Hannah said, trying not to grit her teeth. 'I'll meet you at the Land Rover in a little while. Okay?'

'Er, okay, yeah,' Amy said after a brief pause. 'I think I'll have a quick look at the pet toys while I'm here.'

'Aisle seven,' the shop assistant said, nodding his head to one side. 'Over that way.'

'Thanks, Pete,' Hannah said a while later as the shop assistant effortlessly lifted a large bag of flour into the rear of the Land Rover. The suspension complained at the weight of the flour, and Hannah felt the nose of the vehicle lift a couple of inches. She clicked her seatbelt into place and waved at Pete as he made his way back to the warehouse.

'He seems friendly enough,' Amy said from the passenger seat.

'Yeah, nice bloke,' Hannah replied, pumping the accelerator pedal before starting the Land Rover. It spluttered into life with its trademark cough of smoke. 'That sack of flour in the boot was going to be thrown away. Not good enough for the shops, according to Pete. So we managed to get it for nothing.'

'I would have paid for it, Hannah.'

'Yeah, I know you would have done. But it's so much more valuable when it's free, don't you think?' Hannah turned to look at Amy, hoping that she would see her point. 'We need to get away from the whole capitalism model, and just trade instead. An ideal society wouldn't need money.' From the look on Amy's face, Hannah could see she wasn't convinced. There was plenty of time though. Hannah was just about to put the Land Rover in gear when Amy said something.

'Hang on a sec,' she said, shifting her position in the passenger seat and pulling a tissue out of her trouser pocket. 'Look at me?' Hannah turned her head, and Amy reached out with the tissue to dab something from her hair.

'Did you sneeze?' Amy said, examining the tissue. 'Looks like you've got snot in your hair.' Hannah didn't reply, but put the Land Rover into gear and smirked as she pulled away.

25

E mily scrolled through the report on her laptop while she waited for the Burger Queen to open its doors. Looking at the previous inspection write-up, this was going to be a short visit. Although she didn't eat in fast food restaurants if she could help it, that was more about the food than the way it was prepared. She regarded the familiar red and yellow sign of the restaurant, trying to remember the last time one of them in the huge chain across East Anglia had failed their annual inspection, but couldn't.

She was just scrolling through the latest news on the Eastern Daily News website when she saw some activity at the restaurant door out of the corner of her eye. Emily abandoned the article she'd been reading about an altercation between two rival pizza delivery drivers that had turned nasty, resulting in one of them being burned with melted cheese. At least that proved one of them had a pizza that was hot, Emily thought as she closed her laptop and glanced at her watch. The restaurant had opened right on time, almost to the second, even though it was Saturday morning. She wouldn't have blamed them for opening up a bit late as it was a weekend.

When she walked into the burger restaurant a moment later, the smell of antiseptic hit her nostrils and she could see from the sheen on the floor that it had been freshly mopped.

'Good morning,' a male voice from behind the counter said. Emily looked to see a tall man, standing ramrod straight, looking at her intently. 'Inspection time, then?'

'Er, yes it is,' Emily replied, 'but you're not supposed to know we're coming?'

'We didn't,' the man said. He had a moustache so large that it almost needed its own hair net. 'I saw you outside, reading a Food Standards Agency report on your computer.' Emily was surprised. She'd not noticed him at all, and for him to see the laptop screen he would have had to have been standing pretty much right next to her. 'Anyway, now that you're here, can I leave you with my deputy manager, Billy?'

'Sure,' Emily said.

'Billy?' the man barked turning his head to the side and making Emily jump. 'Billy, on me.'

A door at the back of the shop opened and a young man walked through. Billy, obviously.

'Yes, Boss?' he said, glancing across at Emily.

'Billy, this is…' the moustached man arched an eyebrow at her.

'Emily Underwood,' she replied, giving the new arrival a brief smile. 'From the Food Standards Agency.'

'She's here to do the annual inspection. I'll be in the office if there's any problems.' With that, he swivelled on the spot and marched to the back of the shop before disappearing through the door that Billy had come through.

'Blimey,' Emily said to Billy. 'He's a bit fierce.'

'Oh, don't mind The Major. That's just his way,' Billy replied, leaning forward and crossing his arms on the counter in front of him.

'The Major?'

'Yeah, that's what me and the boys call him. He pretends to be annoyed at the nickname, but I think he likes it really.'

'Is he ex-military then?'

'That's what he says. Twenty years in the Army Catering Corps. Seen more wars than we've had hot dinners, if you believe the stories, but according to his contract he's not allowed front of house so we think he's a wrong 'un.'

'Right,' Emily said, not quite sure how to respond to that statement. She looked at Billy, noticing that he wasn't a bad looking chap. Not bad looking at all. At least that might make the inspection more interesting. Emily reached into her bag and pulled out her protective clothing. When she put her white mesh hat on her head, she realised that Billy was grinning at her. 'What?'

'Nothing,' he replied, still smiling. 'That's very fetching, that is.'

'This from a man wearing a blue hairnet?' Emily countered with a smile of her own.

'Touché,' Billy said, aiming a finger in her direction and miming a pistol firing. 'Very good.' The two of them looked at each other for a few seconds before Billy broke what was turning into an awkward silence, for Emily at least. 'Would you like a cup of coffee?'

'Er,' Emily glanced at the coffee machine on the counter. It looked sparkling clean, but she doubted the coffee that came out of it was up to much. 'Maybe later?'

'Not from there,' Billy replied. 'That's just for the

customers. I've got a Nespresso machine out the back. It does about a million different types of coffee.'

'Go on then. I'll have a medium roast if you've got any? White with two sugars please. In fact, I'm quite partial to a Columbian if you can stretch to that?'

'Right,' Billy's smile faltered ever so slightly. 'You don't know what colour pod that is, do you?'

'I'll have whatever you've got, Billy,' Emily replied. 'Thank you.'

For the next hour or so, Emily made her way through her inspection checklist. As she'd suspected, the place was gleaming, and she couldn't find a thing out of place. Billy left her to it for the most part, absorbed in playing a game on his phone. He didn't want to get in her way, he'd said to her. At one point, The Major put in a brief appearance, sticking his head out of the office door and looking to see if Emily was still there. He harrumphed at her a couple of times before disappearing back into his little cubbyhole. Emily eventually got to the end of the checklist and put a final tick in the 'Outstanding' box for that serial. It lined up with all the other ticks on the list.

'All done,' Emily said, walking over to where Billy was prodding at his phone. She tore off the top sheet of the inspection report. 'There'll be a full report from the Food Standards Agency in the post in the next couple of days, but there's nothing out of the ordinary.'

'Excellent,' Billy said. 'That'll keep The Major happy for a bit, anyway.'

'Will he want to talk to me?'

'Not unless you want to talk to him.' Billy looked over at the door to the office.

'I think I'm good, thanks,' Emily replied. Billy's face broke into a broad grin.

'Can't say I blame you,' he said. 'Thanks for coming

and all that, anyway. Nice to meet you.' Emily thought for a few seconds before replying.

'I wish every visit was like this one,' she said. 'No problems with the inspection, great coffee.' She paused before continuing. 'Good company, even if a little preoccupied.' She flashed a quick look at his phone before peeling one of her business cards off her clipboard. 'This has got my office contact details on it, just in case there's any queries once the report comes in.' *Sod it*, she thought as she turned the card over and scribbled something on the back. 'And that's my mobile number, for, well, just in case.' She could feel her cheeks start to colour at her spur of the moment behaviour. Emily didn't want to look at Billy in case she'd just made an utter fool of herself, but when she did look at him, he looked delighted.

'Well, thank you.'

'No problem, see you around,' Emily turned and walked to the door before she made even more of an idiot of herself.

She strode across the car park, anxious to get to the car and resisting the temptation to look back at the Burger Queen restaurant. Just as she had unlocked the car and thrown the inspection paperwork onto the back seat, she heard a rustling in the bushes. Emily turned to see a man crouching in the undergrowth next to her Mini, half peering out of them at her.

'Great tits,' the man said. Emily's mouth dropped open, and she took a step toward him.

'Sorry, what did you just say?' she said, anger replacing embarrassment in a fraction of a second.

'There,' the man pointed at the restaurant with one hand. 'On top of the roof.' With the other hand he raised a small pair of binoculars that were hanging round his neck on a strap. 'There's a pair of great tits, nesting by the looks of it.' Emily didn't even look over at the restaurant.

'Right,' she said, unsure of herself. 'That's nice.'

Emily got into the car. She would normally have sat there for a while and made some notes on her laptop, but the weird bird spotter in the bushes had made her uncomfortable, no matter how nice his blue eyes were. *What is it with Norfolk?* she muttered to herself as she drove out of the car park.

26

The miserable bastard of a bus driver hadn't stopped at the Thickthorn roundabout last night in the end, and Rupert had ended up going all the way into the city. It wasn't a massive drama, as he'd gone round to Danny's flat to catch up with his dealer and sample some of his wares. One of the things that Danny had learned in prison was how to roll a Camberwell Carrot which was, according to Danny, the only joint in existence to utilise twelve skins. It was conceived in Camberwell, and looked like a carrot. That had been the start of a most enjoyable evening with Danny that had ended with Rupert crashed out on his sofa. The walk back from Danny's flat to the restaurant this morning had been just what Rupert had needed to clear his head.

Rupert wriggled to try and get himself comfortable in the bushes, and raised the binoculars to his eyes. He must have been sitting in the sodding bushes for hours he thought as yet another customer went into the Burger Queen restaurant. Rupert did have a good idea of the way the placed worked, though. There were two of them in there. One of them — with a bloody ridiculous moustache — was obviously in charge of the cooking, and the younger bloke was in charge of taking the orders. Rupert wondered why they didn't change around every once in a while just to mix things up a bit. If he was running the place, that's how Rupert would do it. As he watched, Moustache Man stepped out through the door in the back of the restaurant for another smoke. He was nothing if not regular, and couldn't go for more than an hour without a cigarette. His moustache must be minging if he smoked that much, Rupert thought.

It looked to Rupert as if they'd been having some sort of inspection when he'd arrived there first thing. He was hoping to get in there to do what he needed before any other customers turned up, but there'd been a woman wearing a white coat and one of the stupid white hats. She'd actually clocked Rupert as she'd left, but he'd managed to pass himself off as a bird watcher. It wasn't the best excuse in the world, but it was all he could come up with at such short notice, and she seemed to swallow it.

There were no cameras anywhere near the Burger Queen, which was one of the main reasons he'd chosen this particular restaurant. Rupert was surprised that there weren't any, seeing as it was almost next door to a petrol station, but he'd checked and double checked. There would be one inside, that was for certain, but nothing on the outside walls at all. He had a pair of sunglasses in his pocket, and with a bandana across the lower half of his face he wouldn't be recognisable at all.

It wasn't that Rupert was paranoid, despite what Hannah told him pretty much every day. He knew that all the CCTV cameras were connected to a large database somewhere, probably down in that big donut-shaped place in Cheltenham. He also knew that the software they had running them could detect a face within seconds, despite the politicians saying they couldn't. Keeping his face out of that database wasn't paranoia, Rupert had told Hannah. That was common sense. It wasn't just the cameras that he wanted to avoid on this particular day though — it was everyone. The last thing he needed today was to be spotted by someone who might recognise him. That would be a complete disaster.

What Rupert was about do was controversial to say the least, especially for a man in his position. He knew that he could explain it to the others if he did get caught, but he didn't want to have to. They wouldn't understand, anyway. The only thing that mattered was what was in his head, and he knew that direct action like the activity he was about to undertake was the only way he could truly understand the plight of the animals he'd sworn to protect. It was the only way to see the truth. He'd been over it so many times in his head that, even though deep down he knew it wasn't actually true, he'd convinced himself that it was.

Rupert watched as the single customer in the restaurant left clutching a paper bag full of junk food. For a moment or two, Rupert thought the man was going to sit in his car and stuff his face, but to Rupert's relief he drove off, leaving the car park empty. There weren't any cars in the petrol station either, as far as Rupert could see. This might the best time to act. Rupert glanced at his watch. It was almost two o'clock — that must be the end of the lunch time customers. For the first time in over four hours, there was no-one else about

The young man in the restaurant was filling up a bucket with hot water. If he was about to mop the floor, Rupert reasoned, he wouldn't be expecting any more customers for a while. Rupert contemplated waiting until the bloke with the moustache stepped out for another smoke, but decided against it. It looked as if he was holed up in his little office anyway.

'No time like the present,' he muttered under his breath as he reached into his pocket for his sunglasses and bandana.

A blast of refrigerated air hit Rupert as he pushed the door open. He'd caught a glimpse of himself in the reflection of the door as he'd walked up and realised that he looked more like an armed robber than a genuine customer but it was too late to do anything about that now.

'Afternoon,' the young man behind the counter said. Rupert could see the uncertainty in his eyes, so he held both hands out to show that he wasn't about to pull out a gun. He pointed to the bandana covering the lower half of his face.

'I'm allergic to the sunlight,' Rupert said, his voice muffled.

'Oh, okay.' He didn't look convinced, and seeing as it wasn't in the slightest bit sunny outside this wasn't a surprise, but Rupert didn't really care. He risked a quick look over his shoulder to make sure there was no one else around, but it was just the two of them. 'What can I get you?' Rupert took a deep breath before replying.

'Can I get a large bacon cheeseburger, please?'

'Supersize with extra bacon?'

'Go on then. Cheers,' Rupert replied, his mouth already watering.

27

Hannah parked the Land Rover in the barn on the farm, and between them, her and Amy manhandled the heavy sack of flour out of the back of it and carried it into the kitchen. By the time they had put it into the corner of the small larder next to an already open bag of flour, they were both breathing heavily.

'How the hell,' Amy gasped, 'did that bloke from the warehouse just throw this into the back of the Land Rover like it was a bloody pillow?'

'No idea,' Hannah replied, just as out of breath as Amy, 'but he was quite a big lad in all fairness.' Knowing full well that Amy wouldn't get the irony behind her comment, Hannah allowed herself a brief smile.

The two women walked into the kitchen, where Ruth was sitting at the kitchen table with Matthew. He looked decidedly sorry for himself, so Hannah flashed him a dark look that she hoped would tell him to get a grip of himself. Although, Hannah thought, if he did get a grip of himself, that would probably hurt.

'Ruth, Matthew, everything okay?' Hannah said,

injecting some enthusiasm into her voice that she didn't really feel.

'Yeah, all good,' Ruth replied. Matthew just grunted and got to his feet.

'I'll leave you lot to it, I think.' He made his way to the front door, wincing as he did so.

'Bloody hell,' Hannah said when he closed the door behind him. 'He's milking it a bit, isn't he?' Neither Amy or Ruth replied, so Hannah ignored them and started bustling about the kitchen. 'Bugger,' she said a few moments later. "Amy, could you nip back to the larder and grab the open bag of flour? I'll get the rest of the stuff together for some loaves.

'Sure,' Amy replied. 'No problem.'

Half an hour later, the kitchen was filled with the smell of baking bread. The three women sat at the kitchen table, nursing cups of tea while they waited for the bread to rise.

'My God, that smells lovely,' Ruth murmured. Amy nodded in agreement. There was a total of twenty-five loaves in the oven, as well as some rolls that Hannah had made for their evening meal. They had made the rolls from the new flour as there wasn't as much in the open bag as Hannah had thought there was.

'So, what's Rupert up to in the city?' Amy asked.

'Not sure to be honest,' Hannah replied. 'Some sort of reconnaissance mission.'

'How come it's always the boys that get to have the fun?'

'How'd you mean?'

'Well, it was only them that got to have fun at Pets 4 Homes,' Amy said. 'Neither you or Ruth were involved.'

'That was Rupert's decision,' Hannah said with a side-line glance at Ruth. He'd not thought that she would be up to the job, but Hannah wasn't about to tell the others that.

'Why is it up to him, though?' Amy pressed.

'Yeah, we should do something ourselves,' Ruth added. Hannah looked at them both.

'We could,' she said, slowly. Rupert almost certainly wouldn't like the idea, but so what if he didn't? It wasn't fair, Hannah thought, that he got to make all the decisions. Not very post-modern of him really. A slow smile spread across Hannah's face as she thought about the girls striking out on their own, or more specifically Rupert's reaction to them using some initiative. 'Have you got something in mind?' she asked Ruth.

'Something a bit more meaningful than liberating a bunch of crickets and mealworms maybe?' Ruth smirked, and they all laughed.

Ten minutes later, they had the outline of a plan in place. Hannah looked at the rough checklist that they'd scribbled down. It was, she thought, already a lot better planned than the Pets 4 Homes mission had been.

'I think that might work,' Hannah said.

'Can you imagine the look on their faces if we pulled it off?' Ruth giggled. 'It would show them that we're not just good for baking, wouldn't it?'

'Oh, bollocks,' Hannah exclaimed, leaping to her feet. 'The bloody bread.' She'd forgotten all about it. Rushing to the oven, she pulled the door open and waved her hand at the wall of heat that came rushing out. Peering inside, she could see that she'd got there in the nick of time. The rolls were just a touch on the dark side, but that was probably because they were made out of the new flour that she'd got from the warehouse. The loaves though, all twenty-five of them, were perfect.

Hannah smiled as she slid the tray out with her oven gloves. 'Bloody hell, that was close,' she said as Amy and Ruth came over to admire their handiwork. 'Got them out just in time. We'll leave them to cool and then run them down to the sandwich man.'

'We could all go,' Amy replied, 'and do a spot of our own reconnaissance on the way back.' She pointed toward the plan they'd outlined. 'What do you think?'

A couple of hours later, with the loaves safely delivered to Sam the sandwich man, the three woman were sitting in the Land Rover peering at a farm building in the distance. Hannah had parked in a layby just off the main road, giving them an ideal spot to look at their potential target. The sun was just beginning to disappear below the horizon, but there was still enough light to get a good look.

'Oh my God,' Amy groaned. 'I've eaten too much.'

'Me too,' Ruth replied. 'I've got rotten stomach ache, but I couldn't leave any.'

'See, I told you,' Hannah said to the other two. 'Despite what he looks like, Fat Sam knows his way round a sandwich toaster.'

'My god, doesn't he just,' Amy murmured, rubbing her hand across her stomach. They sat in silence for some moments, lost in their own thoughts.

'Is that it, then?' Ruth whispered, pointing at the low-slung building a couple of hundred yards away. It was a long, thin building that looked as if it would blow away in a strong wind.

'Yep, definitely,' Hannah replied under her breath.

'Why are you both whispering?' Amy asked from the back seat. 'We're miles away. It's not as if they can hear us, is it?'

'Fair point,' Hannah laughed. She pointed at a track leading from the building. 'Look, there's the main access road. We could drive straight down there to the building.'

She looked back at the farm. 'I can't see much in the way of security, can you two?'

'There's a fence, but I can't see anything else,' Ruth replied.

'Me neither,' Amy added.

As they watched, a man came out of the building and closed the door behind him. He got into an SUV that was parked outside, and a few seconds later they watched as he made his way down the track, headlights cutting through the gloom. In another hour or so, it would be pitch black.

'Do you think that's the farmer?' Ruth asked. Hannah bit her lip. Of course he was the bloody farmer.

'Looks like he's done for the day,' Hannah replied, watching as the SUV turned onto the main road and sped away from them. 'I didn't even see him lock the door.'

'We could go and have a closer look?' Amy said. 'See if there are any cameras or lights or anything. If he comes back, we'll just pretend to be lost.'

'Yeah, turn on the old feminine charm and all that,' Ruth added. Hannah didn't say anything, but just started the Land Rover and put it into gear. As the Land Rover lurched forward, Ruth continued. 'We are only going to have a look though, aren't we?' Hannah glanced across at her and realised that the woman was nervous. Perhaps Rupert had been right about her after all?

'Ruth, just relax would you?' Amy replied, putting a hand on Ruth's arm and smiling at Hannah. 'We'll just go and have a little poke round, see what's what. Isn't that right, Hannah?'

Hannah looked at Amy in the rear-view mirror, and the two women exchanged a conspiratorial smile.

'Sure, that's right,' Hannah said. 'We're just going for a look, Ruth. Are you okay? You look really jittery. This whole thing was your idea, after all.'

'Well, not really it wasn't,' Ruth replied. 'I mean, yes it was my idea but I didn't realise we were actually going to do anything.'

'We're not, Ruth,' Hannah said with another smile. 'We're just going for a little look, that's all.'

28

Andy pulled at the corner of the dust cover, and with a flourish like a magician trying to remove a table-cloth from underneath some tableware without spilling it all, snapped his wrist back. He was in his parents' garage, having been dropped off in the city centre by Hannah the day before, and having spent the previous evening vege-tating in front of his Dad's television, was about to spend some quality time with one of the things he loved more than anything else in the world. It might help the dull whisky induced ache at the back of his head go away.

Underneath the dust cover was his most prized posses-sion, and one which he'd kept very quiet about when he joined up with Rupert and the others. He was supposed to have given all his worldly goods to the collective, as a gesture of abandonment of his old ways, and acceptance of the new. But Andy had kept some things back. He still had a bank account with a couple of thousand pounds in that had taken him most of his life to save, and he also had what he was looking at now. What he was running his hand ever so tenderly over.

'Delia,' Andy whispered, almost as if he was in a church. 'Oh, Delia. I've missed you so much.'

Delia didn't reply, and nor was Andy expecting her to. Cars couldn't talk after all, even cars like her. Delia was a pristine, bright yellow MG Trophy 160 convertible which had black and yellow leather trim, a pair of green and yellow fluffy dice hanging from the rear-view mirror, and some of the happiest memories of Andy's short life.

Andy crossed to his father's workbench and picked up a foot pump. He spent the next ten minutes making sure that each tyre was properly inflated. Thirty-six pounds per square inch. Any more and she would squeal on the corners, any less and she wouldn't handle properly. Not that he would be taking her out anywhere, even though according to the voltmeter the battery was fully charged. The solar panel Andy had installed on the garage roof to trickle charge the battery seemed to be doing what it was supposed to.

Two hours later, Andy was content. Delia had been waxed to within an inch of her yellow life, and as he put the dust cover back over her, he felt a pang of regret. She needed a run out, needed to be loved more than he could. Andy's father often said that looking after a car properly was like looking after a woman. They needed love, time, attention, and the occasional slap to keep them in line. Andy wasn't sure about the last one, but the first three of his father's observations were spot on.

Andy turned off the garage lights and wandered back into the kitchen of his old house. His sense of regret started to deepen as he looked around. This was his home, it was the place he had grown up in, made memories in. Most of the memories were about his family, but there were some that they had no idea about but that were just as important to Andy. Such as what happened on the sofa in the front room with Lisa from the DVD rental shop, back when DVD rental shops still existed. The last he'd heard of Lisa she was three times the size that she had been when he'd known her, had three ugly children, and now worked in Tesco on the fish counter. She'd not so much turned Andy into a man that night on the sofa as abused him mercilessly, but regardless of that Andy was eternally grateful.

He wandered into his old bedroom, still with posters from his childhood on the wall, and sat on the bed to just think. At least his parents hadn't turned it into a guest room just yet, although they regularly threatened to in their occasional emails. Andy picked up a photo album that had been a birthday present from his girlfriend at the time he'd left the old world behind. The album was very retro — it had proper photographs that she'd had printed out and everything — and as Andy looked through the early days of their ill-fated relationship, he realised that he had a solitary tear creeping down his cheek.

'For fuck's sake,' he said as he slammed the album shut and put it back into the drawer he'd pulled it from last night. 'That was then, not now.' He got to his feet, unsure why he was drifting back into his past. Not that Andy cared one bit, but Rupert would be furious. As he thought about it while he walked into the kitchen, Andy could see why.

Before he'd joined the collective, Andy had been just treading water. Dead end job — if you could call being an intern at a failed supermarket a job — no real prospects. He didn't do anything back then, just existed. Then the thing with the butcher had happened, and his entire life had changed. At least now Andy's life meant something. He was making a difference, Rupert told him that every day. He had purpose, something to work towards. The only way Andy could achieve that, according to Rupert, was to leave this all behind. His ex-girlfriend, his ex-job, material possessions like Delia. It all had to go so that he could be free, no matter how much it hurt. Well, most of it had to go.

Andy spent a few moments going around his parents' house to make sure that it wasn't obvious he'd been there for a night. He didn't think his parents would mind — every e-mail told him he could come back any time he wanted — but he knew they'd be pissed off with him for coming home when they weren't there. He nipped back to his bedroom and grabbed something to take back to the collective with him, just a memento so that if he got all maudlin again, he would have something to remind him of why he'd left. At least, that what Andy told himself.

By the time he was waiting for the bus back to the farm, Andy had managed to persuade himself to focus on the future, not dwell on the past. There was a lot to look forward to, after all. Amy was, if Rupert was to be believed, about to be initiated into the collective. Their little community was starting to grow, and now that they had a proper base to work from instead of a squat, it could grow into something even more special.

When the bus arrived, Andy headed up for the top deck as usual. He enjoyed being able to look at the city from a different perspective. You could see all sorts from the top deck. To his annoyance, there were some people sitting in the front seats, which was his favourite spot. He would never admit it to anyone, but he liked to pretend he was driving the bus from up there.

29

'You did what?' Emily winced as her flat mate, Catherine, screeched at her from behind the bathroom door.

'I gave him my phone number,' she replied with a smirk. Catherine emerged from the bathroom in a cloud of perfume. She looked, to Emily's annoyance, amazing.

'Seriously?'

'Seriously.'

'Oh my God, what's happened? Has someone kidnapped the Emily who I used to share a flat with and replaced her with an identical one, only more slutty?'

'Shut up Catherine,' Emily laughed, pushing past her and walking into the bathroom. 'Just because I gave the lad my number doesn't make me a slut.'

'Emily, my dear, you are so close to being a nun that giving a man your phone number is virtually prostitution.'

'Yeah, you'd know,' Emily mumbled, pushing the door shut with her foot. A couple of months ago, Catherine had been refused entry to a Holiday Fun hotel in the middle of Norwich because the staff there thought she was on the game. Catherine wasn't, but it was the third night on the trot she'd turned up at the place. Each time with a different man.

Emily took her time putting her face on. Her and Catherine were meeting up with Gary and a few of his friends for a meal later, and at least two of his friends were straight as a die. That was according to Gary though, and Emily had learned that his definition of straight and hers were subtly different. She was looking forward to going out though. It was ages since they'd had a proper night out, her and Catherine.

'If it all works out with burger boy, just help yourself to supplies from my top drawer,' Catherine called through the door. 'There's a selection of sizes in there, but start with the smallest and work your way up.' Emily frowned, unsure for a few seconds exactly what Catherine was talking about. 'If you start off with the largest ones and they fall off, it can put them right off their stride as they're suddenly thinking maybe they're not as large as they think they are.' Condoms, Emily realised. Catherine was talking about condoms.

'I'm good thanks, Catherine,' she called back. 'I'm a way off needing anything like that.'

'Okay, well if that keeps going there's some other supplies in my bottom drawer you're welcome to use to keep the old cobwebs away.' Emily frowned at herself in the mirror. 'Just clean them properly afterwards, yeah? Antiseptic wipes though, not just a rinse under the tap,' Catherine said. Emily's frown turned into a grimace and she half heard Catherine say something else.

'What was that?' Emily asked. Catherine's face appeared at the bathroom door. 'I said, the mains plug for the purple bad boy is in the same drawer. Don't leave it plugged in though. It gets proper hot.' Emily reached out with her foot and closed the door in Catherine's face.

'You're sick,' Emily said as she tried to finish off putting on her makeup without laughing.

A couple of hours later, Emily and Catherine were sitting next to each other at a long table in a new pub called 'Delia's Divas' on Riverside, one of Norwich's more popular nightspots. The unique selling point of the pub was that on the stroke of midnight every Saturday, a bunch of strippers with very skimpy yellow and green outfits came out and did their thing. Emily had never stayed out long enough to enjoy the spectacle, but according to Catherine, they danced along to a song called 'Let's be having you' and always went down well. Much like Catherine, Emily had thought as her friend had explained the spectacle to her.

Everyone had ordered food and were waiting for their first course. Gary was sitting on the other side of Emily, and he and Catherine were trading good natured insults, mostly about how Gary was only gay because Catherine hadn't got to him first. Emily sat there, content to just listen to the two of them riff off each other, when Catherine got up to either sexually harass the waiter or go to the toilet.

'She's a one, isn't she?' Gary said, taking a sip from his beer as Catherine disappeared into the crowded pub.

'Certainly is,' Emily replied, considering telling Gary about the conversation that she and Catherine had earlier. She decided against it in the end on the grounds that a gay man probably wouldn't be that interested in Catherine's collection of sex toys. Especially the mains operated ones. 'So tell me a bit about your friends,' she said, lowering her voice and nodding at the four men sitting opposite them.

They were engaged in a loud conversation about Norwich City's problems at the back, each one of them trying to outdo the other with his opinion. Gary had introduced them all earlier, but it had all been done in a bit of a rush.

'Okay, so left to right,' Gary leaned over to Emily, and she caught a whiff of his aftershave. 'John, Neil, Steve, and French.'

'French?' Emily said. 'Weird nickname.'

'Not really.'

'How come?'

'He's from France.'

'Oh,' Emily said. 'I didn't notice that when you introduced us.'

'No worries. So, again, left to right,' Gary continued, his voice even lower. 'Gay, gay, claims to be straight but actually gay, and straight.'

'Claims to be straight? That's Steve, right?'

'Yeah, nice enough lad,' Gary replied. 'But I'd steer clear if I was you. He's all mouth and no trousers, as far as you're concerned. Talks the talk, but doesn't walk your walk, if you get my drift?'

As Emily looked at the four men sitting opposite, she saw French — the only properly straight one according to Gary — catch her eye and tilt his drink toward her with a smile. He wasn't bad looking, in Emily's opinion. A bit on the smarmy side perhaps, but that could just be the way the light was reflecting off his dark, slicked back hair. Definitely too much gel though, Emily thought as she tilted her glass in his direction. He held her eyes for just longer than was absolutely necessary before returning to his conversation.

'See, he likes you,' Gary said as Catherine returned to the table and sat down with an exaggerated sigh.

'Those toilets are minging,' Catherine said to no-one in

particular before turning to Emily. 'So, what's on the menu tonight then?'

'Er, I've order pâté on toast for a starter, then the lamb shank,' Emily replied.

'No, fool. Not that menu,' Catherine nodded to the other side of the table where the Gary's friends were sitting, 'that menu over there.'

'Oh, right. Well, see the bloke in the red shirt?' Emily said, inclining her head at straight-but-actually-gay Steve, and Catherine nodded enthusiastically. 'The minute you got up to go to the toilet, he was like 'who is she, is she single, she's well fit' and all that. He's called Steve, and he's definitely interested.'

Emily watched as Catherine's eyelids drooped and regarded Steve through half-closed eyes.

'Really?' she said.

'Really,' Emily replied. 'Plus, Gary's seen him in the changing rooms at football and apparently, Steve looks like he could pack a bit of a punch, if you get my drift?'

'Interesting,' Catherine murmured. A couple of seconds later, she got to her feet and whispered something in French's ear. He stood, and the two of them exchanged places. As French sat down next to Emily, he smiled again at her. She tried to keep a straight face as Catherine nestled into Steve's arm, before realising that French wasn't actually too bad looking at all up close.

'Hi,' Emily said, turning her eyes from Catherine 'accidentally' resting one of her breasts on Steve's forearm and turned to her new companion with what she hoped was a demure smile. 'It's French, isn't it?' His face broke into a broad smile. Not too shabby by a long stretch of the imagination, Emily thought.

'Yep, that's me. And you're Emily.'

'You don't sound like you're from France, though,'

Emily said. If anything, he had a broader Norfolk accent than any of the others.

'I'm not,' French replied. 'I'm from Swaffham.'

'Oh," Emily said, taking a sip from her glass of wine. She could hear Gary smothering a laugh beside her. 'Right.'

30

By the time Andy got off the bus at the stop nearest the farm, it was almost nine o'clock. The weekend bus timetable was a nightmare at the best of times and he'd had to wait ages for one to turn up. He was looking forward to seeing the others again, even though he'd only been gone for a single night. Going back to his parents' house had been a good chance to relax a bit and recharge his batteries. One person he was really looking forward to seeing again was Ruth. Even though their friendship was based on the fact that he hadn't slept with her, or even tried to sleep with her, she was growing on him. So much so that, when Hannah and Matthew's bunks had collapsed the other morning, Andy had been lying in bed nursing a painful erection which he blamed on Ruth. Spending half the night listening to the other two shagging hadn't helped though. Maybe it was time, he thought as he made his way across the field toward the farmhouse. Maybe it had been long enough?

When he got to within a couple of hundred yards of the farmhouse, he saw the front door fly open. To his surprise, someone came hurtling out of the door and started sprinting toward him through the early evening gloom. It was only when he heard Ruth's frantic voice screaming his name that he realised who it was. Andy had spent the last few minutes wondering about whether or not to act on his early morning call to glory if it happened again, and here she was running toward him. Perhaps it wasn't going to be as awkward as he'd feared?

As Ruth got closer to him, Andy could see that she wasn't running toward him because she was pleased to see him. If anything, she looked terrified. By the time she got to within a couple of yards, he could see the tears streaming down her face.

'Oh my God, Andy,' Ruth said, flinging her arms around him. 'Thank fuck you're back.' She was out of breath from running, and Andy could feel her thin chest heaving.

'Hey, Ruth,' Andy replied, gently pushing her shoulders back so that he could see her face. 'I missed you too. Is everything okay?'

'No, it's not,' she said. Her face started to wrinkle. 'It's not okay at all. It's Matthew. He's gone bonkers.' Fresh tears made their way down her cheeks.

'What do you mean?'

'He's gone bloody mad.' She tugged at his sleeve. 'Come on, we need to get to the chicken shed. Hannah and Amy are both there, keeping an eye on him to make sure he doesn't do anything stupid.'

'Sorry, wait,' Andy stood his ground. 'Did you just say chicken shed? I didn't know we had a chicken shed?'

'We have now,' Ruth replied, brushing the back of her hand across her face. 'Come on, I'll explain on the way.'

Andy fell into step beside Ruth as she power-walked away from the farmhouse and toward the outbuildings in the distance. One of which was now, according to Ruth at least, a chicken shed.

'So, we'd all gone out. Me, Hannah, and Amy. Matthew stayed behind as he wasn't feeling brilliant after, well you know, after his accident.' Ruth was talking twice as fast as she normally did. 'We met a really fat bloke who made toasted sandwiches out of Hannah's bread. He made us some too. They were lush.'

'Ruth,' Andy said, 'slow down a bit would you? I can hardly understand you.' She looked at him with a wan smile.

'Sorry, it's because I'm all wound up.'

'I know you are, I can see that. Just relax. If Hannah and Amy are looking after him, there's no rush for us to get there, is there?'

'Okay,' Ruth said, slipping an arm through the crook of Andy's elbow. 'I'll try.' She took a deep breath, and then continued just as quickly as she had been before. 'So, we get back and unload the chickens and then go back to the farmhouse to celebrate.' Andy opened his mouth to ask about the chickens when Ruth continued, cutting him off. 'Matthew was acting a bit weird, spaced out like. We just figured he'd had a spliff or two while we were out, but when we told him about the chickens, he started banging on about how he wanted to species identify with them.'

'Sorry, what?' Andy asked.

'Species identify. Like gender identify. That's what he said. He kept going on about how if it was okay to gender identify as a different gender, even if you've got all the right dangly bits for a man, then he should be able to species identify as a chicken if he wanted to. Even though he's not one.'

'Bloody hell,' Andy muttered. 'That doesn't sound

good.' Ruth started to giggle, and then launched into an impromptu impression of Matthew.

'I refuse to be put into a homo sapiens box. To refuse my right to species identify as a non-human is to deny my right to existence.'

'Oh dear,' Andy replied.

'Then he stormed out of the farmhouse, saying we were all just part of the cis-stem and that he wanted to be with his own kind.'

Ruth slowed to a normal walking pace, much to Andy's relief. She was talking so much that she was getting out of breath. 'So, we followed him at a distance. Hannah was saying that Rupert had been stockpiling drugs until he found something that would persuade Amy to have sex with him, and that she thought Matthew had probably found the stash and helped himself to some acid or something. That's where he's gone.'

'That's where who's gone? Matthew?'

'No, Matthew's in the chicken shed. Rupert's in the city trying to sleep with a ginger woman, I think. Or is that Monday night? I can't remember. He's not here anyway.' Andy frowned. He'd been gone for a single night, and hadn't got a clue what had happened since he'd left the day before.

'But where did the chickens come from?' Andy asked. Ruth hadn't explained that bit yet, and it was pretty fundamental to the whole story. At least, the bit of the story with Matthew in it. Not Rupert. Why he was trying to shag a ginger could wait until later.

'We liberated them,' Ruth gasped. 'From a battery farm just outside Norwich. We were only going for a look and we ended up freeing loads of them. Maybe a hundred? We let the ones we couldn't get in the back of the Land Rover go free into the wild.'

'Oh, right,' Andy said. 'Okay, I think. Will Rupert be okay with that?'

'Bugger Rupert,' Ruth replied. Andy was just thinking that he'd rather not when he heard the sound of clucking in the distance. To his inexperienced ear, it sounded like a lot more than a hundred chickens.

Ruth and Andy got to the door of the chicken shed, and Ruth banged on the door with the flat of her hand. A few seconds later, Amy and Hannah slipped out, careful to close the door behind them. Andy caught the scared-looking face of a large red and white chicken staring through the gap as Hannah pushed it shut.

'Ew, what's that smell?' Andy said as a pungent odour hit his nostrils. 'Is that the chickens?'

'No,' Amy replied with a fierce look at him. 'It's me.' Andy looked at her, and her clothes were covered in something very unpleasant looking. 'I had to sit in the back of the Land Rover on the way back from the farm.' She flashed a hostile stare at Ruth and Hannah. 'Covered in chicken shit, so I am.'

'Is Matthew okay?' Andy asked, fighting a smile. From the look on Amy's face, the whole thing was not funny at all.

'He's like a pig in shit,' Hannah said. 'In there with his people, or his chickens. I think they're teaching him how to forage.'

'He is completely and utterly,' Amy said, 'out of his head on something.'

The small group stood talking for a few moments. Andy figured that the best thing to do was to leave Matthew in the shed until he'd come down off whatever he had taken. Hannah was all for manhandling him back to the farmhouse and locking him in the bathroom. Neither Amy or Ruth had really got a clue what to do, but it was obvious to Andy that they were both frightened by the whole thing. They had just decided that leaving him where he was would be the safest course of action when Andy heard a loud 'cluck' from above their head. He looked up to Matthew perched twenty feet above them on the edge of the shed roof, silhouetted against the setting sun.

'Cluck,' Matthew repeated, waving his arms up and down.

'He seems to have settled into his new species quite well, anyway,' Hannah said, crossing her arms over her chest and smiling. This was ridiculous, Andy thought. It was time to stop arsing about. Someone needed to take control of the situation, and it might as well be him.

'Matthew,' Andy shouted. 'Get down off the fucking roof, would you?' Matthew didn't look down at them. Instead, he flapped his arms again with his eyes fixed on the horizon — three, four times in quick succession.

Andy, Ruth, Amy, and Hannah scattered like flies as Matthew launched himself off the roof, still flapping his arms wildly. When he hit the concrete ground in front of the shed, the first sound the others heard was a sickening crack. The next was a deafening, totally un-chicken-like scream. Andy stared at the white shard of bone that was now sticking through a hole in Matthew's trousers.

'Oh crap,' Andy muttered.

31

R upert crouched down in the bushes, wincing as he did so. He'd spent hours doing the same thing earlier in the day, and wasn't very happy about spending any more time hiding in undergrowth, but he didn't have a choice.

He'd been sitting in the front of the empty top deck of the bus when he'd looked over the fields towards the farm he now called home. To his horror, he could see the flashing blue lights reflecting off the buildings at the farm. The bus was too far away for him to be able to work out exactly where the emergency was, but the blue lights were definitely at the farm. He ended up getting off the bus earlier than normal, just in case there were police waiting at his usual stop, and walking a few hundred yards to try to get a clear view of whatever was going on. The problem was that Rupert was still too far away to see anything other than blue flashes bouncing off the buildings, even when he did use the binoculars. He couldn't even see which emergency service it was.

Rupert sat on the damp earth under the bush, crossed

his legs and tried to get as comfortable as he could before reaching into his pocket for a tobacco tin. He opened the tin, pulled out a very fat joint that he'd put together earlier that day, and lit up. As he smoked it, Rupert wondered what the hell was going on up at the farm.

By the time he'd finished the joint, the blue lights had disappeared. He was just considering whether or not to head across to the farm when a pair of white headlights appeared. Rupert watched as they inched their way down the track towards his location. He shuffled back further into the bushes as the headlights got closer. He didn't want to be seen by the bloody pigs. The vehicle behind the headlights appeared through the gloom and Rupert could see that it wasn't a police car or fire engine, but an ambulance.

'What the fuck?' he muttered under his breath as the box-shaped vehicle turned onto the main road. As it made its way past Rupert's hiding spot, there was a sound like an angry chicken from the general direction of the vehicle. 'What the fuck?' Rupert said again as he watched the red lights on the back of the ambulance disappear down the road into the darkness.

Twenty minutes later, Rupert pushed the door to the farm-house open and walked into the kitchen. He looked around — Hannah, Ruth, Amy and Andy were all sitting around the gnarled wooden table with shot glasses in front of them.

'What the fuck's going on?' Rupert asked, looking at them in turn. Hannah got to her feet and walked over to give him a hug. As she pressed herself into him, she whispered in his ear.

'Matthew got to your stash. Don't know what he took, but it fucked him over properly.'

'What?' Rupert exclaimed, pushing Hannah away from him. 'Is he okay?'

'Well, he's still alive, which is a bonus,' Rupert heard Andy say. 'The paramedics gave him something to calm him down a bit. Make him a bit less chicken-like.' Ruth started sniggering, but she stopped the minute Rupert looked at her.

'Does someone want to tell me what the hell's going on?' he asked.

'Sit down, Rupert,' Hannah replied, filling a fresh glass with whisky before topping up the others. She put the glass on the table and gestured to the empty seat. 'Sit down.'

Rupert sat, as instructed, and then sniffed. He sniffed again, more deeply.

'Fuck me, what's that smell?'

Amy sighed and got to her feet. She left the kitchen, not looking at any of the others as she did so. Hannah took a deep breath, and started telling Rupert the whole story. He could feel his anger start to build up when she was telling him about how they'd decided to strike a blow for girl power, even though that wasn't exactly the language that she used. By the time she got to the part where Matthew started going a bit weird, his knuckles were whitening around the shot glass. When Hannah had finished the full story, he put his hands in his lap and clenched and unclenched his fists a couple of times. What he really wanted to was bang them hard on the kitchen table to make them all wake up a bit and realise how fucked up the whole situation was, but instead he said nothing. A few deep breaths later, he got to his feet, leaving the glass on the table.

Rupert walked through to his and Hannah's bedroom, ignoring the tempting sound of Amy in the shower as he did so. Much as he wanted to step into the bathroom and help her with the soap, he wasn't sure that he would be that welcome from the look on her face as she'd left the kitchen. He crossed to the bedside cabinet on his side of the bed and pulled the top drawer open so that he could get to the small money tin inside. Rupert looked at the red metal box, which contained his personal collection of drugs, but he couldn't see any fresh scratches on the lock or other signs that someone had tried to open it.

'You okay?' Hannah's voice came from behind him. He glanced over his shoulder to see her leaning against the door jamb, her bright red hair cascading over her shoulders.

'I don't think he's been at my stash, Hannah,' Rupert said, nodding at the red box. He pulled a small key out of his pocket and unlocked it. Inside the box was just what he expected to see. 'Nope, not been touched.'

'Rupert, we're not kidding. He was off his tits. Convinced he was a chicken, so he was. That's why he jumped. I honestly think he thought he could fly.'

'I don't doubt you, Hannah,' Rupert said, seeing Hannah's earnest expression. 'But whatever he took, it wasn't from here.'

'His leg was a fucking mess,' Hannah sighed, sitting on the edge of the bed and putting her head in her hands. Rupert regarded her, unsure for a few seconds what to do, before crossing to the bed and sitting next to her.

'I can't imagine,' he said, putting an arm around her shoulders as she leaned into him. 'I really can't.'

They sat for a moment before Hannah broke the silence.

'So, what's the plan for tonight, then?'

'Well, I had planned on welcoming Amy to the collective,' Rupert replied with a grin. 'If everyone else is up for it, that is?'

'Matthew will be disappointed to miss out on that,' Hannah said.

'Can chickens feel disappointment?'

'Probably not.'

'Besides,' Rupert said with a glance at the red box, 'from what you told me, he's had more than enough of something.'

Rupert sat at the kitchen table, Hannah on one side of him and Andy on the other. Ruth and Amy were also there, and they were all holding the hands of the person on either side of them. Hannah and Amy had their fingers wrapped together like a cats cradle. In the middle of the table was the red box, its lid open, and the cellophane wrapped contents in plain view. Rupert looked over at Amy, who was staring at the box intently. Perhaps tonight was the night he could finish what he'd tried to start the other night, Rupert thought.

'Friends, lovers,' he whispered before sneaking a glance at Amy, catching her eye at just the right moment. 'Lovers to be. We gather here for one purpose, and for one purpose only. To welcome Amy, our latest arrival, and to celebrate Matthew's sacrifice.' That last point was a bit of a stretch and was something that Rupert had thought of a split second before he'd said it. As he caught the confused looks of the others, he decided to move on. 'We don't have many traditions in this group, but possibly the most important one we do have…' he paused for effect, '…is that when we have a new arrival we open our minds to let them in.'

Rupert's face broke into a broad grin. He knew, or at least was reasonably certain, who needed what. Ruth and Andy both needed something to get them to stop pretending to shag each other and actually do the deed. Hannah and Amy needed something to relax past their boundaries and just let go of their inhibitions. Rupert thought about the small blue diamond-shaped pills hidden away in his trouser pockets. That was all he needed, he thought as he reached toward the red box and selected a package for each of the others. He placed something in front of each of them before leaning back and taking Hannah and Andy's hands back.

'Let us pray,' Rupert said, trying to hide the excitement he felt.

32

Andy looked at the small parcel on the table in front of him. He untangled his hand from Ruth's and unwrapped the cellophane. Inside was a single round white tablet, with something imprinted on the surface. Andy leaned towards the pill to see what the engraving was. It was a bit indistinct, but it looked to him very much like a bird. How appropriate. Andy looked at Rupert to try to work out if this was deliberate.

'This is the hors d'oevre,' Rupert whispered. Around the table, Andy could see that they all had the same pill.

'Sorry, the what?' Ruth asked.

'It's a starter, isn't it?' Andy said. 'Like, something small before the main course.'

'Which is what, exactly?'

'Outside the work, literally speaking,' Amy replied. 'It's French.'

'Oh, okay,' Ruth said, 'but I meant what is it?' She emphasised the word 'is' with a pointed finger at the small white pill in front of her.

'Well, technically it's ecstasy,' Rupert explained. 'But,

according to Danny, it's not just any old ecstasy. It's been genetically engineered into something slightly different. Much softer than normal MDMA. Apparently, this particular little beauty is a very sensual little character.'

'Have you actually taken this, Rupert?' Andy asked, prodding the white tablet with his index finger.

'No,' Rupert replied. 'But I don't need to. I trust Danny implicitly.'

'Is this the same Danny who refuses to have a haircut on the basis that hairdressers are all employed by the government?' Hannah chipped in. She had a cheeky grin on her face as she examined her pill, holding it in front of her eyes between her thumb and index finger.

'Thank you, Hannah,' Rupert said with a sigh. Andy got the impression this wasn't the first time they'd had this conversation. 'Danny's had more drugs than we've had hot dinners. You only have to look at his eyes to know that.'

Andy looked at Rupert, not trusting him or his drug dealer friend for a second. He picked up the pill, put in in his mouth as the others did the same thing, and tucked it into the gap between his cheek and his gums with his tongue. Then he opened his mouth wide, the pill safely hidden from sight, and turned his head from side to side to prove that he'd taken it. This was all part of the ritual. He knew that he could just say that he wasn't interested in taking anything, and that it wouldn't really have been a problem, but the warmth of Ruth's thigh pressing against his was beginning to get to him.

The group sat around the table for about twenty minutes, Andy getting increasingly concerned about the pill lodged between his cheek and gums. Physiology wasn't his strong point, but he was worried about the bloody thing dissolving and him getting the full dose of whatever it was Rupert had given them. He looked over at Amy and

Hannah, who still had their hands clasped together, and realised that they were both starting to feel the effects of the pill. Rupert, who a few minutes after taking the ecstasy had walked over to the counter and put a *Velvet Underground* album on, also had a slightly glazed expression.

'I think I need a bit of fresh air,' Andy said. He looked at the others, but apart from Ruth, none of them seemed to have noticed that he had said anything. He got to his feet.

'I'll come too,' Ruth stood as well.

The two of them made their way to the front door of the kitchen and, totally ignored by the others still sitting at the kitchen table, walked out into the night. It was pitch black outside, and Andy shivered at the sudden change in temperature. He stood in the courtyard in front of the farmhouse and Ruth sidled up next to him. He turned to look at her face, illuminated in the light coming through the kitchen windows.

'Andy,' Ruth said, moving to stand right in front of him.

'Yeah?'

'Can you keep a secret?'

'Of course I can,' Andy replied. 'You know that.' Ruth leaned forward a few inches, and for a second Andy thought that she was going to kiss him. Instead, she just stuck her tongue out. He was just trying to work out what to say when he saw the small white round pill on the end of her tongue. Andy laughed, and manoeuvred his tongue inside his mouth before poking it out as well, balancing his own tablet on the tip of his tongue. They looked at each other for a few seconds, before Ruth raised her hand to her mouth. She threw her pill on the floor as Andy spat his in the same direction. They looked at each other and laughed.

'Guess we've both got a secret now,' Ruth said. 'Not your thing either?'

'Not really,' Andy replied. 'I was going to just say no, but…' His word tailed off.

'But what?'

'I don't know. I guess I didn't want to be the sad one not joining in.'

'Yeah, I get that,' Ruth sighed. 'Me neither, to be honest.' They walked in silence for a few moments, making their way down the track to the main road. Ruth slipped her arm through the crook of Andy's elbow. A hundred yards or so before the junction of the track and the main road, an old tree lay on its side. They walked over to it and sat down, the curve of the trunk pressing them against each other, and sat in silence for a few moments. Andy was churning things over in his head, trying to work out what to say or do next, when Ruth spoke.

'I'm horny as anything, you know that?'

'Oh,' Andy replied. That wasn't what he'd been expecting her to say at all. He paused for a few seconds, unsure what to say. Should he say anything at all? Andy turned to look at Ruth, wondering if he should kiss her or something. She was just staring up at the stars, and made no effort to turn to look at him at all. 'Er, right. Well that's nice,' he said, as he couldn't think of anything else in the moment.

'Rupert knows.'

'Knows what?' Andy said. 'Knows that you're, er, horny?'

'Probably.' Andy looked at Ruth as she replied, but he couldn't see her properly in the darkness. 'I think he knows that we're not actually sleeping together, even though we're pretending to.'

'Maybe we should stop pretending,' Andy said in a low

voice. The minute he'd said the words, he realised that it was his inner voice speaking and that he hadn't actually meant to say it out loud.

'Maybe we should,' Ruth said, and Andy could tell from the tone of her voice that she was smiling. 'God knows I've thought about it enough.' Andy managed to suppress the words 'so have I' so that they stayed in his head.

They sat in silence, both looking up at the stars. Andy sighed.

'Ruth, we're both single. We like each other. So why shouldn't we?' He looked at her, trying to make out her face in the darkness.

'Why shouldn't we what?' she asked, almost in a whisper. 'Go to bed? Properly, I mean?'

Andy paused, again stuck for a response. One obvious answer to that question was 'yes', but he sensed that wasn't the answer Ruth wanted to hear. He decided to say nothing, but to wait to see what she said next. Her reply surprised him.

'Because of her,' she said.

'Who?'

'The one in the picture. I don't know who she is, but she's out there somewhere.'

'Ah, her.'

'The one you're still pining after. Whoever you've not let go.' Ruth's voice had changed, become different somehow. 'I don't want to be a substitute for whoever she is.'

'But you wouldn't be.'

'Andy, don't get me wrong. You're an itch I would love to scratch, and if your hard-on the other morning is anything to go by, the feeling's mutual.' Andy's mouth opened to defend himself but Ruth cut him off. 'Mirror mirror, on the wall, who's got the largest boner of them all? You did a good job trying to hide it, but it didn't work.'

'Er, oh, right,' Andy mumbled. 'I was, I mean…' he paused and took a breath, 'I can't control that.'

'We need to go.'

'Why?'

'Because if we do end up doing the deed, I don't want it to be on a dead tree trunk in the middle of a field.'

33

E mily sat on the sofa in her lounge, sipping from a mug of tea and stabbing at the remote control to try to find something worth watching on the television. She settled on a replay of last night's *Match of the Day*, even though she didn't follow football. There were worse things to watch on a Sunday morning than a bunch of blokes — some of whom were very easy on the eye — running around a field. On the coffee table next to her half-eaten bacon sandwich that she'd called lunch, Emily's phone buzzed. She picked it up and looked at the screen.

Prob won't be back until this eve. C. XXX. Emily sighed at the text message from Catherine and deleted it without bothering to reply.

Last night hadn't turned out how she'd hoped, by a long stretch of the imagination. French, despite looking like a hopeful prospect at the start of the evening, was anything but. By the time the main course had arrived, he'd had almost an entire bottle of wine to himself despite buying it for them both. Emily wouldn't have minded — he'd bought the bottle after all — but he shouldn't really drink wine. Ever. One of the last things he'd said that was intelligible was that he could drink as much wine as he wanted because it didn't affect him. Well, Emily thought as she sipped her tea, it did. He'd got up to go for a cigarette after pudding, and when Gary went to find out where he was, French was fast asleep in the beer garden. Gary had thought it was hysterical and kept making jokes about how French was one of the few blokes he knew who fell asleep before sex, not after it, but Emily hadn't thought that was very funny. Especially as Gary's comments suggested that her having sex with French was going to be on the cards. Catherine had told her not to be so stuck up after they'd waved French off in the company of a very unhappy looking taxi driver, but that hadn't helped either.

Emily had decided to go with what was left of the group to a nightclub on the Prince of Wales Road, and after paying a tenner to get into a ropey looking place with a sticky floor, had stayed about ten minutes. Which was exactly the length of time Catherine took to find herself some poor unsuspecting victim for the evening, and as it turned out, the rest of the night and most of Sunday as well.

'Hey ho,' Emily said to herself as the team in red and white on the television scored yet another goal. She then watched, slack-jawed, as an improbably good-looking foot-baller ran across the pitch in slow motion to celebrate with his fans. 'Bloody hell,' she whispered. 'What has he been eating?'

Now that she had the whole day in front of her, she thought about what she could do. Catherine and she hadn't planned anything, but Emily needed to do something. Besides, even if they had planned anything Catherine wasn't there anyway. Emily picked up her phone from the coffee table and scrolled through her contacts.

When she reached the bottom of the list, she realised how few friends she actually had. Maybe she should take up a few new hobbies, join a group or something. The only problem with that was there wasn't that much she was interested in.

'Right then,' she said, getting to her feet. 'I am going to the gym.' Saying it out loud to herself made it sound more likely that it would actually happen, even if she wasn't sure where her trainers were. It was the footballer's fault, for looking so damn fit. She could go for a run on the tread-mill, then go for a sauna and a swim. One thing she wasn't going to do again was use the bloody cross-trainer. Not after falling off it last time, right in front of the best looking bloke in the whole place.

Twenty minutes later, Emily at least looked the part, even if she wasn't as keen as she had been earlier. She was dressed in a pair of leggings, a loose t-shirt over a sports bra that she'd forgotten she even had. It had been hidden in the back of her wardrobe along with her musty training shoes. Just as she was about to pick up her sports bag and head out, her phone rang. Emily glanced at the screen. It was Mr Clayton, but why he was phoning on a Sunday was anyone's guess. Relieved to have an excuse to postpone her gym trip even if only for a few minutes, she answered the phone and sat back down on the sofa.

'Hi Mr Clayton,' Emily said.

'Emily,' Mr Clayton replied. 'I'm sorry to call you on a Sunday. Hope I'm not disturbing you?' It sounded to Emily like he was calling from the inside of a bathroom. A very crowded one.

'Not at all,' she said. 'I was just on my way to the gym. Could you speak up a bit though? It's very noisy where you are.'

'Hang on a second,' he replied. Emily waited, and

when he next spoke the line was much clearer. 'Is that better?'

'Yep, much better. I can hear you now.'

'Sorry, I was in a pub. I'm outside now, though.' Emily frowned. Why on Earth was he calling from a pub? 'I'm on my way to the football.'

'Oh, okay,' Emily said.

'Norwich are at home to Real Madrid. First leg of the semi-finals.' There was a pause, and Emily wasn't sure if she was supposed to say something. Mr Clayton continued. 'The Champions league?'

'Got you,' Emily replied. 'I did see something about that in the paper. You're going then, are you?'

'Definitely,' he replied. 'I wouldn't miss this one for anything. I'm surprised you're not watching it on the television. It's on BBC and everything.'

Emily reached out with the remote control and turned the television back on. Sure enough, according to the electronic guide, kick off was in less than an hour's time.

'I didn't call to talk about the football though, Emily,' Mr Clayton said. 'Listen, I just had a toasted sandwich at a van that's parked in front of the pub. I think you did the inspection?'

'Are you at the Fat Canary?'

'Yep, that's the one. "Toast With The Most", the van's called,' Mr Clayton replied.

'Is there a problem with it?' Emily asked, relieved that he wasn't phoning her to talk about the football — that would be a bit odd — but she was also concerned about Sam. Emily had a bit of a soft spot for the old boy, and she hoped that he'd not done something to upset her boss.

'Oh no, no problem at all. The sandwich was fantastic. I'm hoping he's still there after the match so I can get another one on the way home,' Mr Clayton said. 'But I was talking to him about his suppliers, and he mentioned one that I'd not heard of before. Can you look them up on the database?'

'What, now?' As soon as the words were out of her mouth, Emily realised she'd been a bit on the sharp side. Even so, it was Sunday. There was a pause on the other end of the line.

'Erm, well not right this minute, but at some point, perhaps?'

'Sure, no problem,' Emily forced a smile onto her face so that she at least sounded a bit less annoyed. 'Let me just grab a pen.'

When Mr Clayton had ended the call a few moments later, saying that they would catch up on Monday, Emily looked at the scribbled name on the piece of paper in front of her. 'Another Way' was the supplier's name, and Emily was intrigued enough to open up her laptop and log into the Food Standards Agency database. Mr Clayton had been right. The supplier wasn't in the database. Emily frowned and nibbled at her pen. The problem was if Sam was using an unregistered supplier for his sandwiches, he could get a reprimand from the Food Standards Agency which could cause him problems with the city council. He could even lose his pitch outside the pub. Emily would need to persuade Mr Clayton to turn a blind eye for a day or two until she could get the supplier registered. Then Sam would be in the clear, at least as far as the council was concerned.

On the television in front of her, the Norwich City line-up was being announced, accompanied by pictures of the players. Some of them were rather nice, she noticed, apart from the short ginger Irish one. He didn't do it for her at all, but there were some good-looking lads in the team. Emily pulled her arms into her t-shirt, and worked her sports bra off, pulling it through a sleeve before slinging the undergarment on the floor. The bloody thing was digging into her anyway. It must have shrunk a bit in the back of the cupboard. She eased her trainers off her feet and put her feet up on the coffee table, wiggling her toes in their as yet unused running socks.

'Going to the gym, my arse,' she mumbled, wriggling into the cushions and promising herself she would at least make it to half time before opening a bottle of wine.

34

Hannah waited for a few seconds before opening her eyes. She could tell that, even though she'd only woken up a few seconds before, it was going to hurt. There was sunlight streaming in through the bedroom window despite the fact the curtains were drawn — she could see the bright light even through her closed eyelids. Next to her, Rupert rolled over, taking most of the duvet with him.

'For fuck's sake,' she muttered, reaching out with her arm and grabbing the duvet. With a jerk, she pulled it back to cover her body. Hannah had been so smashed last night that she'd gone to bed with no clothes on, which she didn't do that often at all. Either that, or she'd just not put them back on after Rupert had finished. Hannah had no idea — she couldn't remember anything after about midnight.

'Morning, sleepyhead,' a voice next to her said. Hannah's eyes snapped open. That wasn't Rupert's voice.

'What?' Hannah exclaimed, blinking in the bright light until she could see Amy's tousled hair and wry smile. 'What the fuck? Where's Rupert?'

'No idea,' Amy said, her smile widening. 'You told him

to fuck off last night. Several times in fact, but he got the message.'

'Why did I tell him to fuck off?'

'Because we were busy,' Amy said.

'Oh my God, were we?' Hannah replied.

'Yes,' Amy's smile faltered. 'Don't you remember?'

'No, I don't think so.' Hannah thought hard for a few seconds. Some vague memories started to come back. Rupert daring Hannah to kiss Amy, and Hannah taking him up on the dare. Rupert getting angry that they wouldn't stop. Rupert storming out of the kitchen. Hannah felt her heart start to flutter in her chest as she realised why she was naked. She had finally done what Rupert had been trying to get her to do for years, and wasn't at all sure how she felt about it. Particularly with a bastard of a hangover. 'Jesus, I remember bits of it.'

'Well, I remember all of it,' Amy said, lifting her arms and putting them behind her head. The duvet slipped down as she did so. Hannah wasn't alone in being naked, and one thing Amy wasn't was shy. 'Every last minute.' Hannah swung her legs out of the bed and looked around for her clothes. They were strewn on the bedroom floor, as were Amy's. She grabbed the ones that she could see were hers and started to get dressed.

'Did we really, I mean, did we do everything?' Hannah asked, scared and excited in equal measures. Had they really done last night what she thought they had?

'Pretty much. I think what I enjoyed the most,' Amy continued beside her, 'was the way you started grinding your teeth when I — '

'Amy,' Hannah cut her off. 'Listen, I'm sure it was lovely and all that, but I don't know how I feel about it. I mean, I'm pretty liberal but even so, I must have been smashed to actually go through with anything. Rupert's been goading me for years to get it on with another woman. He must have pushed me over the edge last night.' She got to her feet and pulled her trousers up over her hips. 'I just don't think it's really my thing, you know?' Amy's smile broadened, and she pulled the duvet up to just under her chin.

'Sure, babe,' she replied. 'It was only sex, that was all.' Amy closed her eyes, but the smile remained on her face. 'Only sex,' she murmured.

Hannah walked through into the kitchen, her heart still racing, and flicked the kettle on. The room was an utter mess. Empty wine bottles and crushed cans of lager littered the table, which had an ashtray that was overflowing with half smoked joints as a centrepiece. Hannah walked past a suspicious looking puddle of something on the flagstones on her way to the fridge. She grabbed some milk and gave it a quick sniff before going to find Rupert. The first bedroom had Andy and Ruth in it, both in their own bunks and both still fast asleep. She closed the door quietly and walked to the next room.

Rupert was in there, lying on the bottom bunk. He was wide awake and staring at the underside of the bed above him.

'Morning,' Hannah said. Rupert waited for a few seconds before replying.

'Morning,' he said, not looking at her, but keeping his gaze fixed on the upper bunk.

'Do you want a cup of tea?'

'Do I want a cup of tea?'

'Yes, Rupert, do you want a cup of tea?' Hannah paused. 'Or not, I don't really care either way.'

'Interesting choice of words there, Hannah. Don't you think?' Rupert turned his head to look at Hannah, the anger in his eyes obvious.

'What is?' Hannah replied. She wasn't really in the mood for an argument, but if they were going to have one, they might as well get it out of the way. One thing Rupert couldn't do was hold a grudge for long but if he was going to be an arsehole about it, Hannah wanted it out of his system. She needed some time to think.

'I don't care, either way,' Rupert said, emphasising the words 'either' and 'way'. Hannah walked to the bunks and sat on the edge of the lower bed.

'You don't own me, Rupert,' Hannah said, reaching out and moving one of his dreadlocks from his face. 'Just like I don't own you. That's how we work, isn't it?' He shuffled over to give her some more room on the bottom bunk, and Hannah ran her finger down his chest. She had an idea of how she could make him a bit less grumpy. 'When I'm with someone else,' she lowered her voice to a whisper, 'I'm with someone else. But when I'm with you, I'm with you.' Hannah slid her hand into his boxer shorts, and Rupert gasped.

'Jesus, you've got cold hands.'

'You're such a romantic, Rupert,' Hannah smiled. He winced as she gripped him. 'Now do you want a cup of tea or not?'

'In a minute,' Rupert replied, lying back into the pillow and grinning.

It was just over a minute later when Hannah walked back into the kitchen, hands washed and mission accomplished. Rupert was happy, at least for the moment. She was waiting for the kettle to boil when he walked up behind her, and wrapped his arms around her chest.

'You are such a slapper, Hannah,' he breathed in her ear. 'Can I ask you something, though?' Oh God, Hannah thought. Here he goes.

'What?' she replied.

'What was it like?'

'What was what like?'

'Come on, you know.' Hannah said nothing. A few seconds later, Rupert prompted her. 'What was it like with Amy?'

'Why do you want to know?'

'Curious. Unless you've been telling porkies, that was your first time with another woman, wasn't it?'

'Yep, it was,' Hannah sighed. She might as well come clean. 'Can you keep a secret?'

'You know I can.' Rupert replied. Hannah turned to face him, looking into his blue eyes

'I've got no idea,' she said. 'I can't remember a bloody thing.' To her annoyance, he started laughing.

'You're joking?'

'Nope,' Hannah replied. 'I remember you getting pissed off when we were snogging, but after that, nothing.'

'Nothing at all?'

'Not really, a few fragments but not much.'

Rupert carried on chuckling, and Hannah felt her irritation start to wane.

'That's a bit of a fail,' Rupert said as Hannah turned back round to make the tea. He kept his arms wrapped around her. 'You're still a slapper, though.'

'And you're not?' she replied.

'Guilty as charged,' he chuckled. 'Talking of slappers, I'm seeing that ginger woman from the University tomorrow night.'

'Are you?' Hannah said, untangling his arms from her so that she could make the tea. 'Any particular reason, apart from the obvious one?' Rupert shot her a sheepish grin.

'I want to get hold of her access card.'

'Access card for what?'

'The animal section at the University. It's locked down, and only some people have got access. We can't get in there to liberate the animals without one, so I need to get hold of hers.'

'I bet that's not the only thing you want to get hold of,' Hannah said.

'Now if that's not the pot calling the kettle black, I don't know what is,' Rupert replied.

35

Rupert kept the smile fixed on his face until he was sure that Hannah couldn't see him. The minute she turned away from him to make the tea, he let it drop. What she had just said was unbelievable. Not only had she ended up in bed with Amy, not only had she told him to fuck off just when it looked as if the two women were actually getting down to business, but Hannah couldn't even remember it. After he'd been thrown out of the bedroom — his own bloody bedroom — he'd spent ages trying to work out how he could at least watch what the two them were up to. He'd thought about sneaking back into the room with his phone camera, but the bloody hinges squealed like a banshee. He'd even gone outside and tried to look through the window, but the curtains were still drawn. He'd been able to hear them, but he couldn't see them.

He didn't mind Hannah and Amy getting together for an evening. Not in the slightest. He'd been trying to persuade Hannah to try something like that for ages. What he minded was the fact that he wasn't involved. Not only that, but he was effectively thrown out of his own bedroom so that they could use it. No matter what Hannah thought, a quick hand-job in the morning wasn't anywhere near enough of an apology for that insult. It could keep, though. He resolved to tuck it away for the future. At least it explained why Amy hadn't been up for anything with him the other night.

Rupert hiked the smile back onto his face as he heard the sound of footsteps in the kitchen. He turned to see Andy walking in, hair all over the place and eyes full of sleep. He was followed by Ruth who looked equally shit.

'Hey, you two,' Rupert said, injecting a note of enthusiasm into his voice. 'You guys sleep okay?'

'Yeah, I guess,' Andy mumbled as he sat at the table. Hannah put a cup of tea in front of him, and he held up a thumb by way of a thank you. Ruth sat down next to him.

'Big night last night, wasn't it?' she said. Rupert couldn't remember her having much more than a single ecstasy tablet at the start of the night, and a couple of joints later on. Ruth looked as if she'd had a lot more than that though, and so did Andy.

'Well', Rupert replied with a pointed look at Hannah. 'We had to welcome Amy to the collective somehow, didn't we?'

'Where is Amy, anyway?' Ruth asked.

'Still in bed, recovering from last night,' Hannah replied with a smile in Rupert's direction. He managed to keep his own smile in place as she continued. 'Isn't that right, Rupert?'

'Yeah,' he said. 'I think she had a good night, though.'

'So, what's the plan for today then?' Andy asked, taking a sip from his tea. 'Is there a plan?'

'Once everyone's up and about, we need to go and sort the chickens out,' Rupert said, 'I guess we need to, I don't know, sweep the floor or something? We need to find out what's happening with Matthew, so someone needs to go up to the hospital and find out how he's doing. Maybe you and Ruth could do that?' Andy glanced at Ruth and nodded.

'Sure.'

'I'm out tomorrow night meeting Lauren from the University. She works in the animal laboratory, so hopefully I'll be able to get her access card thing.'

'Oh, cool,' Ruth said just as the kitchen door opened. They all turned to see Amy shuffle in, her duvet wrapped around her shoulders. Rupert tried to keep an even face as he watched the bitch sit down at the table without a care in the world.

'Morning Amy,' he said. 'Did you sleep okay?' She mumbled something that he didn't catch. Hannah shot him a fierce look as she put a cup of tea in front of the woman before sitting down next to her.

Rupert leant up against the kitchen counter and looked at the small group at the kitchen table. As he watched, Hannah ran her fingers through her bright red hair and sighed. She looked exhausted. Amy, who looked just as tired, was just staring into her cup of tea and Rupert noticed her glance at Hannah from underneath her blonde fringe a couple of times. Despite looking like crap, Andy was by far the brightest in comparison which Rupert was pleased about. He saw Andy developing into a trusted lieutenant, more so now that Matthew was going to be out of action for God knows how long. The rest of them though — and he included Hannah in his assessment — were a bit of a sorry bunch. They needed some new blood, but Rupert knew he had to settle the followers he had back down before he could think of introducing anyone new.

Matthew's leg wasn't the only fractured thing in the group at the moment.

Andy got to his feet and turned to face Rupert.

'Right then, me and Ruth will pop down to the shed and sort the chickens out. Then we'll go to the hospital.' Rupert saw him look at his watch. 'The buses only run once an hour on Sunday anyway.' Ruth scraped her chair back and stood.

'Come on then, lover boy,' Ruth said. 'Take me to the chicken sheds, or lose me forever.' There was an awkward silence as the two of them made their way to the kitchen door, which continued for a few seconds after the door had closed behind them. Amy stirred into life from underneath her duvet which was still wrapped around her shoulders.

'They're not actually shagging, are they?' she asked. Both Rupert and Hannah shook their heads from side to side.

'No, pretty sure they're not,' Hannah replied.

'I don't get why not,' Amy continued. 'I mean, they're both young, free, and single.' Rupert tried not to bristle at the way Amy said the word 'single', but from the look Hannah gave him he realised that it hadn't worked.

'It doesn't matter, does it?' he said with a challenging stare at the pair of them. 'Who sleeps with who?' The awkward silence returned.

'What are your plans for tomorrow then, with this woman from the University?' Hannah said. Rupert, grateful for the change in subject, sat down in the chair that Ruth had left behind.

'Well, I think she's on board,' he said. 'She seemed quite keen the other day when I went over there.'

'Keen on what?' Hannah asked. 'The cause?'

'Not specifically,' Rupert replied. 'I mean, she works in an animal institute so she's probably too far gone to help.

But, she can help us.' He finished his sentence by widening his eyes to give them both the full effect of his most valuable assets.

'So,' Hannah said, with a sigh, 'your plan is to have sex with her, and then steal her access card while she's lying gasping for air on the bed murmuring your name in a post-orgasmic stupor?'

'Yeah,' Rupert replied with a sly grin. 'That's pretty much how I think it'll go down.' He looked at the two women, who were both examining their mugs.

'Okay,' Amy said, looking at him with her lips pressed together in a tight line. 'That sounds like a great plan, Rupert.' Her shoulder moved under the duvet, and he saw Hannah flinch. 'So, you'll be out all night then?'

'Probably,' Rupert replied.

The three of them spent the next thirty minutes or so clearing up the kitchen. The uncertain looking stain on the floor was, according to Amy, spilt beer but she still put on a pair of yellow marigolds to clear it up. By the time they had finished, there were three bin liners full of rubbish stacked up by the front door. Amy, who was looking a lot brighter, was just making a cup of tea when the kitchen door burst open and Andy rushed in, followed by an out of breath Ruth.

'What's going on?' Rupert asked. 'Is everything okay?' He watched as Andy pulled something out of his pocket and placed it carefully on the table. 'What's that?' Rupert leaned forward. In the middle of the table was an egg, a single white feather stuck to it. There was a smear of blood across the brown shell.

'That,' Andy replied, pointing a shaking finger at the egg, 'is what's left of the chickens.'

36

H annah stared at the egg, her mouth half open.
'What do you mean, that's what's left of the
chickens?' she asked, looking at Andy's pale face. Behind
him, she could see Ruth who looked as if she was about to
burst into tears.

'I mean exactly that,' Andy replied. 'There's nothing
else in the chicken shed apart from puddles of blood and
feathers everywhere.'

'It was like a scene from a horror film,' Ruth
whispered.

'What the hell happened?' Hannah heard Rupert say.
She turned to look at him leaning up against the door
frame of the kitchen.

'Well, we were walking up to the chicken shed,' Andy
replied. 'When we were a little way off, Ruth realised that
she couldn't hear anything. The day before, you could hear
the chickens a mile away.'

'Not surprising seeing as Matthew was running
around in there pretending to be one,' Rupert said with
a grin.

'Rupert, shush up and let him tell the story,' Hannah admonished him. 'Andy, just ignore him and carry on.'

'So, we couldn't hear a thing and then when we got to the shed, the door was ajar,' Andy said.

Hannah thought back to the previous evening. She was fairly sure that she'd closed the door and latched it when Matthew had clambered up onto the shed roof, and they'd all gone outside to try to talk him down. She'd been the last one out of the shed, that much she was certain of, but perhaps she hadn't latched the door properly after all?

'Then, when we went in to see what was going on,' Ruth continued, breathless with excitement or fear. Hannah wasn't quite sure which it was. 'It stank inside of blood and, like Andy said, there were feathers everywhere. The only thing left was that.' Ruth pointed at the egg on the table with a trembling finger.

'It's a sign,' Amy whispered.

'What?' Rupert said, moving toward the table. 'How is that a sign?'

'Well, it's a symbol of womanhood,' she replied with a glance at Hannah.

'It looks more like an egg to me.'

'You wouldn't understand, Rupert,' Amy said. 'You're a man.'

'What's that got to do with it, Amy?' Rupert replied, his irritation obvious.

'What do you think it was?' Hannah interrupted them, keen to change the subject.

'Must have been dogs or something,' Ruth said. 'You should have seen it in there.' Her eyes flicked between Hannah, Rupert, and Amy's. 'It was intense. Never seen anything like it.'

'More likely a fox,' Rupert said.

'One fox couldn't do that much damage, could it?'

Andy asked. 'There were at least a hundred chickens in there. Now there's none.'

'Maybe he went back to the fox compound, or wherever it is that foxes live, and got all his mates?' Rupert giggled like a child.

'Could be. Bloody hell, though,' Andy replied.

'Who left the door open?'

There was silence in the room as Rupert asked this. Hannah kept her eyes downcast, not daring to look at any of the others. The silence continued for a few seconds until Ruth finally broke it.

'Does it matter?' she asked, her voice bordering on tears. 'It won't bring them back, will it?' She got to her feet as tears started streaming down her face and fled from the kitchen.

'So Ruth left the door open then?' Rupert said with a grim smile. 'That doesn't surprise me.' Hannah opened her mouth to defend Ruth, but decided against it. Owning up to leaving the door open wouldn't help anyone, least of all her. She decided to wait and see what happened. If Rupert started in on Ruth about it, Hannah could always confess then, but until that moment she decided to keep her own counsel.

'What should we do with the egg then?' Hannah asked. 'Should we bury it?'

'We could eat it,' Amy replied in a whisper.

'Amy, we're supposed to be vegans,' Rupert spat back at her. 'Of course we can't bloody well eat it.' Amy didn't even look at him when she replied, but stared at Hannah instead.

'It'd be like placentophagy,' Amy said. 'Don't you think, Hannah? An act of honour for the chickens that gave themselves for us.'

Hannah, who didn't have a clue what 'placentophagy' was and was afraid to ask, just shrugged her shoulders.

'They got eaten by a fox or something, Amy. I don't know that they necessarily gave themselves for us,' Andy said, echoing Hannah's thoughts. 'But we could bury it if it makes you feel better?'

Half an hour later, the small group were gathered around a very small grave that Andy had dug with a trowel just outside the back door of the farmhouse. Ruth had managed to compose herself and rejoin them. Amy held the egg, wrapped in tissue paper, in her hands as Rupert watched her with a look of disdain on his face.

'This is ridiculous,' he muttered.

'Shh,' Hannah replied. Rupert was right in a sense, the whole thing was a bit silly.

'Are you going to say a few words, Amy?' Ruth said in a soft voice.

'No,' Amy replied with a sharp look at Rupert. She knelt down and placed the egg into the small hole before covering it over with earth. Hannah watched her lips moving as she said something to herself while shaping the earth into a small mound. The burial complete, Amy brushed the soil from her hands and turned without a word to walk back into the farmhouse. Ruth and Andy followed her in, leaving Hannah and Rupert outside.

'That was bloody stupid,' Rupert said. 'It was a sodding egg from a random chicken. She buried it like it was her pet hamster or something.'

'Don't be so cold, Rupert,' Hannah said. 'I think Amy was doing it more for Ruth than herself, anyway.'

'Bloody women,' Rupert mumbled before following the others into the farmhouse. Hannah stayed behind for a few seconds, gathering her thoughts. Rupert really was a prick. The more she thought about it, the more she realised that he was getting worse. Or getting better at being a prick, depending on how you looked at it. Hannah crossed to the back door and before walking through it, turned to look back at the small grave. Where there had been a small mound of earth a few minutes before, there was now a solitary footprint from one of Rupert's boots.

'What a tosser,' Hannah whispered as she opened the back door.

37

The day after the egg funeral, Andy and Ruth had walked down the track towards the bus stop. As they walked, he asked her what she thought about the weird atmosphere in the room before they'd left the farmhouse.

'It was definitely a bit heated,' Ruth had said. 'Did you see the way that the three of them looked at each other?'

'Or not,' Andy replied. 'I don't think Rupert looked at Hannah once.' Ruth had paused before replying.

'Do you think they've had a barney?'

'Who? Hannah and Rupert?' Andy said.

'Yeah.' Ruth rubbed her hands up and down her arms. Even though it was sunny, it was still cold for the time of year. 'Should have brought a coat.'

'We can nip back and get one if you want?'

'No, it's all good,' Ruth replied with a look over her shoulder at the farmhouse. 'I don't want to go back there.

'Maybe Hannah and Amy had some sort of argument over Rupert after we'd gone to bed.'

'I don't think so,' Ruth replied. 'I can't see the two of them arguing over him, unless they were both trying to get the other one to sleep with him.' Andy smiled at her response.

'Is he that bad, from your perspective?' he asked.

'He's worse,' Ruth said. 'Much worse.' For a second, Andy had been tempted to defend Rupert but he thought better of it.

After a shorter than usual wait for the bus, Andy and Ruth were sitting on the top deck heading into Norwich. They were both subdued and had been sitting in silence for a while. Despite managing to get the front seats at the top of the bus, Andy didn't even feel like pretending to drive, and from the look on Ruth's face she didn't either. He tried to brighten her mood anyway by miming steering the thing, but it didn't seem to have much effect on her. Instead, they sat in silence until the bus reached the hospital. As he got off the bus, Andy looked at the sprawling modern buildings in front of him.

'Blimey,' he said. 'This is a bit of a change from the old one.'

'Have you not been here before?' Ruth asked.

'I have, but it was at night and it was only for a checkup.' He thought back to the last time he'd been here and shook his head to try to drive the memories away. Ruth looked as if she was just about to ask him about it, and that wasn't a question he wanted to answer so he set off in the direction of the main entrance.

The Norfolk and Norwich Hospital was a large complex of buildings, all built within the last ten years. The previous hospital in the centre of the city — that Andy had known quite well when he was a kid — had since been converted into a whole bunch of expensive apartments. The only thing left of the original building that Andy was in fact born in was the Victorian facade. Its replacement on the outskirts of Norwich was an imposing steel and glass monstrosity that, despite the fact it consistently remained in 'special measures', was impressive enough to look at in Andy's opinion. He and Ruth walked past an elderly man in a wheelchair, complete with an oxygen cylinder strapped to the back of it, who was having a furious argument with a doctor about a parking space. Andy caught snatches of their disagreement as he and Ruth walked past them.

'It's not for patients, this parking area,' the doctor was protesting.

'But if you didn't have any patients, you wouldn't have a job,' the elderly man countered. 'That's why I'm parking here.'

'But if you didn't have any doctors, then you'd be...' the doctors voice trailed off, and Andy started to chuckle.

'Dead?' he whispered to Ruth, who started laughing as well.

'Well that would solve the parking problem,' she muttered under her breath.

They walked through the main doors of the hospital into a large open space. On either side of the entrance hall was a variety of shops and businesses. About the only thing Andy couldn't see was a McDonalds. He approached the woman behind the main reception desk. She was dressed almost entirely in brown, even down to the colour of her glasses, and looked very similar to Andy's old english teacher. He shivered at the memory and looked again at the woman. She was about the right age to actually be his old english teacher, but surely not?

'Hello, we're here to see Matthew...' Andy paused, realising that he had no idea what Matthew's last name was. He turned to Ruth. 'What's his last name?'

'Dunno,' she replied.

'What was he admitted with?' the receptionist said with a kind smile. 'That'll help me narrow it down a bit. We've got over 800 patients here, but I don't think there'll be that many Matthews on the same ward.' She tapped at the keyboard in front of her, staring at the computer screen.

'He broke his leg,' Andy replied.

'Jumped off a shed by accident,' Ruth added. Andy glanced at her, not sure if that information would help.

'Do you mean the Chicken Boy?' the woman said with a grin, looking up from the screen. 'He's in orthopaedics. Ward S3.' She turned as another receptionist walked behind her desk. 'Paula, these people are here to see the Chicken Boy.' The other woman looked at Andy and Ruth, and walked off laughing.

'There's eight hundred beds in this hospital,' Andy whispered, 'and they both know about Matthew thinking he was a chicken. How does that work?' Ruth shrugged her shoulders in response.

'How do we get to Ward S3 please?' Ruth asked the woman behind the desk.

'Sorry, yes,' the receptionist replied. She launched into a complicated set of directions to a set of lifts that were, from the sounds of it, right at the other end of the hospital. Ward S3 was on the fifth floor, but that was okay, the woman explained. The windows didn't open.

'Right, thanks,' Andy said, keen to get away from the front desk. 'How do we know we've got the right lifts though?'

'Oh, you can't miss them,' the receptionist replied. 'They're right opposite the McDonalds.'

38

Like most other people with a nine to five job, Emily really didn't like Monday mornings. She was sitting in the main briefing room in the Food Standards Agency, listening to what was known as "Morning Prayers". There was — to her relief — no actual praying involved. It was just a run down of the priorities for the inspection teams in the week ahead and any active investigations.

Mr Clayton was just finishing a description of reports of a feral group of chickens who appeared to have moved into a playground in one of the council estates on the outskirts of Norwich. The media had got hold of the story, and the Eastern Daily News were running a series of articles on their website about the unexpected invasion. The chickens were, according to the locals, in a pretty sorry condition. Many of them looked battle-scarred, and were in what one of the local residents described as 'a right old state'. Emily knew the estate quite well, and suspected that many families had had an unexpected treat for their Sunday lunch. If some of the chickens hadn't ended up with a couple of strips of bacon across their backs and an onion up their arse the day before, she would be very surprised.

'Of course, it would help if half the bloody estate wasn't feeding them,' Mr Clayton muttered as he finished the morning meeting. The small group of attendees got to their feet and started heading for the door. Emily was just about to follow them out when Mr Clayton turned his attention to her. 'Emily? Could I grab you for a second?'

'Sure, Mr Clayton,' Emily replied with her sweetest smile. If there was any way she could get out of doing outreach visits to a council estate playground overrun with chickens, she was game.

'The sandwich van. Can we have a chat about it?'

Emily realised that, even though she'd sat through the entire football match the day before, she had no idea who had won.

'Of course,' she replied. 'What did you think of the match? I ended up watching it on the telly.'

'Wow, that second goal was something else,' Mr Clayton's entire face lit up, and Emily surmised that Norwich had won. Thinking about it, she vaguely remembered a very buff lad running round in what may have been a yellow and green shirt, but she'd been concentrating too hard on his slow-motion legs to remember. Emily listened for a few moments to Mr Clayton describing Norwich City's impressive front line and solid defence. As far as Emily could recall, their defence wasn't the only solid thing she'd seen on the television. 'Anyway,' Mr Clayton continued, managing to get off the subject. 'The sandwich van.'

'Yes,' Emily replied, bringing her concentration back to the matter at hand and away from footballers' legs. 'That's run by a lovely chap called Sam. He's a really nice bloke, he is. I know the van looks a bit ropey, but the inspection was faultless.'

'I don't dispute that, Emily,' Mr Clayton said, raising a hand to stop her. 'I'm more than happy to give the man a bit of a break based on the fact that his sandwiches are just to die for, but there's a problem with one of his suppliers.'

'Yeah, you said,' Emily replied. 'I looked them up and they're definitely not registered. But, I was thinking, maybe if we could get them registered really quickly then the council wouldn't be that bothered about it?' She looked at Mr Clayton with what she hoped was a sad puppy face, but from his frown she wasn't convinced she'd got it quite right.

'Are you okay?' he asked. 'You look a bit, er, unwell?'

'I'm fine,' Emily replied, making a concerted effort to put her face back to normal.

'Okay, anyway I quite agree with you about a swift inspection,' he continued after a brief pause. That wasn't what Emily had been expecting him to say. 'But that's not the problem. The supplier is based on a farm outside Norwich.'

'Okay,' Emily said. There were a lot of farms outside Norwich.

'Hill Top Farm.'

'Oh,' she replied.

'Where the thing with the butcher happened.'

'Yes, I know, thank you,' Emily replied, trying to keep her voice even.

'I'd allocated the visit to you before I realised which farm it was, so I'll quite understand if you want me to reallocate it to someone else.'

Emily paused before replying. She looked at Mr Clayton, who was regarding her with a compassionate expression.

'No, that's fine. I can go. No problem,' Emily lied through her teeth. She could feel her heart thudding in her chest just at the thought of going back to the farm, but she didn't want to show any signs of weakness to Mr Clayton.

'Why don't we both go?' he asked. Emily looked at him, surprised. If she did have to go back to the bloody place, having someone with her would probably be a really good idea. The only problem would be that if she did go a bit odd, it would be her boss with her when she did.

'Really?' she replied a few seconds later, having made her mind up that Mr Clayton would probably understand

'Yes,' Mr Clayton said. 'It would do me good to get back out into the field, and you'd have someone with you. Just in case.'

Emily spent the rest of the morning finishing off paperwork in the office, and after lunch, met Mr Clayton in the foyer of the Food Standards Agency. In between filing reports, Emily had given a lot of thought to returning to Hill Top Farm. She wasn't nervous as such, more curious to see how she would feel when she got there. One thing that still concerned her was if she went wibble when they actually got there, but Emily figured that she would work that one out if it happened. After she had lunch — a home made cheese and onion sandwich at her desk — Emily met Mr Clayton in the foyer of the Food Standards Agency hoping that her breath didn't smell too bad. They made their way to Emily's red Mini in the underground carpark, and a few minutes later they were on their way out into the countryside.

'Blimey,' Mr Clayton said, looking out of the car window. 'There's some money round here, isn't there?' Emily glanced out of the window. They were just passing Cringleford, a suburb of Norwich well known for large grandiose houses and elderly, equally grandiose residents.

'I bet they don't have feral chickens in their playgrounds round here,' Emily replied.

'I doubt they've got playgrounds at all,' Mr Clayton said. 'Children would be far too noisy and annoying for this area, I would have thought.' They drove on in silence for a few moments until they were almost in open countryside. As Emily turned off the main dual carriageway, they passed a large road sign with the words 'London - 95 miles' in bright white letters. Above the word 'London', in crudely painted off-white letters, was the word 'That'. Emily's attention was distracted by the graffiti and she had to brake hard at the roundabout at the top of the slip road as a double decker bus — with no intention of slowing down — came careering round the roundabout.

'Sorry,' Emily said as the Mini came to a juddering halt. To her surprise, Mr Clayton started laughing.

'Did you see that?'

'What, the double decker bus? I did, but perhaps slightly late.'

'No, not the bus. The muppets sitting at the front of the top deck?'

'No,' Emily replied, putting the Mini into gear and pulling onto the roundabout. 'I was too busy trying not to get wiped out by the bus.'

'One of them was pretending to drive the bloody thing,' Mr Clayton said, still laughing. 'If that's not 'Normal for Norfolk', I don't know what is.'

'Yeah, okay,' Emily replied, ignoring the comment. Just because Mr Clayton had lived in Norfolk for over thirty years, he still wasn't local. Which made his comment — in Emily's opinion at least — bordering on racist. She didn't say anything else, but concentrated on the road in front of her.

'Are you sure you're okay about this visit, Emily?' Mr

Clayton said. Emily took a deep breath, thinking that she'd rather not have this conversation while she was driving. Or at all, in fact. 'You don't have to do it, you know?' he continued.

'I'm fine, Mr Clayton, thank you,' Emily replied in a grim voice before forcing a smile onto her face. 'If anything, it'll do me good. Help me put everything behind me.' She flashed him a quick look, making sure she was still smiling when she did so, before returning her attention to the road.

'Well, as long as you're sure,' Mr Clayton replied. Emily pressed her lips together.

'I'm sure,' she said.

They drove on in silence for a few moments, leaving the suburbs of Norwich behind them. To Emily's relief, Mr Clayton didn't mention the farm again, but was absorbed with his mobile. At one point, she glanced down at his phone to see him looking at what she thought was dresses, presumably on the internet. Emily considered starting a conversation about the man's wife — perhaps she had a birthday or something coming up — but she thought better of it. She knew next to nothing about his personal life apart from the fact he was married and had no particular wish to find out about it. A few minutes later, the lights of Norwich a pale orange glow in the distance, Emily slowed the Mini as she drove along the road that ran next to the Hill Top Farm.

'Where is this place, anyway?' Mr Clayton said a few moments later, tearing himself away from his phone.

'The track's just up here, past that tree.'

'What, the one that looks like a swastika?'

'Yeah, that one,' Emily replied with a sigh.

39

'Jesus wept, Rupert's something else, isn't he?' Hannah said from her position at the kitchen table. Amy was making toast and had managed to burn at least four slices already. Rupert was in the shower, lathering himself up in preparation for meeting the woman from the university later on.

'He certainly is,' Amy replied. 'I can't believe he stepped on the bloody grave. What a thing to do, and as far as it being an accident…?' She let her voice trail away. Amy shrugged the duvet she was still wearing around her shoulders onto the chair, and Hannah realised that Amy was wearing one of Rupert's shirts.

'Do you want another cup of tea?'

'That sounds nice,' Hannah replied. 'Thanks.'

The two women waited for the kettle to boil, neither of them saying a word. Hannah looked out of the window, noticing Amy glance across at her a couple of times. It was obvious she wanted to say something, but Hannah decided to wait and see if she would or not. A moment later, Amy put a couple of mugs of tea on the kitchen table and sat down. She shuffled her chair a few inches until she was sitting opposite Hannah, their knees almost touching.

'Are you okay?' Amy asked in a whisper, glancing at the kitchen door. Hannah could hear the shower still going, so at least Rupert wasn't about to walk in on them.

'Okay about what?'

'About what happened on Saturday night?'

'Sure. Why wouldn't I be?' Hannah asked. Amy leaned forward.

'You just don't seem to be, that's all. Are we cool?'

'Of course we're cool.'

'I was just thinking, if Rupert's out tonight…' Amy let the rest of the sentence hang, looking at her from underneath her fringe. Hannah sighed, not quite sure how to approach the situation. In the end, she decided to just be honest.

'Can we not?'

'Not tonight, or not ever?' Amy replied. Hannah tried to remember exactly what had happened on Saturday night. If Amy knew about Hannah's teeth grinding, well that wasn't something she did very often. So, she must have enjoyed it. In fact, given the physical state that she had to be for her teeth for grind, Hannah must have enjoyed it a hell of a lot.

'Just not tonight?' Hannah replied with a sheepish grin. Amy tried to hide the disappointment on her face, but it was obvious enough to Hannah.

'Sure.' The two women looked at each other in silence for a few seconds. Hannah could tell that Amy wanted to say something else, but wasn't sure how to phrase it. The silence continued and was just beginning to get uncomfortable when, to Hannah's relief, there was a sharp rap on the farmhouse door. She got to her feet and when she opened it, she saw a thin, bald man in a suit standing on the doorstep with an uncomfortable looking younger woman behind him. The man was holding up an identification card, and for a horrible moment, Hannah thought that they were police, even if they looked unlike any coppers she'd ever met before.

'Hello,' the man said. 'Is this Another Way?'

'Who's asking?' Hannah jumped as Rupert's voice boomed from the other side of the kitchen. He walked over to the front door with only a towel wrapped about him and stood next to her. 'Who are you two?'

'My name's Mr Clayton, and this is Miss Underwood,' the visitor gestured at the woman behind him. Hannah could have been imagining it, but the poor girl looked terrified. 'We work for the Food Standards Agency. Could we come in?'

'No,' Rupert barked. 'What do you want?'

'Rupert, really,' Hannah pushed Rupert to one side, dislodging the towel. He grabbed it just before it fell to the floor. 'Of course you can come in.' Ignoring Rupert's angry glare, she beckoned them into the kitchen. 'Would you like a cup of tea?'

Ten minutes later, they were sitting around the kitchen table, sipping from mugs of tea. Amy had disappeared the minute Hannah had answered the door, and Rupert was at least dressed.

'So,' Mr Clayton said. 'It's come to our attention that you're supplying some premises in Norwich with food. Specifically, bread.'

'Where did you hear that from?' Rupert asked, his arms folded tightly across his chest.

'That's not really the point,' Mr Clayton replied. 'But you are supposed to have a license, you see. To supply food for public consumption.' Rupert laughed before replying.

'Yeah, yeah, whatever,' he said, waving a hand dismissively. 'That's not going to happen.'

'Well, then you can't supply anyone with anything,' Mr Clayton said. Hannah was just about to reply when Rupert cut her off.

'Well, why don't you two just get the hell off of my farm. We don't answer to you, we don't need a license from you, and there's nothing you can do to us. So why don't you take your suit, and your butch little silent assistant, and do one.'

Mr Clayton's eyebrows shot up, and Hannah put her hand on Rupert's forearm as she felt him tense up. The last thing she wanted was a punch being thrown, no matter how unlikely that was.

'Who are you calling butch?' the blonde woman said with a frown. It was the first words she'd said since they'd arrived.

'Emily,' Mr Clayton said in a low voice.

'Oh, it speaks,' Rupert barked, pointing at her. 'You. I'm calling you butch.'

'Fuck off,' Emily retorted. Hannah stifled a smile. That wasn't what she was expecting the woman to say.

'What did you say?' Rupert said.

'You heard.'

'You can't tell me to fuck off. It's my farm. I should be telling you two to fuck off.' Rupert's eyes darted between the two visitors. 'In fact, fuck off the pair of you before I go and get my shotgun and get all Tony Martin on you.'

'Are you threatening us?' Mr Clayton had found his voice at last, even if it was shaking.

Hannah took a deep breath.

'That's enough, the lot of you,' she shouted. 'Enough,

you hear?' She held out her hands, palms down over the table. 'Everyone just relax. There's no need for any of this.'

'She started it,' Rupert said, glaring at Emily.

'Rupert, enough,' Hannah said, again fighting a smile.

They all sat in silence for a few seconds, Rupert's stare alternating between Mr Clayton and Emily. To her credit, Emily didn't take her eyes off him once. Hannah knew how intense Rupert's eyes could be, and when he was in a temper, they were a hundred times worse.

'Right, can I make a suggestion to you all?' Hannah said. They all turned to look at her. 'Rupert, why don't you pop down to the sheds and make sure they're closed up?' Rupert opened his mouth to protest but he closed it again without saying anything. 'Mr Clayton, why don't you go and wait in the car?' Hannah turned to look at Emily and smiled at her. 'So that me and Emily can sort this out between us.'

There was a another silence. Eventually, Rupert scraped his chair back and got to his feet.

'Fine,' he said. 'I've got better things to do than talk to these muppets anyway.' He shot a dark look at Mr Clayton, who was examining his fingernails, and walked out of the kitchen slamming the door behind him.

'Mr Clayton?' Hannah said in as sweet a voice as she could muster. He looked up, and Hannah noticed a thin sheen of perspiration on his forehead.

'Has he really got a shotgun?' he asked.

'Oh God no,' Hannah replied, laughing. 'I wouldn't trust him with a breadknife, let alone a shotgun. He wouldn't know which end was which. You'll be quite safe in the car.'

'Are you sure, Emily?' he asked, getting to his feet. Hannah saw Emily force a smile onto her face.

'Yeah, it's all good.' She tossed him a set of car keys. 'Just wait outside and we'll work it all out.'

Hannah and Emily sat in silence until Mr Clayton had left the kitchen through the front door. When he closed it behind him, Hannah blew a deep breath out of her cheeks.

'Jesus wept, bloody men,' she said, grinning at Emily even though — technically speaking — she was just as much to blame as either Rupert or Mr Clayton, if not more so.

'Sorry,' Emily said, returning her smile. 'That was kind of my fault. He just, well, he just wound me up.'

'Yeah,' Hannah said. 'He does that sometimes.' She watched as the woman sitting opposite her looked around the kitchen.

'I love what you've done with this place,' Emily said. 'It looks so much better than it did.'

'Have you been here before?' Hannah asked. Emily looked at her, a dark expression crossing her face.

'Once or twice,' she replied.

40

'I bloody hate hospitals,' Andy muttered as he and Ruth waited for the hospital lift, the smell of Big Macs wafting through the air.

'I'm not that keen on them either,' Ruth replied as the lift arrived with a pathetic 'ding'. 'Which floor is his ward on again?' she asked once they had walked into the lift. Andy looked at the panel on the wall. There was a series of floors, all the way from a basement to a tenth floor.

'Fifth, was it?' he said. 'I think that's what the old bag behind the counter said.' Ruth pressed the button for the fifth floor, and they both stood in silence until the lift started going up. To Andy's surprise, it stopped at the first floor. The doors opened, and a surly looking man dressed in a navy-blue porter's uniform peered through them at Andy and Ruth before walking into the lift, dragging a trolley behind him. The trolley wasn't a standard hospital one, but a functional looking thing with what Andy could only describe as a white canvas wrapped frame over the top of it. The porter fumbled with a key ring on his belt and selected a key which he inserted into the lift panel. He turned it before stabbing the button for the basement with a fat finger. The lift descended, the doors opened and the porter left after removing his key, pulling his strange trolley behind him. Before the doors closed, Andy peeked out at the corridor outside. The walls were unpainted, and silver pipes snaked down the ceiling. He didn't think this was a part of the hospital that the general public were supposed to see. During the short journey, the porter had not said a word to either Andy or Ruth, or even made eye contact with them. As the doors sealed themselves shut, Ruth turned to Andy.

'Was that what I think it was?' she asked. Andy turned to her and realised that she had gone as white as the canvas that had been over the top of the porter's contraption.

'What, a hospital trolley?'

'No, it wasn't. I think it was one of those things that they cart dead people around in. I've seen them on the telly, on Holby City and that.' Andy saw her look up the display of the lift which read '-1' in unblinking orange lettering. 'I think we're in the morgue.'

'Shit,' Andy said, stabbing at the button for the fifth floor. 'That's not good.' The doors closed, and after what felt like ages, the lift started to rise.

'That was a body under there, that was,' Ruth whispered. She took a step closer to Andy until she was standing in front of him with her back to him as they watched the numbers climb up the floors. 'I've never been that close to a real live dead body before.' Andy leaned forward and blew on the back of her neck very softly. Ruth jumped, her shoulders jerking upward as she did so. 'Oh Christ, did you feel that?' Andy started laughing, and Ruth turned around and slapped at his arms. 'You're a bastard, you are,' she said with a grin as they arrived at the fifth floor.

They both stepped out of the lift into a bright white corridor. Andy wrinkled his nose at the smell of antiseptic with an underlying trace of urine before following Ruth down the corridor toward the ward entrance. Happy to let her take the lead, he walked behind as she approached the nurses station inside the doors of the main ward.

'Hi,' Ruth said to the beak-nosed nurse behind the station. 'We're here to see Matthew? Broken leg?' The nurse looked up at them and broke into a broad smile which made her nostrils flare.

'Oh, are you? That's nice. He's in that bay over there.. The nurse pointed a bony finger across the ward before nodding in the opposite direction. 'Or he might be in the Day Room down that way. I'm not sure.' She paused for a few seconds, the smile fixed to her face. 'He's free-range, you see.'

They found Matthew in the Day Room, sitting in an uncomfortable looking armchair, leafing through a dog-eared copy of *Cosmopolitan*. His left leg was encased in a fibreglass cast and propped up on a threadbare armchair opposite him. A thin, yellowed pillow under Matthew's leg was the only nod to comfort that Andy could see.

'How you doing, mate?' Andy asked as they walked into the room. Matthew looked up from his magazine and gave them both a wan smile.

'I've been better,' he replied, wiggling his toes. 'Good to see you both though, thanks for coming in.'

'No worries,' Ruth replied before Andy could say anything. 'They treating you alright?'

'Apart from all the fucking chicken jokes, it's fine,' Matthew said. 'I should be out in a couple of days, according to the doctor that came round earlier. At least, I think he was a doctor. He could have been a work experience student for all I know. He didn't look old enough to have a paper round, let alone have done ten years at medical school or however long it is they do.'

'That's just you being old, that is,' Andy laughed.

'Course it is,' Matthew replied, throwing the paper onto the floor with a look of irritation. 'Easy for you to say, mate. Is Hannah okay? I kind of hoped that she might be coming in to see me.'

'Hannah's fine,' Ruth replied. 'The others are all good as well. The new girl, Amy, seems to be making herself at home anyway.'

'Good stuff. Tell Hannah I'd like to see her if she can get in.'

'Will do.'

'So, any gossip then?' Matthew asked.

'Not really, mate,' Andy replied.

Andy and Ruth had talked on the bus about whether or not to tell Matthew what had happened to the chickens, but they'd decided between them to wait until he was home. Andy glanced across the room at the door to make sure that it was shut. He didn't want to be overheard.

'Listen, what happened Matthew?' Andy asked. 'The other night?'

'Well, I fell off the roof, didn't I?'

'Yeah, but why?'

'Think it's called gravity, Andy.'

'Matthew, that's not what he meant,' Ruth said, kneeling down next to him and taking his hand in hers. 'Come on, we're your friends. We're not taking the piss.' Andy thought for a second about kneeling on the other side of the armchair, but decided that would just be a bit weird so decided to stay where he was. Matthew looked at Ruth for a few seconds before replying in a whisper.

'I've got no bloody idea,' he said, speaking so softly Andy had to lean forward to hear him. 'One minute I was in the kitchen with you lot, the next I was in the back of a bloody ambulance.'

'Do you not remember any of it then?' Andy asked.

'Nope,' Matthew replied. 'Not a bloody thing. I remember earlier in the day, arseing about in the farmhouse. I had a bread roll in the middle of the afternoon because I was peckish, and I remember Amy giving out to me for using up the last of the quorn strips from the fridge when she and Hannah got back with the chickens. After that, nothing.'

'Nothing at all?' Andy asked.

'Nope. Not a sausage.'

'So what's next then?' Ruth asked. 'I mean, are you going to come back to the farm? Because if you are, then we'll need to organise that.'

Matthew looked at them both, flicking his eyes from Andy to Ruth. From the look on Matthew's face, Andy was pretty sure what Matthew's response would be before he even opened his mouth.

'I don't think so,' Matthew said, confirming Andy's suspicions. 'I'm thinking about going back to Mum and Dad's place until this thing comes off.' He gestured at the cast on his leg. 'I'm not going to be much good to anyone with this, am I? Besides, Mum's already made up my room and once she's made her mind up on something, that's that.'

Andy glanced over at Ruth, who was — in his opinion — quite deliberately not looking at him. From the way she had her lips pressed together, she looked as if she was trying not to laugh.

'So, when are you being released then?' Andy asked.

'Day or so, hopefully,' Matthew replied. 'I've got to wait for some more blood tests to come back, and they want me to see a psychiatrist.'

'A psychiatrist?' Ruth said. 'Whatever for?'

'Something to do with the fact I thought I was a chicken.'

'We didn't say anything, Matthew,' Andy said, concerned that his mate thought they'd grassed him up. 'Not to the paramedics or anyone.'

'I know,' Matthew replied with a sad smile. 'Apparently I was going on about it right up until the point they put me to sleep for the operation to fix my leg. That's why everyone keeps taking the piss. I can't wait to go home. At least then I can go for ten minutes without someone making a sodding chicken joke.'

41

Emily's eyes wandered around the inside of the kitchen, taking it all in. When she had first walked in, she had been so nervous that she thought she was going to pee herself. It was only when the prick with the dreadlocks called her 'butch' that she snapped out of it. Emily was pretty sure that she was going to get into trouble with Mr Clayton for telling the bloke to fuck off, but there was nothing she could do about that now. One thing she did know was that she wasn't going to discuss her previous visits to this particular farmhouse with the girl with red hair.

'There you go, pet,' Hannah said as she put a fresh cup of tea on the table in front of her.

'Thank you,' Emily replied.

'Do you want biscuits?'

'No, I'm good, thanks. I've not really got a sweet tooth.'

'Okay, cool. So,' Hannah paused for a few seconds. 'What's the deal with this licence thing, then? I suppose we should sort that out.'

'It's pretty straightforward really,' Emily replied,

grateful that Hannah wasn't going to question her about anything else. 'Could you tell me exactly what you're supplying though?'

'It's only bread,' Hannah said. 'We've not actually sold any, but we would like to at some point. All we did was give some to a bloke who runs a sandwich van. To see if he liked the bread.'

'Sam? Parks up outside the pub on match days?'

'Yeah, that's him. Do you know him?'

'I do his inspections. I always give him five stars,' Emily grinned, 'in return for one of his sandwiches.'

'Oh my Lord, they're to die for, aren't they? He made me and the others a sample using our bread. It was lush.'

Emily reached into her bag and pulled out a sheaf of paperwork.

'It's pretty straightforward, the license. Plus, if all you're doing is baking bread, it's even easier. The minute you start with any sort of animal products, it opens up all sorts of problems.' Emily put the paperwork on the kitchen table.

'We won't be doing that, we're all vegans. Well, mostly vegan.' Hannah said. 'That's the whole point of us being here, you see.'

'How many of you are there?' Emily asked.

'There's me and Rupert — you've met him,' Hannah smiled, 'and there's Amy and Ruth. There's another couple of lads as well, but one of them's in hospital with a broken leg.'

'Oh dear,' Emily said, frowning. 'How did that happen?' Hannah paused before replying.

'He, er, he fell off the shed roof. Trying to fix a leak.'

'Right.' Emily wasn't at all convinced that Hannah was telling the truth. It was the way she spat the words out, almost as if she'd just thought of them, but it didn't matter to Emily. 'So what, you all just live here in a group?'

'Yeah, that's pretty much it. None of us are that interested in a traditional set-up, so here we are.'

'That sounds interesting,' Emily said, even though she thought it was anything but.

'Our ultimate plan is to be as self-sufficient as possible. Growing our own food, making our own rules, not being dependent on society but living off to the side of it. That's why we gave the sandwich man some bread as a sample. Market testing.'

Emily frowned, not sure why anyone would want to live 'off to the side of society'. There was a definite contradiction in Hannah's argument though. How could they claim to be not dependant on society if they were selling to it? Deciding not to raise the question, Emily looked around the kitchen again, and realised that apart from a kettle, there was no technology anywhere. No radio, no television, no computers. What on Earth did they do for fun?

'Okay,' Emily said, slowly. 'Cool. So, this paperwork. If you just run through this section and fill it out, then someone from the Food Standards Agency will come out and do the inspection.' She pointed at some of the boxes on the paper to illustrate her point.

'Will that be you?' Hannah asked.

'It might be, it depends who the visits are allocated to.' Just as she said this, Emily's stomach gurgled. She pressed her hand to her abdomen. 'Sorry, I didn't have much for lunch.'

'Are you sure you don't want a couple of biscuits?'

'No, honestly. I'm fine.' Emily replied. Hannah got to her feet, an excited look on her face.

'Why don't I make you a sandwich? You could try out some of our bread.' Before Emily could protest, Hannah was bustling around the kitchen. She threw the fridge door open and peered inside. 'Hmm,' Hannah said. 'Bit thin on the ground in here. Do you like hummus?'

'Er, well, I do,' Emily replied. 'Is it home-made?' she continued, hoping that the answer would be no. Beyond chickpeas and sunflower seeds, Emily hadn't got a clue what actually went into the stuff. Hannah turned to look at Emily.

'No, don't be daft,' Hannah said. 'It's from Waitrose.'

'In that case, I'd love some,' Emily replied, stifling a laugh. 'Not that I'd mind if it was home-made you understand, but…'

'Honestly, don't worry. I get you.' Hannah pulled a plastic tub out of the fridge and collected together a knife and a breadboard. As she did so, Emily got to her feet and ran a practiced eye over the kitchen. It was clean enough, that was for sure. Certainly clean enough for an inspection. Looking around, Emily couldn't see anything that made her nervous from a Food Standards Agency point of view.

'Hannah, this inspection? I can't see anything here that would be an issue. Obviously I'd need to go through everything, but there's nothing jumping out at me.'

'Oh, thank you, Emily,' Hannah said, a broad smile lighting up her face. She reached into a bread bin, and Emily saw her frown for a second before she pulled a brown crusted roll out. 'These are mine,' she continued, her smile back in place. 'What do you think?'

Emily leaned forward and examined the bread. It looked like a brown crusted roll, exactly the same as any other she'd seen.

'That looks lovely,' she said, not wanting to offend Hannah's feelings. It was obvious to Emily from the excited expression on Hannah's face that she was proud of it, even though it was only a roll.

A few minutes later, Emily was sitting back at the kitchen table, a cling film wrapped hummus roll in her hands.

'So, are we good then?' Hannah asked, pointing at the paperwork still on the table. 'We fill that lot out, send it in, then you come out and do the inspection?'

'That's pretty much it, yeah,' Emily replied. 'I'll have a chat with Mr Clayton on the way back to Norwich, and ask that it gets assigned to me. But I don't think you'll have anything to worry about from what I've seen. If I do find anything, well, there's always a way round things if it keeps Sam in business.' Hannah laughed before replying.

'Excellent,' she said. 'I knew we'd be able to work it out between us.' Her eyes dropped to the roll. 'I hope you enjoy that, anyway.'

'I'm sure I will. I don't suppose there's much point asking for a phone number so that we can schedule the inspection, is there? I don't suppose you've got phones here, have you?'

To Emily's surprise, after glancing toward the door, Hannah dug deep into one of her pockets and pulled out a brand-new iPhone. She pressed the button to turn it on, crossed to the kitchen window, and turned to Emily.

'We've got phones, even though Rupert doesn't like them,' Hannah said, peering at the screen. 'Just can't get a bloody signal inside the farmhouse, that's the only problem.'

42

R upert sat on the roof of what had been until very recently their chicken shed. He looked out over the farm, and then down at the concrete floor below him. As he took a deep drag on the joint in his hand, he wondered what it would be like to do what Matthew had done and just launch himself off it.

'That must have bloody hurt,' Rupert muttered as he picked a small piece of tobacco from his lip. 'Idiot.'

Across the still air of the early evening, he heard the kitchen door to the farmhouse close. Rupert looked up, breathing twin streams of smoke out of his nostrils, and peered at the farm. He could see the butch one from earlier walking across to her red car, no doubt to join her slack-jawed colleague. The two of them represented everything that he hated about the society he so badly wanted to leave behind. He hummed the tune of a Leonard Cohen song as he finished off his joint. He couldn't really remember all the words, but they were something about being sentenced to twenty years of boredom for trying to change the system. That was their life, right there. Twenty years of boredom.

Rupert got carefully to his feet, not wanting to repeat Matthew's antics, and climbed back into the shed through a small skylight with a ladder underneath. Ten minutes later, he was back at the farmhouse.

'Hey you,' he said to Hannah as he walked into the kitchen. 'I hope you sent the bastards packing.'

'Yeah, I did, kind of,' Hannah replied, her bright red hair glinting in the early evening sunshine that flowed through the kitchen windows. For a second or two, Rupert thought about seeing if she was up for a bit of nonsense before he went out, but he wanted to keep his powder dry for the woman from the University.

'I'm off into the city, anyway. Any chance of a lift?'

'You could have got a lift from those two,' Hannah replied with a wicked grin. Maybe she would be up for some nonsense, Rupert thought for a few seconds before dismissing it. 'They're going back to the city.'

'Yeah, right,' Rupert snorted. 'Like that would actually happen. Excuse me, Mr and Mrs Establishment, please could you give me a lift into the dark heart of the society you represent?' Hannah laughed in response.

'Maybe not then. Give me ten minutes and I'll run you in. I just need to tidy this stuff away.'

'Aw, did you make me a sandwich to take in with me?'

'Er, no,' Hannah replied. 'I made a roll for the woman from the Food Standards Agency. She was starving.'

'You did what?' Rupert asked, trying not to sound too annoyed. It was enough them coming in here and throwing their weight about, without Hannah feeding them his food as well.

'Oh don't be a sourpuss, Rupert,' Hannah replied, not looking at him. 'The poor girl was hungry. Are you that self-centred that you begrudge a woman a sandwich? She's just trying to make her way in the world, just like we are.'

'But she works for the Food Standards Agency.'

'So what?'

'Establishment, Hannah. They're establishment.'

'I don't care, Rupert,' she retorted, waving a dismissive hand at him. 'The Food Standards Agency aren't exactly the bad guys, are they?'

Rupert looked at Hannah, who finally met his eyes. He could tell from the determined look in them that this wasn't a battle he was going to win.

'Okay, okay,' Rupert said, raising his palms. 'You're right, to a degree.' He saw her frown at his last comment, so smirked at her to let her know that he was only messing. At least, that was what he wanted her to think.

'So, what's your plan for this evening, anyway?' Hannah asked, wiping crumbs from the counter top with a damp sponge. 'What's her name again? Laura?'

'Lauren,' Rupert corrected her. 'Lauren from the animal testing slaughterhouse at the university.'

'Well if you're going to get riled up about the establishment, maybe you should start with her?'

'Oh, don't you worry about that. She doesn't know what's in store for her tonight. Danny sorted me out with some assistance on that front.'

'What do you mean?' Hannah asked in a sharp voice, turning to him with her arms crossed. 'You're not going to bloody drug her, are you? You do know you can go to prison for that?'

'No, Hannah,' Rupert replied with a sigh. 'I wouldn't do that. Please, give me some credit.' Danny didn't have any Rohypnol anyway, otherwise he might have taken some along just in case Lauren turned out to be less enthusiastic than he thought she would be. 'He's given me a few little diagonal blue helpers.'

'Help me out here, Rupert. What are you talking about?'

'Sildenafil.'

'In English?'

'Viagra,' Rupert replied with a grin. 'Tonight, Hannah, I will be a sexual superhero.'

'You serious?' she laughed, but it wasn't a nice laugh at all. 'What, you're going to pop a bunch of boner pills? Have you suddenly developed performance anxiety?' Hannah wiggled her little finger at him and laughed again.

'No,' Rupert said, keeping his voice even. 'I've got no worries about performance. You should know that, of all people?'

'So what's with the Viagra then? Is it to stop you doing a Friday special?'

'What's a Friday special?'

'It's when you finish early.'

Rupert decided to ignore Hannah's barbed comment.

'If it means we both enjoy the evening, then where's the harm?' he said. Hannah refolded her arms across her chest and looked at him with a face like thunder. 'Are you jealous?' Rupert asked.

'Am I jealous? No sodding way am I jealous. The poor woman's welcome to your enhanced little erection. It doesn't matter how long it lasts for, she'll still be listening to you snoring thirty seconds after you're done.'

'You are too. You're bloody jealous,' Rupert barked. He could feel the tension building up in the back of his head and knew that Hannah was winding up him up on purpose. The best thing for him to do would be to walk away, but he couldn't. For a second, he thought about crossing the kitchen and giving Hannah a good slap, but he didn't think that would go down too well no matter how satisfying it might feel. Besides, she was standing next to the kitchen knives. 'So, it's alright for you to skulk around shagging Matthew or Amy when you think I'm not looking but it's not okay for me to use my own gifts to further the cause?'

'Your gifts?' Hannah said, her voice a full two octaves higher than normal. 'Did you just say that with a straight face?'

'Oh fuck off, Hannah,' Rupert barked. Enough was enough. 'Help yourself to some of the Viagra. It works on women as well. You can chop one of them down the middle and share it with your carpet-munching friend while I'm out.'

The two of them stared at each other for a few seconds. Rupert was — inside his head — daring Hannah to reply to what he had just said. He'd not meant to blurt that particular phrase out, but once it had been said, it couldn't be unsaid. Rupert and Hannah turned as the internal door to the kitchen opened. Amy was standing in the door frame. She didn't look happy.

'Rupert,' Amy said, almost in a whisper. 'That really is quite crass, what you just said.'

'Oh, well, I am so fucking sorry,' Rupert said, knowing that he was being unreasonable but not really caring. He watched as Hannah walked across the kitchen toward Amy and stood next to her. Bitches, the pair of them. 'So can I get a lift into Norwich or not?'

'Rupert,' Hannah replied with a glance at Amy. 'You can get the fucking bus.'

43

Andy was pleased to leave the hospital and get back out into the fresh air. Ruth had suggested stopping at the McDonalds on the way out for some cheese bites and fries, but Andy wasn't hungry in the slightest. They walked toward the bus stop, both lost in their own thoughts. It was Ruth who finally broke the silence when they were both sitting on the uncomfortable bench.

'I can't believe he's not coming back,' she said, glancing across at Andy.

'Well, he's only going home to recuperate,' Andy replied. 'He'll probably be back once his leg is sorted out.'

'Nope, he won't,' Ruth said. 'I don't think we'll see him again to be honest.'

'What makes you say that?'

'Did you see the look in his eyes? He looked, I don't know, broken.' Ruth's voice tailed off as she said this, and Andy looked at her. She was chewing her lip hard, and Andy wondered for a moment if she was about to start crying.

'It's only his leg that was broken,' he said, trying to put a light tone in his voice. It didn't work, and Andy saw a tear form at the corner of Ruth's eye. 'Hey, come here,' he said, putting his arm around her and pulling her toward him. 'You don't need to be upset.' Ruth brushed the tear away and snuggled into him. They sat in silence for a while before Ruth broke the silence again.

'Do you think you'll stay?' she asked Andy. Surprised, he pulled away from her, leaving his hand on her shoulder.

'Where's all this come from, Ruth?' he said. 'This isn't like you. I'm not going anywhere.'

'You will, at some point,' she replied. 'You always do.' Andy opened his mouth to protest before he realised that she wasn't talking about him, but about men in general. He decided to keep silent and let her carry on when she was ready. A few minutes passed before she continued.

'My Dad always told me he wasn't going anywhere, but he did.' Andy waited for a few seconds before replying.

'Oh, sorry. I didn't know that,' he said.

'He just walked out one evening and never came back,' Ruth continued. 'He said he would only be a couple of hours, that he was only going for a few drinks on Riverside with some friends. My Mum tried to talk him out of it. She said that he was too old to be going to places like that Riverside and that it was for youngsters. Not pervy old men like him.'

Andy stifled a smile. From the way that Ruth had described her mother, he thought that she would probably get on quite well with his own mum. Andy realised that he knew nothing about Ruth's family. He didn't know if she had any brothers or sisters, or anything like that. Ruth sat in silence, chewing at a fingernail.

'So, what happened?' Andy said a moment later.

'That was the last time we saw him. He walked out, and never came back.'

'He didn't say anything?'

'He called Mum a fat old trout as he closed the door.'

'Oh,' Andy replied. If nothing else, that was a memorable last line. 'That's crap that is,' he said, not sure what else to say. Andy couldn't even begin to imagine why a man would just walk out on his family like that, never to return. He couldn't see his own father doing that, nor did he ever think that he would be able to just do one.

'So, are you still in touch with him at all?' he asked. Ruth gave him a strange look before replying.

'Well, we've tried to get in touch,' she said in a small voice. 'But we never actually managed to get through to him. We nearly did, a couple of times. But apparently he didn't want to talk to us.'

Andy took a deep breath, realising that he was now — in a sense — acting as a representative for the entire male gender.

'Well, I guess it's not really possible to really know what's going through someone's head when they decide to do something like that.'

'I'm pretty sure I know what was going through his head,' Ruth replied, staring straight ahead and not looking at Andy.

'Can I ask what?' he said after a few seconds. Ruth looked at him with a sad face before replying.

'Probably something along the lines of 'oh fuck, I've fallen in the river and can't swim'. Some fisherman hooked him just outside Great Yarmouth. That was the furthest Dad ever got away from Norwich, that was.'

'I thought you said you tried to get in touch with him?'

'We did, but I'll tell you something. Janine the Psychic

— the one at the end of Yarmouth pier — she's shit, she is.'

'Ah,' Andy said. 'Right.' They sat in another long, uncomfortable silence, until Andy was saved by the appearance of the number 24. 'Look, here's our bus.'

44

Emily managed to drive her Mini as far as the end of the farm track before she started hyperventilating. By the time she had turned onto the lane that ran down the side of the field, she could feel the tips of her fingers starting to go numb. This hadn't happened to her in almost a year. The first time was when she was at college and there was an unfortunate incident in one of the assemblies that left none of the sixth form in any doubt about what she looked like naked. That had just been a picture on a screen, an early version of revenge porn that her amateur photographer ex-boyfriend ended up getting expelled for, but the panic attack she'd had at the time was an horrific one and it was the first of many. From the bloating Emily could feel in her stomach to the trembling in her thighs, she knew this one was shaping up to be just as bad, if not worse.

'Are you okay, Emily?' Mr Clayton asked. Took him long enough to bloody notice, Emily thought. She breathed in through her nose and out through her mouth, just like her old therapist had taught her.

'I'm cool,' she said, quickly, not trusting her voice. 'Just pulling over.'

She pulled the Mini into a layby and turned the ignition off. Emily glanced at Mr Clayton, who was looking at her with a concerned expression on his face.

'Are you sure you're okay?' he asked. Emily nodded her head, flapping her hands in front of her face before cracking open the door to let some fresh air in the car.

'Panic attack,' she gasped. 'It'll pass.'

'Ah, okay,' Mr Clayton replied. 'Got it.' To Emily's relief, he then just sat there looking at his phone until her heart had stopped thudding in her chest and returned to something approaching normal.

'Sorry,' Emily whispered a few minutes later. 'That's not happened for a while.'

'Don't worry, Emily,' Mr Clayton replied. 'I used to get them a lot back when I was drinking.' She looked at him, surprised. Emily didn't know he was a drinker. 'I thought I was having a heart attack in Sainsbury's once. Awful, it was.'

'I don't drink Mr Clayton,' Emily said. 'Well, not much.'

'Oh no, that's not what I was saying,' Mr Clayton cracked a smile. 'But I did. Oh my God, did I put it away. Been almost a year now.' He raised his voice a couple of octaves. 'Hello, my name is Chris, and I'm an alcoholic.' His smile broadened, and Emily realised that she hadn't known what his first name was until just now. He didn't look like a Chris, but equally she wouldn't be able to come up with a more likely first name for him.

'Do you mind if we just take a few minutes?' she said. 'I mean, I'm feeling better, but I'd just like to take a moment.'

'Not at all, Emily. We can take as long as you need.' He

returned his attention to his phone, and Emily noticed that he was still shopping for dresses.

Twenty minutes later, Emily was completely back to normal. She'd spent a few minutes wandering around the trees next to the layby, wondering if she was going to be sick or not, but hadn't. Other than the fact she smelt of sweat, all was good.

'Shall we crack on?' she said as she sat back in the driver's seat. 'Sorry about that.'

'Don't be,' Mr Clayton replied, looking up from his phone. 'Not a drama.' He tucked his mobile back into his pocket as Emily started the car. 'I was thinking, according to the schedule your next visit is the Cathedral Tea Rooms.' Emily's heart sank. The last thing she wanted to do was another inspection, especially that place. The last time she'd been there, she'd got into a bit of a barney with the Bishop. It hadn't ended well. 'I live near the cathedral, so why don't you drop me off there. I'll do the inspection so you can head home. Have a large glass of wine, and then Netflix and chill?' Emily stifled a laugh, fairly sure that he didn't really understand the Netflix reference. She had a horrible thought for a second that maybe he did understand the phrase and was about to invite himself over to her flat to 'Netflix and chill', but he just stared at the strange shaped tree next to the layby. 'Looks like one of the nazi things, that tree, doesn't it?' Emily didn't reply as she put the car into gear.

It took them about half an hour to get to the cathedral — ten minutes to get into Norwich, and another twenty to get through all the 4x4 vehicles that swarmed around the entrance to the posh school on Cathedral Close.

'I bet they've only got them for the school run,' Emily

muttered as she manoeuvred her way around yet another driver who seemed to think they were in a tank and that parking in the middle of the road was acceptable.

'Yeah, you're probably right,' Mr Clayton replied. 'You can drop me here if you want?' He pointed to the side of the road.

'I was going to park up and come in with you,' Emily replied. 'I've got a roll to eat, and was thinking about grabbing a cup of coffee and sitting in the gardens.' As soon as she'd said this, she wondered if she'd made a horrible mistake. Mr Clayton — her boss — had just offered to do an inspection for her and she'd responded by saying she was going to get a coffee and sit outside eating her roll while he was doing it. Emily opened her mouth to try to explain when Mr Clayton cut her off.

'Excellent idea, Emily,' he said. 'That sounds like just what you need.'

'Oh,' Emily replied. That wasn't what she was expecting him to say. 'I mean, I can do the inspection and then get a coffee?'

'Nope,' Mr Clayton replied. 'I'm all over it like a tramp on chips.'

Emily eased her Mini into a tiny parking space just outside the cathedral. They both squeezed themselves out of the car and were just about to walk over to the tearooms when a thin, well-dressed woman with peroxide blonde hair approached them.

'Excuse me,' she said in a high-pitched whine,' Could you move that please? I need to reverse out, and you're in my way.' The woman turned and pointed at an enormous SUV that was parked half on the pavement and half on the road. An elderly lady was struggling to get her shopping basket past the black vehicle, and in the passenger seat a young boy with bright ginger hair regarded the old woman with amusement. Emily was just about to reply when, not for the first time that day, Mr Clayton interrupted her.

'You shouldn't have it if you can't drive it,' he barked at the SUV driver before walking off, leaving her open-mouthed. Emily flashed a quick grin at the woman and mouthed 'sorry' before she set off after him.

45

Hannah sat at the kitchen table, grateful for the peace and quiet. Rupert had left, grumbling like mad about the fact that she wouldn't give him a lift into the city. Hannah wasn't having any of it. As far as she was concerned, he was going into the city to try to shag some poor woman from the university on the basis that he wanted to get her access card. Knowing Rupert, Hannah was pretty sure that the primary reason he was going to the city was to get his end away with someone new and unsuspecting, and stealing the key card was a secondary bonus. So, he could get the bus. His comment about carpet-munching had just confirmed to Hannah how much of a cock he could be.

'Whatever,' she sighed, getting to her feet and crossing to the kettle. She flicked the switch to boil the kettle and make a cup of tea just as Amy reappeared in the doorway from the bedroom, wrapped back up again in a duvet.

'Has he gone?' Amy whispered.

'Yep,' Hannah replied.

'Thank fuck for that,' Amy said, her voice back to

normal. She padded across to the table, her bare feet slapping on the stone tiles. ' I don't know how you put up with him.'

'Used to it,' Hannah replied. 'In one ear, and out of the other most of the time.' Amy didn't look convinced. 'Do you want a cuppa?'

'That'd be nice. Cheers.'

Hannah made them both a cup of tea, and they sat opposite each other at the kitchen table. Amy seemed quiet, not saying much at all, but that gave Hannah a chance to think about Rupert. He was probably sitting at the bus stop, fuming about the fact that she'd refused to give him a lift into the city. If she knew him — which she did — he was probably muttering about how the bus timetable didn't meet his requirements. What would be really funny was if he sloped back into the farmhouse in a couple of hour's time, his tail between his legs, having got absolutely nowhere with the woman from the university. Not so much blown, as blown off.

'What's the grin for?' Hannah heard Amy ask. She hadn't realised that she'd been smiling.

'Nothing, just thinking,' Hannah replied.

'About anything in particular?'

'Not really,' Hannah replied, not wanting to share her hope for Rupert's disappointment with the woman. 'Stuff, that's all.' She looked across at Amy, who gave her a lop-sided smile in return. Hannah looked at Amy's smile, and a vague recollection of kissing her last night popped into her head. What Hannah wasn't expecting was the way her stomach lurched at the memory. She got to her feet.

'You okay?' Amy asked. 'Your face just went a bit weird there for a second.'

'No, I'm good,' Hannah replied. 'I was just thinking

about a large glass of wine and an equally large joint. You in?' Amy glanced at her watch before replying.

'It's not even four o'clock,' Amy said with a wry smile. 'Isn't that a bit early?'

Thirty minutes later, Hannah was completely buzzed. In the ashtray on the table, the tail end of a joint smouldered away. Hannah had put far too much of Rupert's stash into it, but she didn't care. Two glasses of wine sat on the table between her and Amy, both glasses barely touched. Hannah watched through hazy eyes as Amy carefully licked a cigarette paper, sticking it to another one with exaggerated care. The look of concentration on her face was something else.

'Now stick the third paper across those two' Hannah said, aware that her voice was a fair bit deeper than normal. 'Like I showed you earlier.' Amy looked at her with equally glazed eyes.

'This is a lot more difficult than it looks.'

'It's easier if you do it before you smoke any.'

'Yeah,' Amy replied, licking another cigarette paper and pressing it together with the other ones. 'There we go, that looks okay.' Hannah watched as Amy licked the seam of a cigarette with the tip of her tongue and undid it like a zip to empty the tobacco from it. She bunched the loose tobacco into a line on the papers, and reached for Rupert's bag of grass. She pulled out a very generous helping of weed.

'He won't mind if we have a bit more, will he?' Amy asked.

'He's not here,' Hannah replied with a grin, prodding the ziplock bag on the table with Rupert's drugs in. She watched as Amy piled weed into the joint she was putting together. 'Jesus, go easy. That'll kill us both.' Amy looked at Hannah with a lopsided smile.

'At least we'll die happy,' Amy said as she licked the cigarette papers and rolled the joint together, running her fingers over the seams. 'Do you want to smoke this now, or save it for later?'

'I think we should have it later. It's pretty loaded.' Hannah's eyes flicked back to Rupert's pile of drugs on the table. 'Do you think he was right?' she asked Amy.

'About what?'

'About the Viagra?' Hannah pointed at a small bag full of small blue diagonal pills on the table.

'What, working on women as well?' Amy asked, her voice almost a whisper. They stared at each other for a few minutes until Hannah broke the silence.

'Yeah.'

'We could do an experiment. In the interests of science,' Amy replied, opening the bag of pills and pulling two out. Hannah watched as Amy pushed a blue pill across the table before teasing another one out of the bag and pushing it next to her own glass of wine. 'Shall we?'

In response, Hannah picked up the pill and put it on her tongue before picking up the glass of wine and downing it in one, the pill disappearing as she did so.

'Your turn,' she said to Amy. With a grin, Amy did exactly the same thing.

Hannah and Amy sat in silence for a while, both waiting to see what happened. To Hannah's disappointment, nothing much at all seemed to be going on. Maybe Rupert was wrong? She looked at the fattened joint on the kitchen table a couple of times, wondering if she should suggest sparking it up. The only problem with that was it would almost certainly signal an end to the day, even though it was still early. She looked across at Amy, who was picking at something on the table with her fingernails. Had the two of them really gone to bed together? The only issue Hannah had with that scenario was not being able to remember it, and the fact that she'd just popped some Viagra wasn't exactly giving off negative signals about a repeat performance. Shaking her head, she got to her feet and made her way to the kitchen sink. She washed the cups up and put them on the drainer.

When she had rinsed the cups, Hannah turned around to see Amy standing a few feet behind her. Hannah leaned back, appreciating the solid feel of the counter behind her. She realised that her head was spinning ever so slightly, but whether that was from the weed or the Viagra she didn't know. Hannah could feel a slight ache in her teeth and made a conscious effort to relax her jaw.

'Amy?' Hannah asked. She paused before continuing. 'Why are you wearing a duvet?

'Why not,' Amy replied. Hannah realised from Amy's dreamy voice that she was just as off her head as she was.

'Have you still got Rupert's shirt on?' Hannah asked. Amy didn't reply, but just shrugged her shoulders and slipped the duvet off. As it slipped to the floor, Hannah realised that Amy wasn't wearing a stitch of clothing. She kept her eyes fixed on Amy's.

'What do you think?' Amy asked in a whisper.

'I think you'll catch your death dressed like that.'

Amy didn't reply, but just took a few steps forward, slipped her hand round Hannah's neck and entwined her fingers in her hair.

46

E mily took a tray from the counter in the Cathedral Tea Rooms, and put the roll that Hannah had made for her earlier onto it before walking up to the counter.

'Could I get a coffee, please?' she asked the elderly woman in an apron who was standing next to the till.

'Of course you can, my dear,' the woman wheezed. 'What type would you like?' Emily paused, not sure what to say in reply. She glanced behind the woman to see if there was a proper menu, but Emily couldn't see anything. The Tea Rooms wasn't the sort of place to have a wide variety of coffee choices though, so she decided to play it safe.

'What are the options?' she asked with a smile.

'Well,' the woman replied, 'you can have black, or white.' She took a deep breath, and Emily was reminded of the time Catherine had a really bad chest infection and sounded like an asthmatic. 'It's up to you.'

'Oh, thank you. Could I have a white coffee then, please?'

Once the coffee had been delivered, which took far longer than it could have done, Emily turned to find somewhere to sit down. Spying a table on the other side of the room, she was crossing toward it when her foot got caught in a walking stick that was leaning against one of the chairs. She was trying to keep her footing when she crashed into a man walking back toward the counter carrying a tray. Both their trays flew up into the air, and Emily's coffee went flying. Straight toward her. Almost as if it was in slow motion, the contents of the cup poured onto her blouse.

'Oh, for fucks sake,' Emily exclaimed as the almost hot liquid soaked into her clothes. She glared at the man who had walked into her and realised that he was dressed a bit strangely. He was wearing some sort of long purple dress with loads of fancy buttons, and he had a big gold cross hanging around his neck. Oops. That was what Emily had seen bishops wearing on the telly. Emily wasn't sure, but she thought the dress was called a cassock or something like that.

'Oh my word,' the man said, his voice smooth and reassuring. Definitely a bishop. 'My goodness me, I am so sorry.'

'No, I'm sorry, er…' What was the right thing to call a bishop? 'My fault entirely. I tripped on that walking stick.' The bishop glanced at the offending article.

'That's not a walking stick, that's my crozier. Therefore, this entire incident is absolutely my fault. Phyllis?' he called out, and the woman behind the counter looked up. 'Phyllis, could we get some cloths please?'

'Yes, My Lord,' the old woman replied. Emily looked at the man in front of her. He might be a bishop, but she wasn't going to call him 'My Lord'.

While Phyllis was bustling around looking for a cloth, Emily reached down and picked up her roll from the floor. There was another one, also wrapped in clingfilm, so she picked that up as well.

'Ah, that one's mine,' the bishop said, taking it from her and putting it on a table next to them. She looked at him while they waited for Phyllis, trying to ignore the coffee dripping down her cleavage. He looked like a kind old boy, maybe mid-sixties. Lots of laughter lines around his eyes. When he saw her looking at him, they deepened as he smiled at her.

'So, are you just visiting then?' he asked.

'Yeah, kind of,' Emily replied. 'I mean, I've been here before but I just wanted to get a coffee.'

'Yes, but now you seem to be wearing it,' he replied. 'I'm so sorry.' Emily tried to interrupt but he carried on talking, holding out a hand for her to shake. 'I'm just visiting as well. I'm Doctor Wells.'

'Emily,' Emily said, shaking his hand. 'Pleased to meet you.' It was a bit lame, but she couldn't think of anything else to say. Behind the counter, Phyllis was getting flustered, presumably at her inability to find any cloths. 'So, er, you're a bishop then?'

'What makes you say that?' he replied with a self-deprecating glance at his cassock. Before she could reply, he continued. 'I am, guilty as charged. I'm not the Bishop of Norwich though. We haven't got one at the moment. That's why I'm visiting. We're called 'flying bishops', and go round the various dioceses that don't have any senior leadership.'

'Oh, good,' Emily said. She had no idea what dioceses were, but figured that they must be something to do with churches. Or cathedrals.

'Here you are, My Lord.' Phyllis had finally managed to find a cloth. She passed it to Doctor Wells, and Emily noticed that the beds of the old woman's fingernails were dark blue. She'd seen that once on the television as well in an old episode of *999 - What's Your Emergency?*, and knew that it wasn't a good sign. Something to do with oxygen, or more specifically, not enough of it. As she looked at the old woman in front of her, Emily realised why so many of the people in the tearooms were so elderly. They were hedging their bets as they got closer to the inevitable.

'Thank you, Phyllis,' the bishop said before turning to Emily. 'Now young lady, let's get you sorted out.'

Doctor Wells dabbed at Emily's blouse with the cloth. His first few dabs were tentative, but they became progressively harder as he realised that none of the coffee was coming off.

'It's okay,' Emily said, slightly uncomfortable. 'I'll just head back to my flat and get changed.'

'My dear, no. You must let me do what I can. If I can't get this stain out, then you have to send me the bill for the dry cleaning.' He continued pressing the cloth against her blouse, but all that it seemed to be doing was to spread the brown stain across the material. 'Hmm,' the bishop said. 'This isn't really working. I think I need to put some more elbow grease into it.'

Emily flinched as Doctor Wells reached out his hand — the one without the cloth in — and cupped her left breast. He pressed the cloth harder against the material, and she felt him adjust his hand on her tit.

'Everything okay, Emily?' Mr Clayton's voice came from the direction of the till. She turned to see her boss standing behind Phyllis. Emily stared at him, imploring him with her eyes to help. She was standing in the middle of a church tea room, with a bishop whose hand was now very firmly on her chest. To her relief, he strode across to where they were standing and put his hand on the bishop's arm.

'Bishop Wells, I'm so sorry if young Emily here has been bothering you. She was just leaving. Weren't you, Emily?' Mr Clayton looked at her with an inscrutable expression.

'Yes, I was,' Emily replied with a sigh of relief. 'Just on my way off now.' It might have been her imagination, but she was pretty sure that the bishop rubbed his thumb against her nipple as he let go of her breast. 'Sorry about the coffee, and all that. I'll just be on my way.'

Emily picked up her roll from the table and walked toward the exit. As she did so, she glanced around the Tea Room. None of the other customers seemed to have noticed her interaction with the bishop.

'I should have kneed him in the bollocks, bishop or no bishop,' Emily muttered to herself as she left the tea rooms and walked over to her car. She looked at her phone to see if Catherine had texted her — they'd made some vague plans earlier to go out that evening — but there was nothing so she started the car and headed for home. Within a few hundred yards, she was stuck in a traffic jam. Muttering to herself, she balanced her roll on her knees and unwrapped the clingfilm. She was going to wait until she got back to the flat before eating it, but Emily was starving. Scrunching the roll between her fingers, she took a large bite.

'Oh for Christ's sake,' Emily muttered through a mouthful of bread. She wound the window down before spitting the bread out of the open window, not caring what anyone else stuck in the traffic jam thought. Frowning, Emily looked down at the roll on her lap. It had what looked suspiciously like egg mayonnaise in it — not the hummus she'd been looking forward to. 'Bollocks,' she said as she wrapped the clingfilm back round the bread. Not only was she still starving, but she hated egg mayonnaise and would now have the taste of it in her mouth all the way to her flat.

47

O ne thing that Andy wasn't expecting to see when he pushed open the farmhouse door was Amy. More specifically, he wasn't expecting to see Amy as naked as the day she was born, with her tongue down Hannah's throat.

'Oh my goodness,' he said, stopping so suddenly that Ruth ran into the back of him. 'I'm so terribly sorry, I didn't mean to, er, I didn't mean to interrupt. I would have knocked if I'd known that…' his voice tailed off as Amy and Hannah unentangled themselves from each other. From the look in both their eyes, and the thick sweet-smelling fog in the kitchen, they'd both been at the weed. Quite a lot of it. He felt Ruth's hands on his upper arms and her chin leaning into his shoulder.

'Gosh,' she whispered in his ear. 'I wasn't expecting that.'

'Neither was I,' he whispered back.

'Andy, Ruth,' Amy said with a far-away smile. 'It's lovely to see you.' Behind her, Hannah wiped her mouth with the back of her hand and stared over Andy's shoulder at the field outside.

'It's lovely to see you too, Amy,' Andy replied, concentrating hard on looking at her face and not letting his eyes drift down, or further down. 'We're, er, we're just passing through. To the bedroom.'

'Yes,' Ruth said, pushing him in the small of the back. 'To the bedroom. That's where we're going.' She paused before continuing. 'We'll leave you guys to it.' Andy stumbled forward.

'Sorry again,' he called over his shoulder as Ruth propelled him toward the bedroom.

'Bloody hell,' Ruth said in an excited whisper when the bedroom door was closed behind them. 'Did you see that?'

'Did I see what?'

'Shut up, you fool,' Ruth laughed, swatting at his arm with her hand.

'Nipples like clothes pegs,' Andy mumbled under his breath.

'What?'

'Nothing,' he replied.

'Did you know about that?'

'About what?'

'About those two?' Ruth looked at him, incredulous. 'Them being, well, involved?'

'News to me,' he replied. 'Didn't see that coming when I walked in the door.'

'Do you think Rupert knows?' Ruth asked. Andy paused for a few seconds before replying.

'If he knew, he'd have been in there filming it on his phone. Mind you, Hannah's been shagging Mathew for ages and Rupert doesn't seem that fussed about it.'

Ruth crossed to the lower bunk bed and sat on it, crossing her legs.

'Bloody hell,' she said, blowing her cheeks out. 'How fucked up is this place?'

'What do you mean?' he replied, frowning. 'They were only kissing.'

'Andy,' Ruth said, trying to shout and whisper at the same time. 'Amy was naked, in case you hadn't noticed.'

'She was?'

'Oh, shut up,' Ruth smiled, getting to her feet. 'You couldn't take your eyes off her.' Andy opened his mouth to protest but she continued. 'Do you think it's safe to go for a pee?'

'What do you think's going to happen if you do, Ruth?' Andy replied. 'They might kidnap you, take you to their secret lesbian lair and perform sexual acts on you until you're begging for mercy?'

'Sexual acts until I'm begging for mercy?' Ruth said, her smile slipping a notch. 'Chance would be a fine thing.'

'Oh get a grip, Ruth,' Andy said, trying to stop a note of irritation creeping into his voice.

'Maybe you need to get a grip, Andy,' Ruth replied, flashing a look toward his groin. 'That might help your eyes get back into their sockets.' By the time he had thought up a witty reply, she had already turned her back on him and left the room.

Andy sat on the bed that Ruth had just vacated and leaned forward, putting his head in his hands and his elbows on his knees. Deep down, Ruth's comment about this place being fucked up had hit home. Rupert was rapidly losing control of what was going on in his little empire. One of their number was in hospital with a broken leg, never to return. In the meantime, Rupert's supposed partner seemed to be sleeping with anyone she could while he was off furthering the cause. Which, if he was to be believed, involved him sleeping with a random woman from the university. The only two of them who weren't sleeping with anyone were he and Ruth, and she had made it quite clear that she only wanted that to be temporary.

By the time Ruth came back from the bathroom, Andy had just about managed to push the image of Amy and her improbably erect nipples to the back of his head. He shuffled up on the bunk to give Ruth room to sit down. They sat in silence for a few seconds.

'Sorry,' Ruth said. 'That was uncalled for.'

'S'okay,' Andy mumbled in reply. She leaned into him, and he put his arm around her shoulder. As she wriggled to get herself comfortable, Andy couldn't help but think about Amy and Hannah. He'd never actually seen two women kissing in real life before, and it had made quite an impression on him for some reason. Too much porn when he was a teenager, he supposed.

'Have you ever thought about going back?' Ruth asked.

'Back where?' Andy replied, his mind still on what he'd seen in the kitchen.

'Back to, well, out there I guess.'

'What, leaving the farm, do you mean?'

'Yeah,' Ruth sighed. Andy wondered whether he should tell her about his weekend in his old house, but he thought better of it.

'Sometimes, I suppose,' he said, 'if I'm honest.'

'What would you do?' Ruth asked him.

The last thing that Andy would do is go back to working as an intern in a supermarket. The problem was, he didn't really have much on his resume apart from that and a long gap when he'd been on the farm.

'I've got no idea,' he replied. 'What would you do? If you left?' Ruth paused before replying.

'I'm not sure. Maybe work as an exotic dancer, or a high-end prostitute,' she said with a sly grin. 'At least then I'd get laid once in a while.'

'A high-end prostitute? In Norwich?' Andy said, returning her smile. 'I don't think so.'

'Alright then,' Ruth replied with a laugh. 'I'll be a low-end street hooker doling out blow jobs for twenty quid a pop off Rose Lane.'

'Twenty quid?'

'What, you think I'm selling myself short?'

'I was thinking maybe a tenner.'

'Fuck off,' Ruth laughed, slapping his arm and standing up. 'I need a drink, and I wouldn't mind a smoke as well. Do you think it's safe to go out there?' She nodded her head toward the kitchen.

'I might have to come with you, make sure it's safe?'

'No, you only want to come with me in case they're scissoring on the kitchen table,' Ruth replied. Andy wasn't one hundred percent sure what 'scissoring' was, but he had a vague memory of watching it once on a borrowed DVD in the solitude of his bedroom.

They crept into the kitchen like burglars, but there was no sign of Hannah or Amy. Andy grabbed a half-full bottle of whisky from the cupboard, and a couple of cans of coke from the fridge. While he was hunting for some clean glasses, Ruth picked up the bag of weed on the table and some cigarette papers.

'What do you want to do?' she asked Andy. 'Stay here or go back to the bedroom?' Andy didn't reply, but reached into his pocket for his wallet. He opened it and fished out a twenty pound note which he unfolded and put on the table. Looking at Ruth, he took a deep breath and smiled, saying nothing. She looked at the twenty pound note, and then back up at him, a slow smile creeping across her face.

'Bedroom it is, then.'

48

J ust here, please mate,' Rupert said to the cab driver. 'If you could turn left at the burned-out tree, I'm at the end of the track.' The cab driver — a taciturn, dark-haired man with a deep Norfolk accent — stopped at the end of the track. The early sun was reflecting off the deep puddles in the track. It looked as if it was going to be a really nice day. Not that Rupert cared, all he wanted to do was curl up in bed and sleep.

'Not going up there, mate,' the driver said. 'Look at it. Couldn't get a cow up there without breaking its legs.'

'Come on, it'll be fine,' Rupert replied. 'It's not as bad as it looks.'

'Nope,' the cabbie replied, shaking his head. 'Not going to happen. It's here, or you can come back into the city with me.'

'Fuck's sake,' Rupert muttered under his breath. 'How much is that then?'

'Eight pound fifty, fella,' the taxi driver said. Rupert dug into his pocket and counted out exactly eight pounds and fifty pence. As an afterthought, he added a single twenty pence coin to the money in his hand.

'Keep the change,' Rupert said as he handed the money over. 'Fella.'

As the cab driver was counting up the fare, Rupert inched his way out of the cab, wincing as he did so.

'Are you okay, mate?' the driver asked. Rupert paused, caught out by the other man's sudden concern. 'Only it looks like you've had a right kicking.'

'Yeah,' Rupert replied, wincing again as he got to his feet on the track leading to the farm. 'You could say that. All good though.'

Rupert made his way up the track back to the farmhouse. He paused a couple of times to get his breath, and to try to ease the pain, staring as he did so at the faint lights of the farmhouse. Even though it was only just after dawn, the kitchen light was on.

'Don't worry about the bloody electric bill, will you?' he asked no-one in particular. Not far to go now, Rupert thought as he lurched his way toward the welcoming front door.

The inside of the kitchen was musty with the smell of stale booze and cannabis. Rupert looked around and tutted at the state of the place. There was an empty bottle of whisky on the table, two glasses — one of which was on its side and had leaked whisky into the wood — and an ashtray with the remnants of several joints. He must have missed out on an impromptu party, he thought as he walked past some broken glass on the floor to open the windows and let some fresh air in. When he stretched for the window handle, a sharp jolt of pain racked its way down his back.

'For fuck's sake,' he grimaced. Moving more carefully, he reached out and opened the window before returning to the table. There was a joint in the ashtray that looked as if it had barely been smoked, so he fished it out and sparked it up. That might ease the pain a bit. He carefully eased himself into one of the chairs.

Rupert examined the end of the joint as he smoked it. Whoever had put it together — Hannah from the look of it — had overloaded it with weed. Normally, this would have annoyed Rupert. It was his weed after all, but considering how much pain he was in, he didn't really care. Just as he crunched it out into the ashtray, the door opened and Amy walked in. Her eyes were still full of sleep, and her long blonde hair was tousled. That wasn't what got Rupert's attention though. It was the fact she wasn't wearing a stitch of clothing.

'Morning Rupert,' she said, crossing the kitchen floor to the kettle. Rupert watched her, his eyes wide.

'Bloody hell,' he whispered as she stood on tip toes with her back to him to get some mugs from the top cupboard.

'Do you want a cup of tea?'

'Er, go on then,' he replied. Amy fussed about with mugs and teabags, keeping her back to him. That was a shame, Rupert thought. He much preferred the view from the front, although what he was looking at wasn't too shabby. Rupert was just admiring the curve of her buttocks when she reached down and scratched one of them with a long red fingernail.

'For God's sake, Amy,' Hannah's voice came through the door to the hallway. 'Would you put some clothes on? Morning Rupert,' she called as she walked into the bathroom.

Amy turned to face Rupert and walked over to him, putting a mug of tea on the table. As she leant forward to put the mug down, her breasts were inches from his face.

Without a word, Amy padded out of the kitchen, Rupert's eyes fixed on her backside as she did so.

'Bloody hell,' he said again as the sound of the toilet flushing filtered through the bathroom door. A few seconds later, Hannah walked into the kitchen. At least she had some clothes on, even if she looked as tired as Amy.

'Good night then?' she said, taking a seat opposite him at the table. 'Looks like it was from your face.'

'Looks like it was here, too,' Rupert replied, letting his gaze float toward the ashtray, whisky bottle, and broken glass on the floor.

'That was Andy and Ruth, not us. We just had a few smokes and went to bed,' Hannah said, running a hand through her red hair.

'Together?' he asked. Hannah didn't reply, but just looked at him. Her forehead wrinkled ever so slightly as she opened her mouth before closing it again.

'I'll clear up in here a bit,' she said, getting to her feet. The change in subject wasn't lost on Rupert.

He watched Hannah as she moved about the kitchen, tidying up as she did so. When Rupert was sure that she wasn't about to turn around, he gingerly got to his feet.

'What are your plans for the day, anyway?' he asked.

'Baking,' Hannah replied over her shoulder, both hands in the sink. She took out a sud-covered glass and put it on the drainer. 'Me and Amy are going to use up the rest of that free flour we got from the warehouse. She knows someone at Snetterton Market who'll take as much as we can bake.'

'What about the Food Standards Agency?'

'What about them?' Hannah asked. 'You're not bothered about them, are you?'

'Not in the slightest.'

'Well neither is the bloke at Snetterton Market, so we're good.'

Rupert made his way to the door, trying to walk as normally as he could despite the pain in his back. He was almost there when he heard Hannah say something behind him. He turned round to see her leaning up against the counter, drying her hands on a tea-towel.

'Sorry, I missed that?' Rupert said.

'I said, we were together,' Hannah was looking at him with an expression that he'd not seen before. Her eyes looked sad, but at the same time she was smiling. 'We are together.'

Rupert felt the anger flash in his chest. If it wasn't for his injuries, he would have crossed over to Hannah and grabbed her round the neck to ask her what the hell she meant by that. Instead, he just turned his back on her and walked into the bathroom. He needed a shower, then he needed sleep. There would be plenty of time to sort Hannah out later.

49

Andy lay in bed, watching the sunlight streaming in through the curtains. Next to him, breathing deeply with her back to him, was Ruth. He wanted to get up, but didn't want to wake her up. But it wasn't just that, he didn't really want to talk to her just yet. Andy knew that within the next few minutes, he would have to get up anyway as his bladder was fit to burst, but he stayed where he was for the time being, appreciating the peace and quiet.

'You're awake,' Ruth whispered a few minutes later. It was a statement, not a question.

'Nope, I'm still asleep,' he whispered back.

'You're not, I can hear you blinking.'

'You cannot.'

'Yes I can. Every time you blink, there's like a little click.' Ruth turned over and put her arm on his chest. As she snuggled into him, he felt her hand sliding down and into his boxer shorts. It wasn't there for long. 'No morning glory, then?' she asked.

'Sorry,' Andy replied. 'Not this morning.'

'Not last night, either.'

'No, sorry,' he said, thinking back to the previous evening. It hadn't been his finest hour.

They had retreated to the bedroom, smoked a joint, and finished off most of the whisky. Ruth had offered to demonstrate her exotic dancing skills. Andy — who had never been to a strip club in his life — had been more than happy with that plan. It turned out that Ruth wasn't bad at all, even though Andy didn't have a reference point to work with. She had discarded most of her clothes, and pulled him to his feet.

'Your turn,' Ruth had whispered as she knelt in front of him and unbuckled his trousers. A few seconds later, Andy heard her say something else. 'Oh.' It wasn't a gasp of anticipation, more a sigh of disappointment. A few moments later, they were back in the kitchen finishing the whisky. Andy had offered to 'finish her off' another way if she wanted him to. That was when she had thrown the glass at him.

'Has that ever happened before?' Ruth asked, breaking Andy's recollections of the previous evening.

'No,' Andy replied. 'Never. It must have been the wacky baccy and booze that got to me.'

'Well you're not stoned or pissed now, are you?' Ruth said. 'But Mister Happy still isn't very happy. He wanted to change the subject, and soon. 'Can I squeeze past you? I need a pee.' In response, Ruth's hand pressed down on his bladder.

'Ouch, stop it,' he gasped. In response, Ruth just giggled and pressed again. 'Seriously, stop it or I'll piss the bed.' He reached out and grabbed the skin just above her bony hips, knowing that was where she was most ticklish. They wriggled together on the single bunk bed for a moment, both laughing, with her trying to prod his bladder and him trying to tickle her. Andy managed to get the upper hand, and sat astride her with his hands pinning her wrists either side of her head.

'Okay, okay,' Ruth laughed. 'You win, big man.' He leaned down and kissed her on the end of her nose.

'I do like you, you know that?' he said. Ruth's smile disappeared and she looked at him.

'So show me.'

Andy didn't reply, but levered himself off Ruth and made his way to the bathroom.

'Bollocks' he said when he heard the sound of the shower running. He hopped from foot to foot, wondering what to do, before deciding that he could nip outside and go down the side of the farmhouse somewhere. The only problem with that plan was that he was only wearing a pair of boxer shorts. Andy walked into the kitchen, the pain in his bladder overriding the thought of the cold outside, and saw Hannah and Amy bustling around. Neither of them noticed him, but the fact they were both in here meant that it must be Rupert in the shower. He wouldn't mind if Andy nipped in for a pee while he was in the shower, so he walked back to the bathroom door and opened it.

'Don't mind me, mate,' Andy called out to Rupert before walking to the toilet and relieving himself noisily. 'Bloody hell, I needed that,' he said before turning round.

Rupert was standing with his head underneath the shower, water steaming. Andy gasped when he saw Rupert's back. It was covered with bright red raised welts, some of them bleeding.

'Mate, what the fuck happened to you?' Andy said. Rupert turned and looked at him from underneath a sopping wet dreadlock.

'Is it bad?' he asked. 'I can't see.' Andy took a step toward the shower and examined Rupert's back.

'Looks bloody nasty,' Andy said, reaching out a finger

but stopping just short of touching Rupert's skin. He glanced down at Rupert's buttocks. There were several nasty looking bruises on each cheek. 'What are those, on your arse?'

Rupert turned the shower off and grabbed a towel from the rail.

'I think they're bite marks,' Rupert replied. 'Mate, can we chat in the bedroom?'

A few minutes later, they were both in the farmhouse's main bedroom. Rupert was wearing the towel round his waist and had put on a loose-fitting shirt. Andy watched him wincing as he eased the shirt on and wondered if he should offer to help, but decided against it. Rupert looked at the bed and the rumpled sheets on top of it. His face hardened, and he walked awkwardly to the bed, picking up a bundle of female clothing and throwing them across the room.

'Fucking bitch,' he hissed through gritted teeth. 'After everything I've done for her.' Andy said nothing, not wanting to get involved and not liking the look of pure hatred on Rupert's face. An image of Hannah and Amy from when he and Ruth got back last night flashed back into his head, and Andy had a good idea what Rupert was so pissed off about. He'd never seen him look this angry before, though.

'So those marks, Rupert?' Andy asked, partly to change the subject and partly out of genuine concern. He didn't know how long it would be before Ruth came looking for him, or one of the others came back in, and Andy wanted to find out what had happened.

'They're from a whip, Andy,' Rupert replied, turning his ice-blue eyes on him. 'I would have thought that much was bloody obvious.'

'That woman from the university?'

'Yeah, Lauren "butter wouldn't melt" from the lab,' Rupert snorted. 'Started off okay, then she got all weird on me. It was all "why don't we try this" and "trust me, it'll be fun". Next thing I know I'm face down on the bed tied up like a pig for the slaughter.' He rubbed at his wrists with his hands. 'Then she starts laying into me with a horse crop.'

'Jesus Christ,' Andy said. 'Wasn't there anything you could do?'

'Did you not just hear what I said? I was tied to the bloody bed. The only good thing that came out of the whole sodding evening was that according to Lauren and her gigantic un-lubricated index finger, I've got an entirely normal prostate.'

'But surely…' Andy wracked his brain for the right thing to say. 'Didn't you have, I don't know, a safe word or something?'

Rupert took a couple of steps toward Andy, who tried not to flinch.

'I'll show you something you haven't seen.' Rupert pulled his bottom lip down to show Andy his teeth and gums. Andy leaned forward and could see a painful looking blackened area at the base of Rupert's gum line.

'What's that?'

'That,' Rupert replied, letting go of his lip, 'is what happens when you try to bite through a ball gag.'

50

E mily yawned and pulled her dressing gown tighter around her abdomen. It looked like it was going to be a nice day, but it was still chilly. She sipped her tea, enjoying the warmth of it, and flicked through the channels to find something to watch.

When she'd got back last night, Catherine had been nowhere to be seen. Emily had tried calling her, but there was no reply so she'd sent a couple of texts to see where her flat-mate was. It had been long after ten o'clock, when Emily was already curled up on the sofa with a hot chocolate and a good book, by the time Catherine replied.

Sorry, busy xxx

She took another sip of her tea and had just settled on a re-run of *Real Housewives of Cromer* — a surprisingly entertaining show about the wives of some of Cromer's top fishermen — when Emily heard the front door open. A few seconds later, Catherine walked into the lounge. To Emily's annoyance, her flat-mate looked immaculate apart from a faint dark shadow underneath each eye. Considering what she'd probably spent most of the night doing, it wasn't fair that she looked so refreshed.

'Morning babe,' Catherine said, dumping her coat onto an armchair and plumping herself on the sofa next to Emily.

'Morning,' Emily replied, turning the volume to the television down a bit. 'Did you have a good night?'

'Fucking awesome.'

'You're such a lady,' Emily laughed. 'What was his name?'

'Which one?' Catherine asked before giggling. 'It doesn't really matter. I can't remember either of them. Would you be a darling and make me a cuppa? I'm knackered.' With a pretend 'tut', Emily got to her feet and wandered into the kitchen. She might as well make herself another cup at the same time.

'Do you want some toast?' Emily called through the kitchen door.

'No ta,' Catherine shouted back. 'Maybe in a bit.'

Emily made the brews and walked back into the living room. Catherine had changed the channel to the local news and was watching the weather forecast. 'Local news will be on in a minute,' she said.

'It'll all be about the football match this afternoon,' Emily grumbled.

'The city was buzzing last night from it though. Everyone's really excited about the whole thing.'

'Yeah, my boss is going. The picture on the screen changed and, sure enough, the lead piece on the local news was all about the football, and the fact that Norwich City were only ninety minutes away from a Champions League trophy. The only thing in City's way were Bayern Munich. The excited reporter on the screen was standing outside Carrow Road where, despite the early hour, he'd managed to find a couple of Norwich fans who were there about ten hours early for the match. From the look of them, they were from quite a long way out in the sticks. They watched the painful interview for a few moments. The male fan was doing all the talking, while his female companion just stared open-mouthed at the camera. Catherine turned the volume down and started telling Emily about last night.

'So, I met these two lads in the Murderers. Right old laugh, they were. The pub had an Oompa Loompa band on to warm people up for the game.'

'Pretty sure it wasn't an Oompa Loompa band, Catherine,' Emily said, turning and giggling at her flat-mate.

'They were too.'

'What, they were all four-foot-tall, and orange with green hair?'

'No,' Catherine replied with a frown. 'They were fat, sweaty, and German.'

'Well, they're not Oompa Loompas then,' Emily said. 'I think you mean it was an Oompah band.'

'What's the difference?'

Emily was just about to reply when she saw a very familiar face on the screen.

'Pause it, pause it,' she said loudly, startling Catherine who fumbled for the remote control. 'That's him.' Catherine prodded at the remote, and the screen froze.

'That's who?'

'The bloke who felt me up at the cathedral. I was going to tell you about it, but you weren't here. He grabbed my tit yesterday.' On the television, the kind face of Doctor Wells stared back at them, frozen in a rictus grin. He was wearing his purple cassock, and Emily could just see the top of the gold cross he'd been wearing around his neck.

'He did not.'

'He bloody well did.'

'Emily, he's a bloody bishop,' Catherine said with an exasperated sigh. 'Bishops don't go about grabbing women's tits.'

'Well that one does, I'll tell you that for nothing,' Emily replied. 'I would have kneed him in the bollocks but he had this long dress thing on. Rewind it, back to the start.' It took Catherine a couple of goes, but she managed to find the start of the piece.

'This had better be good,' Catherine muttered as she pressed 'play' on the remote control and a female news-reader with a bright orange face started talking.

'Is she an Oompa Loompa?' Catherine whispered.

'Shh,' Emily hushed her. 'Listen.'

'In a devastating accident at Norwich Cathedral, visiting bishop Doctor Aaron Wells fell to his death from the top of the spire yesterday evening,' the news reader said with an earnest stare at the camera. 'It's still not clear what actually happened, but live at the scene is our roving reporter, Bob Rutler.'

'Bloody hell,' Emily said.

'Well that'll teach him to grab your itty bitty little tittie,' Catherine replied. Emily was just about to respond when the reporter started his piece.

'Thank you, Amelia,' he said, stroking his unkempt beard. 'I'm live at Norwich Cathedral at the scene of the tragic death of visiting bishop, Doctor Aaron Wells.' Over his shoulder, Emily could see a policeman standing by some tape, picking his nose and examining the results. 'I've got some witnesses to this horrible accident.' In the back-ground, the policeman was just raising his index finger to his mouth when the camera jerked around and settled on a familiar looking couple.

'Weren't those two at Carrow Road a few minutes

ago?' Catherine whispered. 'They're not even out of breath, and that's a good mile away that is.'

'Shh,' Emily replied as the man on the screen started talking.

'So, me and my partner Marie were here yesterday evening. We're from Potter Heigham, but we've got season tickets in the Upper Barclay so decided to make it a weekend in the city.'

'Partner my arse,' Catherine whispered. 'Looks more like his sister to me.'

'Would you shut up,' Emily barked in a low voice.

'Probably both,' her flat-mate replied, rolling her eyes. On the screen, the reporter was trying to steer the man away from the difference between Jarrolds of Norwich and Lathams of Potter Heigham — both very different department stores — and back to the matter at hand.

'So, what did you see?' the reporter asked.

'Didn't see nothing,' the man replied. 'Just heard it.'

'What did you hear?'

'It was like when Marie dropped the Christmas turkey on the floor,' the man replied. 'Big wet slap, so it was.' The man's companion smiled.

'Ew,' Catherine said. 'She's got no teeth.'

51

Hannah brushed her flour covered hands against her apron, and turned the dial on the oven to get it warmed up. Behind her, Amy was clattering trays around, each one with a collection of round, flat, dough pancakes. Between them, they'd managed to use up the majority of the free flour. The trays had what would eventually be hundreds of bread rolls on them.

'We good?' Hannah said to Amy.

'I think we're more than good,' Amy replied. 'Karl the Cat Man's going to love these.'

'Is that your mate at the market?'

'Yeah. He's called Karl, and he likes cats.'

'I'd never have guessed,' Hannah said with a grin. 'What does he do?'

'He's got a van thing, sells pulled pork rolls with a difference.'

'So what's the difference?' Hannah asked as she walked over to the sink to rinse her hands.

'It's not pork,' Amy replied. Hannah thought about

asking what the meat was, if it wasn't pork, but decided against it.

'You've seen all those "Missing Cat" posters that pop up on telegraph poles?' Amy continued. 'Well, that's a pretty good sign that Karl's in town.'

'Oh,' Hannah said. 'Not sure I like that to be honest.'

'Hannah, he's going to pay us fifty pence a roll. We won't get that anywhere else.'

'Cats? Seriously?' Both women turned at the sound of Rupert's voice. He was standing at the door to the kitchen, a towel wrapped around his waist. 'That's okay is it, selling rolls to a bloke who murders defenceless cats?' Hannah looked at Rupert. She'd known him long enough to recognise when he was properly pissed off.

'I think she was joking, Rupert,' Hannah said, trying to keep her voice even.

'Killing and eating cats is a joke now, is it?' he replied. 'Although, to be fair, I cannot see either of you two having a problem with it.'

'A problem with what?' Hannah asked. 'I've never killed anything in my life, you know that.'

'Eating pussy,' Rupert replied with a dark look.

'Oh, that's enough, Rupert,' Hannah shot back. 'Seriously, that's enough. You can't walk back in here after spending the night with that woman from the university and have a go because me and Amy spent the night together.'

'Yes, I can,' Rupert said. 'What I was doing last night was trying to further the cause. To do something to make people sit up and take notice.'

'Bollocks,' Hannah laughed, and Rupert's face got even darker. 'You just wanted to shag a ginger woman, and anything else is a bonus.' Rupert started walking over to where Hannah was standing, but she moved away from him and stood next to Amy. Hannah didn't like the look on his face, and figured that there was safety in numbers. To her relief, he didn't try to follow her. If anything, he looked as if he was walking really awkwardly, almost as if he was hurt.

'Are you okay?' Hannah asked. He might be being a cock at the moment, but she still cared for him.

'No, I'm bloody not,' he replied. 'It was a scam. I got beaten up, kind of.'

'You serious? What happened?'

'I don't want to talk about it,' he replied. 'Not to you two, anyway.'

'So did you get the key card?' Amy said. When Rupert turned to look at her, Hannah saw the fury on his face.

'No, Amy,' he hissed. 'I did not get the bloody key card. I was lucky to get out of there at all.' The three of them stood in an awkward silence for a few moments before Hannah spoke.

'Amy, could you give me and Rupert a moment please?' Amy didn't reply, but just walked off, her hand brushing against Hannah's as she left. Hannah waited until the kitchen door had closed behind her.

'Sit down, Rupert,' she said, gesturing toward a chair. 'You're making me nervous.'

'I'd rather stand.'

Hannah sighed, and sat down.

'What's going on?' she asked, putting her head into her hands. She realised too late that they were still covered in flour. 'What's going on with us, Rupert?'

'You tell me,' he replied through gritted teeth.

'One of the things about us, Rupert, is that we don't own each other. It's always been that way. So why are you suddenly like this?'

'Hannah, give me some credit,' Rupert said. 'This is different.'

'How is it different?' Hannah asked. 'Because she's a woman?' She looked at Rupert, but he was avoiding her eyes. He took a couple of steps over to the counter and put his hand into the almost empty flour sack, pulling out a handful of flour from the bottom.

'Is this what you're using?' he said, examining the flour in the palm of his hand.

'Rupert, don't change the subject,' Hannah sighed. 'Just talk to me, would you?' He didn't reply. Instead, he brought the flour much closer to his face and examined it. Rupert used the index finger of his other hand to smooth out the small pile of flour in his palm, and squinted at it carefully. 'Rupert? I'm talking to you?'

'You're not talking to me,' he said, brushing the flour back into the sack. 'You're talking at me.'

'How is it different with me and Amy? That's a question, Rupert. That's not me talking at you, that's me asking you a question.'

'You know it's different, Hannah.'

'Because she's a woman?'

'No, it's not that.'

'So what is it then?' Hannah asked. 'It's just sex, for God's sake.'

'No it's not!' Rupert slammed his hand onto the kitchen counter, making Hannah flinch. 'It's not just sex.'

'Well what is it then?'

'Oh for God's sake, Hannah. I've watched the two of you together.' Hannah opened her mouth to protest but Rupert cut her off. 'Not together in that sense, but just when you're with each other. Amy's constantly staring at you, touching you, admiring you. She was like that before the two of you even got together, but you were just too thick to see it.'

'That's bollocks, Rupert.'

'No, it isn't,' he replied, walking over and standing behind her, putting his hands on her shoulders. Hannah reached up and put one of her hands over his. 'But do you know what the most hurtful thing is?' His voice was soft, almost a whisper.

'What?'

'It's that you're starting to look at her in the same way,' he continued. 'You've never looked at me like that.' He leant forward and hugged her from behind.

Hannah relaxed back into his arms, rubbing the back of his hand with her thumb. They'd argued before, and always been able to work it out, although Hannah knew it was going to be difficult this time. She sighed and closed her eyes. Behind her, Rupert jerked his arm and Hannah felt the crook of his elbow at the front of her throat getting tighter and tighter. She opened her mouth to say something, shout, scream even, but the pressure on her neck was so tight that she couldn't make a sound other than a strangled gasp. Hannah tried to get her fingers in between his arm and her neck, but his hold was too tight. Her peripheral vision started to go grey, and it felt as if she was looking through a tunnel at the kitchen window. Hannah was just on the verge of passing out when she heard Rupert's voice whisper in her ear.

"I. Want. Her. Gone.' Rupert spat the words out, and Hannah felt flecks of saliva landing on her cheek. He released his arm and she lurched forward on the chair, taking a deep breath as he stamped his way toward the kitchen door.

52

R upert closed the kitchen door quietly behind him and stepped out into the courtyard. That would give the traitorous little bitch something to think about. He strolled down the track toward the sheds, not because he needed to go there for anything, but to give Hannah a chance to throw Amy out on her ear. He figured he would give them half an hour, maybe an hour. It wasn't as if Amy had arrived with much stuff to pack away anyway. By the time he got back, she would be gone and he could take Hannah to bed to show her what she'd been missing while she was messing about with Amy. Rupert grinned with anticipation at the thought, even though he knew it would probably make his back bleed. She wouldn't be able to see the wounds on his back with her face shoved in the pillow anyway.

Rupert thought back to the flour in the sack. There was something not quite right about it. It wasn't white, for one thing, although some wholemeal flours weren't. It had been difficult to work out exactly what colour it was tinged with, but eventually he had settled on purple. But he couldn't work out why a bag of flour would be tinged purple. At least, he couldn't until he saw the pig shed that Matthew had jumped from. Like a coin being dropped into a slot machine, his brain worked it out.

'Claviceps,' he muttered to himself. 'It's bloody claviceps. That's why he jumped.' Rupert's grin broadened into a wide smile as he laughed loudly. 'Fucking ergot.'

When Rupert had been studying chemistry at the university, one of his little side projects had been trying to re-create an experiment done by Albert Hoffman in the 1940s - creating lysergic acid. He and one of his fellow students had spent ages trying to grow the highly toxic mould known as claviceps purpurea so that they could synthesise it into LSD, just like their hero Hoffman, but the lecturer had other ideas when he found out. It turned out that the lecturer objected so much to them trying to make hallucinogens in his laboratory that he threw them both off the course, and ultimately from the university.

Rupert hurried into the old abattoir to get a notepad. He needed to make some notes, get some ideas down on paper. If his suspicions were correct, Matthew had launched himself from the top of the pig shed while he was tripping out of his head. That meant — and this was the bit that he wanted to write down — there were hundreds of highly hallucinogenic rolls in his kitchen. He was sitting in the abattoir, scribbling down some thoughts about what he could do with them when the door swung open. Rupert looked up to see Andy standing at the entrance.

'Hey,' Rupert said, flipping his notepad shut. 'You okay?'

'I'm fine mate,' Andy replied. 'I was going to ask you the same thing. Is everything okay?'

'Yeah, all good,' Rupert shifted his shoulders from side

to side to show Andy how well he could move, trying to ignore a tearing sensation on one of his shoulder blades as he did so. Perhaps that hadn't been a good idea. 'Bit sore but I can move okay.'

'No, not with your back,' Andy said. 'With you and Hannah?'

'What do you mean?' Rupert gave Andy a sharp look.

'I mean, it's not really any of my business but —'

'You're right, it's not.'

'— she seems really upset, that's all,' Andy finished.

Rupert remembered the feeling of satisfaction that he had when he was choking the life out of Hannah. He knew that if he had carried on, she would have lost conscious-ness within a few seconds. Did she realise how close she had just come to dying?

'We've just had a bit of an argument, that's all,' Rupert replied. 'Nothing to worry about, mate. What's she said?'

'She's not said anything,' Andy said. 'Her and Amy were in the bedroom shouting at each other when I left.'

'Could you hear what they were shouting?'

'Not really, you know how bloody thick the walls are. I did hear Hannah screaming "pack your stuff" at Amy at one point though. That's when I thought I'd better come down and find you.' Rupert looked at Andy's concerned face and had to suppress a smile.

'It's probably just a lovers' tiff, Andy.'

'Sounded like it was a bit more serious than that. Do you think we should both go back to the farmhouse, make sure everything's okay?'

'No, Andy,' Rupert replied. 'Let's leave them to it. Hannah's been feeling bad about what's been going on with her and Amy.' He ignored Andy's frown and contin-ued. 'She was telling me about it this morning, about how it wasn't her kind of thing and she was going to tell Amy to leave her alone.'

'Oh,' Andy said. Rupert looked at the other man and could see the confusion on his face. 'It's just, well, I wasn't going to say anything but I did see the two of them last night.'

'Doing what?'

'Oh, I didn't see anything like that. They were just kissing, that was all.'

'Was Amy kissing Hannah, or was Hannah kissing Amy?' Andy paused before replying.

'Well, they were kissing each other. I think.' Rupert let a frown play across his face. 'Although, thinking about it, maybe it was Amy kissing Hannah?' Andy said, and Rupert changed his frown to a smile to let Andy know that was the correct answer.

'There you go,' Rupert said. 'She's predatory, that's what she is. Hannah's had enough of it. From what you've said, things have escalated.'

'Right, okay,' Andy mumbled. He didn't look convinced, but Rupert didn't really care as long as Amy was gone when he got back. He flipped open his notebook.

'Andy, sit down, mate,' he said. Andy scraped a chair across the floor and sat next to Rupert. 'Look, I've got an idea,' Rupert said. 'There's a problem with the bread, but I think I know how we can use it to our advantage.'

'What sort of problem?'

'It's laced with ergot.'

'Er, you might have to help me out a bit with that one.'

'It's a fungus that grows on cereals,' Rupert replied. 'Highly toxic. Have you heard of St Anthony's fire?'

'Oh yeah, I know that.' Rupert looked at him, surprised. 'That was one of my mum's favourite films, that was. Didn't it have Demi Moore in it?'

'What the fuck are you talking about?'

'I'm sure it did. I think she got her tits out in it. Or was that *About Last Night*? I'm not sure now, it's ages since I've had to watch any of those films. But it was definitely Demi Moore. I remember because the first time I saw it, I'd not seen breasts in real life before. My dad thought it was hysterical, the way my mum was trying to block the screen.'

'It's not a film, Andy. It was a mass poisoning outbreak in the middle ages.'

'Oh,' Andy said. 'Right.' Rupert paused before continuing.

'Ergot is a hallucinogen. It's what LSD is made out of, kind of,' he explained. 'That bag of flour is essentially one large bag of acid, and Hannah's made a whole bunch of bread rolls out of it.'

'So that's why Matthew jumped off the roof,' Andy said. 'He was off his tits after all.'

Rupert slapped Andy hard on the shoulder, wincing as he felt something else tear in his back.

'Yes, Andy,' he said, 'that's exactly why Matthew jumped off the roof. Now how much fun do you think we could have with those bread rolls?'

53

Emily sat in her lounge, channel surfing to see if there was anything on worth watching. Catherine had long since disappeared to bed for the day, claiming to be exhausted and a bit sore. Emily didn't really want to hear any of the sordid details of why Catherine was sore, so she hadn't asked, even though she knew Catherine was dying to tell her.

The news about the bishop had affected her more that she'd thought it would. On the one hand, he was a randy old pervert who had touched her up in a church restaurant, on the other hand he was dead. She thought back to the previous day, and the incident with the coffee. Had the bishop realised what he was doing? Perhaps he was being a gentleman, and trying to dab the coffee from her blouse without realising? Not wanting to think ill of the dead, Emily had just about convinced herself that it had all been a horrible mistake and that she had just imagined his thumb rubbing across her nipple.

One thing Emily was sure about was that she wasn't going to spend the day lounging around the flat feeling sorry for herself. She flipped open the lid to her work laptop and turned it on, changing the television channel to a daytime soap as she waited for it to boot up. When the computer had finally whirred into life, she opened up her visit schedule to see what was coming up next week. If she spent a bit of time now preparing for the visits, she could treat herself to an extended lunch break or two next week.

The only visit that had been added since the last time she had checked the schedule was one to Hilltop Farm. Mr Clayton had scheduled it in for Thursday. Emily remembered her conversation with the woman with red hair, and Emily's promise to make the inspection as smooth as possible. One way of doing that would be to drop off the paperwork in advance so that there weren't any surprises. The only problem with that would be that it would mean another visit to the farm, and this time on her own without Mr Clayton for support. Remembering her panic attack in the layby, Emily made a decision.

'Right, time to face that demon head on,' she muttered to herself as she closed the laptop screen.

Twenty minutes later, Emily was sitting in a traffic jam. It looked as if most of the occupants of the other cars were dressed in green and yellow, and she realised she'd driven straight into football traffic. The big game was this afternoon at Carrow Road — the Champions League final. Emily remembered a big argument about where the game was going to be held with the opposing team complaining like mad that Norwich City would have home advantage. If Emily remembered correctly, an ex-politician called Ed Balls who was now the President of FIFA had over-ruled their complaints.

Emily looked to her right and saw a middle-aged man

in the car next to her in the queue. He was wearing a green and yellow wig, his face painted in the same colours, and he was waving at her. He looked like a grotesque clown, and was far too old for face paint, but she managed an insipid wave back at him. The man responded by slapping his car door with the flat of his hand and shouting 'come on you yellows' at the top of his voice.

She re-tuned her radio to Canary FM to listen to the pre-match build up. If nothing else, it would give her something to talk to Mr Clayton about next week. Whether or not she would listen to the game itself was something she could decide nearer the time, depending on how the visit to the farm went. Eventually, the traffic started to ease and Emily managed to get out of second gear. A few minutes later, she was in open countryside and heading toward Hilltop Farm.

When she saw the tree shaped like a swastika, Emily slowed down and pulled into the layby that she and Mr Clayton had sat in a few days before. She took a few deep breaths, willing herself to go through with the visit to the farm. She didn't have to go anywhere other than the farmhouse, not the pig sheds, not the abattoir. Emily only had to go as far as the farmhouse.

She looked at the track leading from the tree up to the farmhouse itself. The last time she'd driven up the track, it had taken the poor blokes running the drive-through car wash near her flat ages to get rid of all the mud. Emily had felt so bad she'd ended up paying them twice what they advertised for a full wash. For that reason, and the memory of her head smacking off the car window as she'd hit a particularly bad pothole, she decided to walk up the track. It would give her a chance to get some fresh air as well.

By the time Emily got to the farmhouse, she was breathing heavily. It had been more of a trek than she thought it would be. Standing in front of the front door, she rapped her knuckles on it hard, knowing that if she hesitated she would bottle it and be back at the car in no time at all.

'Bloody hell,' Emily grimaced, flexing her fingers. 'That hurt.' She was just about to knock again when the door opened a couple of inches. It was constrained by the security chain, and a familiar red-haired woman was peeping through the gap. Behind her, another woman who Emily didn't recognise was looking anxiously over her shoulder.

'Hi, Hannah?' Emily said, remembering the woman's name at the last moment.

'What?'

'I'm Emily Underwood, from the Food Standards Agency? We met the other day.'

'What do you want?' Hannah replied. Her demeanour was totally different to the other day when they had first met.

'Can I come in?' Emily asked.

'It's not really a good time, Emily.' Behind her, the other woman spoke urgently in Hannah's ear.

'Let her in, Hannah,' she said. 'It's not safe out there.'

Hannah opened the door, and beckoned to Emily to step into the kitchen. As the door closed behind her, she looked around the inside of the farmhouse. At the kitchen table, a third woman was sitting. She was thin, almost to the point of being gaunt, but was just finishing off a bread roll. Emily thought the poor girl looked as if she needed it, but admonished herself as she thought this.

'Hi,' the woman said, her mouth still full of roll. 'I'm Ruth.'

'Hello,' Emily replied.

'This is Amy,' Hannah said, gesturing toward the

woman who had been behind her when she had opened the door.

'Hello, Amy,' Emily said before turning back to Hannah. 'Is everything okay, Hannah? You seem, I don't know, really tense.'

'Like I said,' Hannah replied. 'It's not really a good time. Me and Amy were just leaving.'

'Oh, sorry. I can come back later if that's easier? I don't want to get in your way.'

'No, no point,' Ruth said from her seat at the kitchen table. 'They're leaving for good. Not coming back.'

'Ah, I see,' Emily said, not sure how else to respond to the statement. Hannah wasn't joking when she said it wasn't a good time. Emily was just trying to think of something to say when she heard the door handle to the kitchen door creaking.

'You forgot to put the bloody chain on,' Amy snapped at Hannah as the door started to swing open. Emily turned to see a very familiar face walk into the kitchen.

54

Andy lay curled in a foetal position on the cold flag stones of the kitchen floor, trying not to be sick. The pain in his testicles was intense, and he could hear shouting filter through the agony. The last thing he'd been expecting when he walked through the kitchen door was a swift and expertly executed knee to the groin from his ex-girlfriend, Emily Underwood.

He felt a hand on his shoulder shaking him, and Rupert's voice cut through the pain.

'Andy, are you okay?' Rupert said. Andy took a couple of deep breaths and forced himself up into a sitting position. He blinked once or twice and used the sleeve of his shirt to wipe tears from the corners of his eyes. 'That looked nasty, that did,' Rupert continued. Andy nodded in reply, not trusting himself to speak just yet. He looked around the room to see Ruth sitting at the kitchen table, picking at some crumbs on her plate. Hannah and Amy — who Andy was sure he'd seen just before Emily had floored him — were nowhere to be seen.

'Emily?' Andy wheezed. 'Where is she?'

'That woman from the Food Standards Agency?' Rupert replied. 'She's long gone, mate. Kicked you in the bollocks and did one. You know her then?'

'Ex-girlfriend,' he said.

'That's her?' Ruth exclaimed, getting to her feet and wobbling slightly as she did so. 'That's the one?' She sat back down heavily. 'I feel a bit odd.'

'I don't know I'd call her "The One", but she's my ex-girlfriend, yes.'

'Come on, mate,' Rupert said, putting a hand underneath Andy's elbow. 'Up you get, it'll help with the pain.' Andy wasn't convinced that it would, but he struggled to his feet with Rupert's help.

'Fuck me that hurt,' he said, rubbing his groin.

'It looked like it did,' Rupert chuckled. 'You went down like a sack of flour, mate.'

'Where did Hannah and Amy go?' Andy asked. 'They were here, weren't they?'

'Sod the pair of them,' Rupert snarled. Andy looked at him, surprised at his sudden change in expression. A few seconds ago he'd been laughing, even if it was at Andy's expense. Now he looked like he wanted to thump something. Andy glanced across at Ruth to see if she'd noticed, but she was sitting at the table, staring at her fingers.

The internal door opened, and Hannah and Amy walked into the kitchen. Each of them had a bag with them. Hannah was trailing a small suitcase on wheels, and Amy was clutching a rucksack. Andy saw that Amy was holding onto the strap of her rucksack so tightly that her knuckles had turned white, matching her face. She was terrified.

'Rupert,' Hannah said, her voice wobbling as she spoke. 'We're leaving.' Ruth made a peculiar sound in response, and Andy glanced at her for a second before turning back to look at Rupert.

'Good,' he replied, glaring at Amy. 'Go on then Amy, off you fuck.'

'It's not just Amy who's leaving, Rupert,' Hannah said. 'We're both going.'

Andy looked between Rupert and Hannah, trying to work out what on Earth was going on. Hannah had her chin tilted toward Rupert, almost in a gesture of defiance. Rupert was looking at her open-mouthed.

'What?' Rupert said, and Andy's head swivelled back to look at Hannah.

'You heard,' she replied as Amy took a step closer to her. Andy turned to Rupert.

'You're not going anywhere,' he said, picking up a large knife from the counter and using the tip of it to get a bit of something from underneath one of his fingernails. Even though Rupert seemed to be using the knife for the benefit of his personal hygiene, the threat was obvious — even to Andy.

'Rupert, stop being such a drama queen and put the bloody knife down. We're going, and you can't stop us. So that's that.'

Rupert was just opening his mouth to reply when Ruth let out a deafening scream, startling them all. She leapt to her feet, screamed again, and lurched toward the kitchen door. Ruth pushed it open and ran out into the courtyard.

'She didn't take that very well, did she?' Amy said in a quiet voice over Hannah's shoulder.

'Oh, shut up you daft cow,' Rupert said, returning his attention to the tip of the knife and his fingernails. 'Ruth's off her tits. How many of your rolls has she had?' He directed the question toward Hannah.

'Two, I think,' Hannah replied. 'Why?'

'They're full of ergot.'

'What's that?' she asked.

'It's a hallucinogenic fungus,' Andy replied, pleased to be able to contribute something. 'Acid, basically.'

'That's why Matthew thought he was a chicken. He'd had one of your rolls,' Rupert explained, sneering at Hannah.

'Jesus Christ,' Hannah shouted, dropping the handle of her suitcase. 'Come on, we need to catch her before she does something stupid.'

A few moments later, Andy, Hannah, and Amy had formed a rough triangle around Ruth who they'd managed to surround in the middle of the field behind the farmhouse. They all stood with their arms outstretched, Ruth in the centre of them. Every few seconds, Ruth flapped her arms in the air and squawked.

'Easy, easy,' Andy said in a soft voice. 'It's okay Ruth, we're all here.' She just stared back at him, eyes wide. He took a step toward Ruth, and she moved away from him. 'Hannah, Amy,' he called out. 'We need to get her back to the farmhouse where she'll be safe.' Out of the corner of his eye, Andy could see Rupert looking through the kitchen window, a broad smile on his face. Nice of him to help out, Andy thought as he took another step toward Ruth. Again, she moved away from him.

Between them, they managed to work out the best way of shepherding Ruth back toward the farmhouse. They had to take it in turns, one of them moving toward her, one of the others moving away to give Ruth space to move into. It took a good twenty minutes, but eventually they had manoeuvered her toward the courtyard at the front of the farmhouse. A couple of times, Ruth tried to make a bid for freedom and run through their makeshift barrier, but she didn't manage to get through. The only place Ruth had left to go was through the open farmhouse door. Andy realised that how they could get her into one of the bedrooms was something that they would have to work out when they got there. Perhaps Rupert would help out?

'Tighten it in,' Andy whispered, glancing at Hannah and Amy who were both standing in the courtyard with their arms wide. Together, they started taking small steps toward Ruth to tighten the circle around her.

Ruth's head jerked from side to side, looking at each of them in turn. Her eyes were vacant, pupils so dilated that Andy couldn't see any of the colour in them. She made a bizarre squawking noise before turning and running full pelt through the kitchen door, arms flapping as she did so.

Andy ran in after her, wondering how they were going to get her into a bedroom. He was closely followed by Hannah and Amy. To his relief, when he entered the kitchen, he saw Ruth standing in the middle of the room with Rupert holding on to her shoulders.

'Jesus wept,' Andy said with a sigh of relief. 'That was a bloody nightmare.' At least Ruth would be safe now. They could barricade her in a bedroom until the ergot wore off. She might feel like shit for a while when she eventually came down, but she wouldn't be able to jump off anything higher than the bunk beds.

Ruth gasped, and Rupert let go of her. She turned round to face Andy, and he saw the handle of Rupert's knife buried to the hilt just below her sternum. A dark red stain was spreading across her lower chest.

'Oh fuck,' Andy whispered.

55

E mily sat in the seat of her red Mini, tears streaming down her face.

'Bastard,' she muttered as she searched in the well of the car for an unused, or at least not very well used, tissue. 'Absolute bastard.' Seeing Andy come in through the door of the farmhouse, without a care in the world, had thrown her completely. He was pretty much the last person she expected to see as after he'd disappeared, Emily hadn't heard a word from him apart from a solitary bloody letter. Not a single phone call, e-mail, or text message. Just a letter. She figured that he'd left the country, gone to live overseas somewhere, but it turned out that he'd been living just down the road. On the farm where they'd both so nearly come to a sticky end. 'Bastard, bastard, bastard.' Emily sniffed and dabbed at her eyes with the single fragment of tissue she'd found on the floor.

Kicking Andy in the testicles was what she had been planning to do the next time she saw him from the minute Emily had realised he'd left. She smiled wryly as she remembered her knee coming up without her even thinking about it, almost as if it was some sort of reflex action. Emily fished in her pocket for her phone and tapped out a text message to Catherine.

Just seen Andy. The reply came back within seconds.

OMG. Where?

On the floor clutching his bollocks.

No way! Where are you? Emily was just thumbing a reply when there were a couple of loud knocks on her car window. Jumping, she dropped the phone and it slithered down into the space between her seat and the centre console. The one bit of the car that was an absolute nightmare to retrieve the phone from, and the place she always seemed to drop it. She turned to see Andy standing next to the car, hand raised to knock on the window again.

'Fuck off, Andy,' Emily shouted through the closed window as she fumbled for the ignition key. One thing that she didn't want to do was to talk to that bastard ever again.

'Emily, please,' she heard him. 'Help me, please.' His voice was high pitched, frantic, but Emily didn't care. She found the key and turned it, the engine bursting into life. Emily revved the engine and turned, intending to give him the bird as she sped away from the layby and hopefully running over his toes, when she saw the bloody handprint on the window. She took her foot off the accelerator and put the car back into neutral. As the engine noise dissipated, she wound the window down an inch. 'Please, Emily, you have to help me.'

''What's going on?' she replied, examining his face. He was wide-eyed, distraught, and his hands were covered in blood. Even though he was a complete and utter bastard, the thought of Andy being injured made Emily feel sick. 'Are you hurt?'

'No, it's not me,' he said, 'it's Ruth. She's been stabbed.'

Emily thought back to the thin woman in the kitchen and pressed the button to unlock all the car doors.

'Get in,' she barked.

Andy ran around to the passenger side of the car and threw himself into the seat. His door hadn't even closed before Emily spun the car into a sharp u-turn and headed for the entrance to the farm track.

'So what happened?' she said, not taking her eyes off the road. Emily knew she wouldn't be able to hammer the car down the track — not without snapping something — but she wanted to get to the farmhouse as soon as possible.'

'Ruth's off her head on bread rolls,' Andy replied, his words so fast they ran into each other. 'We got her back into the farmhouse but then Rupert stabbed her — or she ran into him. Not sure which.'

'Where?' Emily asked, trying to concentrate on both Andy's rapid narrative and the pot-holes in the road. Her mind span as she tried to work out what the hell was going on.

'In the kitchen.'

'No, you idiot. Where on her body?' she asked. Andy pointed at his sternum.

'Just here. That soft bit that really hurts when you press it too hard.'

Emily's mouth flattened into a thin line. She'd seen enough episodes of *Holby City* to know that was one of the worst places to get stabbed. All sorts of important stuff were in that bit. There was a first aid kit in the boot of the Mini, but Emily doubted there would be much in it for a knife wound to the chest.

'Emily,' Andy said. She risked taking her eyes off the road for a second to look at him.

'What?'

'I'm sorry,' he replied. 'For everything.'

'Not the time, Andy,' Emily said. 'Not the time.'

When Emily pulled into the courtyard, she saw
Hannah's distinctive red hair behind the wheel of a
battered old Land Rover. It looked as if she was trying,
without much success, to get the thing started. Emily threw
herself out of the car and ran toward the farmhouse door,
Andy a split second behind her. When she got inside the
kitchen, Ruth was lying on the stone floor, her head
cradled in Amy's lap. Andy hadn't been messing about —
there was a wooden handle sticking out of Ruth's chest.
The injured woman was as white as a sheet, and for a few
seconds, Emily thought she was dead. Then Ruth moaned
softly and took a shallow breath.

'Jesus Christ,' Emily said. 'Andy, get some towels or
something.' As he ran across to the cooker to grab some
tea-towels, Emily knelt down next to Ruth.

'Ruth, can you hear me?' she said. There was another
soft moan in response. Emily pressed her fingertips against
Ruth's neck, searching for a pulse. It looked a lot easier on
the television, but she finally found a weak, thready pulse.
At least it was there.

'What do we do?' Amy said, and Emily looked at her
tear-stained face.

'Tea-towels,' Andy said, pressing some stained cotton
towels into Emily's hands. 'Should I get a bowl of hot
water or something?'

'She's not having a fucking baby, Andy,' Emily snapped
back at him. 'She's been stabbed.' Emily suddenly realised
that Rupert was nowhere to be seen. 'Is Rupert still about?'

'No,' Amy replied with a sob. 'He took off over the
fields when he saw what he'd done.'

'Okay,' Emily said, relieved that he wasn't still lurking
about the farm somewhere. She didn't know how Ruth had
ended up with a knife in her chest apart from what Andy

had told her in the car, but Emily didn't want to take any chances. 'Andy, have we got something we can use as a stretcher? We need to get her to the car.'

'What about an ambulance?' he replied.

'Too slow,' Emily said. 'My car's outside, let's just get her in it.'

56

Hannah gave up on the Land Rover, or more accurately, the Land Rover gave up on Hannah. She turned the key one more time, but the engine just coughed a terminal cloud of black smoke from the exhaust as the battery died. She was just getting out of the car when she saw Andy running across toward her.

'We need a stepladder,' he gasped as he pushed past her into the barn. 'Come on, give me a hand.' Hannah followed him and between them, they manhandled a rusty old stepladder from the barn and toward the kitchen door. 'Stretcher,' Andy explained as they manoeuvred it through the front door.

Hannah looked down at where Ruth was lying on the kitchen floor. She looked a lot paler than she had done when Hannah had rushed to the Land Rover to try to get it started. Rupert had just disappeared, which was fine by Hannah considering the large knife he'd managed to embed in Ruth's chest. Hannah hadn't seen what actually happened as her view had been blocked by Andy. Had Rupert stabbed Ruth, or had she just run into the knife? From the colour of Ruth's face, it didn't really matter.

The woman from the Food Standards Agency was kneeling next to Ruth, pressing a wad of tea-towels around the handle of the knife. She was calm, methodical, and looked as if she had everything under control. It was only when Emily turned to look at Hannah that she saw the abject fear in the other woman's eyes. At least she had a vehicle that worked, though.

'Come on, give me a hand,' Emily said as Andy laid the step ladder down next to Ruth. 'Let's get her out to the car, nice and easy.'

Between them, they slid Ruth onto the stepladder as carefully as they could. She moaned a couple of times while they were trying to get her central on the makeshift stretcher, and flapped her arms weakly once or twice before Emily folded them over her stomach.

'Right, everyone grab a corner. We'll lift on three,' Emily instructed them, and Hannah put her hands on the ladder. 'One, two, three.'

A few moments later, they had slid Ruth off the stepladder and onto the back seat of Emily's Mini.

'I'll get in the back with her,' Hannah said to Emily who nodded in response before jutting her chin in Andy's direction.

'You coming, then?' she asked him.

'Yeah, I'll come,' he replied and turned to Amy. 'Sorry, Amy. You'll have to stay here. There's no room.'

'Go, just go,' Amy replied, waving her hands at the Mini. Hannah slid herself into the back seat and eased Ruth's head onto her lap, making what she hoped was a reassuring shushing sound as she did so. There was no response from Ruth.

Hannah tried to cradle Ruth's head as best she could as

Emily made her way back down the track toward the lane. A couple of times, Hannah leaned forward to warn Emily of some particularly vicious potholes that had caught her out on more than one occasion.

'Thanks,' Emily muttered in reply. After what felt to Hannah like ages, they reached the lane and Emily accelerated. They'd not even got a mile down the road when Hannah felt the car braking, and looked through the windscreen to see a tractor in the middle of the road in front of them.

'Oh, you have got to be kidding me,' Hannah heard Emily say. The tractor driver trundled past a passing place a few yards later. He obviously had no intention of letting them past.

'Stop the car,' Andy barked, his seatbelt already undone. The car ground to a gentle halt and Andy leapt out, sprinting after the tractor and launching himself onto the step next to the cab. What followed would have been comical if the situation wasn't as dire as it was. Andy was hanging onto the side of the tractor with one hand, miming being stabbed in the chest with the other. He then used his free hand to point toward the Mini. The tractor driver turned and looked over his shoulder before shouting something to Andy who jumped down from the cab. The tractor then turned sharp right and straight through a hedge into the field next to the lane.

Andy ran back to the Mini and got in.

'Nice one,' Hannah said. 'I didn't think he was going to move over.' As Emily sped up and passed the tractor, Hannah saw the driver's concerned face looking back at her.

A few moments later, they were on the dual carriageway that led back to Norwich. Hannah could hear the engine complaining as Emily drove at God knows what speed toward the city. Ahead of them, a line of blinking orange lights across the road could be seen in the distance.

'For fuck's sake,' Hannah heard Andy say. 'The ring road's shut again.'

'Which way?' Emily replied, her desperation obvious.

'We'll have to go through the city. Past the football stadium,' Andy replied.

'Isn't there a match on?'

'Yeah, but it's on now so everyone will be in the stadium.'

Hannah leaned her head back against the seat, stroking Ruth's face as she did so. Her skin was clammy, and Hannah looked down to see her mouth moving.

'Hang in there, Ruth,' Hannah said, leaning forward. 'You'll be okay.' She put her ear to Ruth's mouth to try to hear what she was saying. A few seconds later, she repeated Ruth's words to the others. 'She says she can't breathe.'

'Maybe open the windows?' Andy replied. 'That might help.' Hannah couldn't see how it would, but she wound down one of the rear windows a few inches.

The Mini's tyres squealed as Emily took one of the roundabouts that led to the city centre far too fast. Hannah's head cracked off the window, and she tightened her grip on Ruth to stop her being thrown about the back of the car. In front of them, there was a white glow in the sky from the lights at Carrow Road.

'Should we stop at the stadium?' Hannah asked Emily. 'They'll have ambulances and stuff, won't they?'

'St John's Ambulance, maybe, and a physiotherapist or two with a magic sponge,' Emily replied. 'The hospital's only a few minutes further — I say we just go for it.'

'Okay,' Hannah said. 'You're the boss.' She wound the window down a bit further to let some more air into the car and looked out of the window. A few hundred yards ahead was a police car parked at the side of the road. Hannah glanced at the speedometer over Emily's shoulder. They were doing almost ninety miles an hour — in a thirty mile an hour zone.

'Shit,' Hannah heard Emily mutter. 'Police.' The car didn't slow at all as they sped past the marked police unit. It could have been her imagination, but it looked as if the two policemen in the front seats of the car were both fast asleep.

Just as Emily careered through two sets of red lights at the end of the road, a massive cheer went up from the stadium. Hannah didn't really follow football, but it sounded to her like Norwich City had just scored.

As the roar of the crowd faded into the distance, Hannah saw Ruth's lips moving again.

'What did she say?' Andy asked a few seconds later.

'She says she can't feel her wings,' Hannah replied.

57

Andy jumped as the door to the hospital interview room opened. On the sofas in the room, Hannah and Emily were both fast asleep, and he'd been fighting to stay awake in what had to be the most uncomfortable armchair in the world. He looked up to see a policewoman walking in — not a member of the hospital staff with news about Ruth — and glanced at his watch to see that it was almost four in the morning.

'Any updates?' Andy asked the policewoman as Emily started to stir into life.

'No, nothing yet.'

'Oh, okay,' he replied.

'I remember you two,' the policewoman said. 'From last time up at the farm. That thing with the butcher.'

'Yeah,' Emily yawned. 'I remember you too. Chief something Antonio, isn't it?'

'That's me,' the policewoman replied with a warm smile. 'It's Chief Superintendent Antonio, but you can call me Jojo.' On the sofa next to Emily, Hannah was still out for the count, her red hair hiding her face.

Jojo sat on an armchair opposite Andy's, and looked at him, still smiling.

'It's really nice to see that the two of you are still together, after everything that you went through with that butcher. A lot of couples don't have the strength to survive that sort of thing.'

'Oh, we're not together,' Emily said. She looked a lot more awake than she had done a few moments ago, Andy noticed. 'He's an utter bastard.'

'Ah,' Jojo's smile slipped for a second or two. 'I see.' She reached into her pocket and pulled out a notebook, flipping it open. 'Talking of utter bastards, we've not been able to locate this Rupert chap yet. He seems to have disappeared into thin air. Any ideas where he might have gone to lay low?' She looked at Andy, still smiling, but he could see the steel behind her eyes. Jojo was not a woman to be messed with and Andy was pleased that, at least for the time being, she was on their side.

'No, no idea at all,' he replied. 'Sorry. He was quite a private bloke really. I never got to find out much about him at all.'

'Well, every copper in East Anglia is looking for him so we'll pick him up soon.' Andy thought back to the two sleeping policemen that Hannah had pointed out as they'd made their way here the previous evening, and didn't hold out much hope. 'The knife that he used to attack Ruth with is now in our lab, so we can match it to him when we get him.' Jojo's smile broadened. 'She's in good hands, your friend. You did a good job getting her here. Nothing else you could have done, so for the time being, try to relax. She's come this far, and in my experience, people usually do okay if they get here in time.'

The policewoman got to her feet and left the room, glancing back at Andy and Emily as she left with another smile. As the door closed softly, Andy stood up and looked at Emily. Her hair was all over the place, and she had a crease down one cheek from the cushion she'd been using as a pillow, but Andy's heart lurched as he looked at her.

'Emily,' he whispered, glancing across at Hannah who was still fast asleep.

'Yeah?' she replied.

'Can I ask you for something?'

'What, another knee in the bollocks?'

'No, I'm good on that front thanks.'

'Then what?' Emily asked. They looked at each other for a few seconds.

'Can I have a hug?'

'Seriously?'

'Yeah, very seriously.'

'You're still a bastard.'

'I know.'

Emily got to her feet and walked over to where Andy was standing. He crossed his hands in front of his testicles, just in case.

'This doesn't mean we're friends again,' Emily said as she wrapped her arms around his shoulders.

58

Norwich Castle was surrounded on all sides by a sea of people wearing yellow and green, most of them staring up at the battlements two hundred feet above their heads. There must have been thousands of people there — it looked as if the entire population of Norwich had come out to watch their football team celebrate winning the Champions League. Occasional chants broke out among small groups of supporters, often taken up by other members of the crowd before petering away. The Champions League final had been held a couple of weeks earlier, and had ended with a surprise one-nil win to Norwich and the German cup holders going home with one less trophy on the coach. In the dying seconds of the game, Norwich's only home-grown player — a solid lad whose last name was so complicated he only had 'Luke' on the back of his shirt — had made a goal line clearance that had instantly elevated him to hero status in the eyes of Norwich City's faithful army of fans.

In the crowd, a Canary FM reporter was making his way round the supporters, trying to find some who would be sober enough to speak live on the radio. He wasn't having much luck at all. Bob Rutler thought he had found one loved-up young couple who looked reasonably sensible. They were standing outside the Murderers Pub, hand in hand, and watching the football team pass by on an open-top double-decker bus. The reporter had got as far as finding out that their names were Emily and Andy before they confessed that they knew nothing about football but had just come out to soak up the atmosphere. He left them to it and wandered off to try to find someone else.

The ancient medieval castle stood on a commanding mound that elevated it above the rest of the city, and the view from the top was considered by most to be the best available of the city's skyline. At the bottom of the castle, in an area cordoned off for their exclusive use, the first team milled about and enjoyed their moment of glory. At the top of the castle, a massive firework display was planned, and all the players were looking forward to waving at the crowd from the top as the fireworks exploded above their heads. It wasn't every day a team like Norwich City won the Champions League, and they were determined to enjoy it to a man.

A small door at the base of the castle was opened, and a member of staff beckoned to the team to make their way over to it. The players pushed each other playfully as they made their way over to the door, and through it to the narrow winding staircase that led to the roof of the castle, some two hundred feet above the crowds below.

With the striker — a hulking brute of a player called 'Bodders' — who had scored the winning goal leading the way, the team, their manager, and coaches started to trudge their way up to the roof of the castle. He wasn't called Bodders because that was his name. He was called Bodders because he was partial to several pints of

Boddington ale both before and after playing. Bodders turned to his team mate, Luke, who was right behind him.

'Bloody hell, mate,' Bodders said. 'These are a bit on the steep side, aren't they?'

'What's up, Bodders?' another team mate called from further down the staircase. 'Can you not get your massive head through the door at the top?' A ripple of laughter filtered up from the rest of the team.

'Yeah, yeah, whatever,' Bodders replied before pausing and putting his hand to his stomach for a moment.

'You alright mate?' Luke asked him.

'All good, just a touch of indigestion.'

'That's why I didn't have one of those sandwiches.'

'Yeah, I noticed that,' Bodders replied. 'How come?'

'Too much fat on the bacon.' Luke replied.

'Fair enough. Did you see the bloke that was serving them, though?'

'Come on Bodders,' a voice came from below. 'I'm feeling a bit weird mate. Need some fresh air.' There were a few calls of 'me too' from the other players.

'Okay, okay,' Bodders replied before looking at his hands as he carried on climbing the stairs to the top of the castle. He turned to Luke, taking his attention from his fingers for a few seconds. 'Hey Luke, did you see his eyes? They were the most amazing blue colour I've ever seen.'

AUTHOR'S NOTE (2)

Hi.

Nathan Burrows again. So, what did you think of *The Baker*? I'm really hoping that you enjoyed reading it as much as I enjoyed writing it.

Perhaps you could do me a favour? If you did enjoy *The Baker*, maybe you could leave a review for it? It would be a massive help to me as an independent author, and would increase the chances of other readers enjoying the book as well.

The final book in the *Rub-a-Dub-Dub* trilogy is *The Candlestick Maker*, and is available now. I've included the first couple of chapters here for you to enjoy!

Stay in touch, and we'll speak soon.

Nathan B.

JACK BE NIMBLE, JACK BE QUICK...

THE
CANDLESTICK
MAKER

NATHAN BURROWS

1

It was fair to say that Jessica was a big girl. Some people would use the term bubbly, perhaps cuddly, or even plus size if they were trying to be particularly polite. Her mother told anyone who would listen that Jessica had big bones or that her size was in her genes. The fact that both her parents were stick thin seemed to pass everyone by.

Other less kind people would just use the term fat. Like her ex-boyfriend, which was the primary reason he was an ex-boyfriend. He couldn't, according to Jessica and her friends from Flab Fighters, appreciate the unique pleasure that only a woman of Jessica's size could offer. The anonymous people on the other end of the computer that Jessica was staring at now were a different breed altogether. They not only appreciated women of Jessica's size, they positively worshipped them.

Jessica hadn't turned her webcam on just yet. She had a set routine that she had to go through before she hit that magic switch. First, she had to make sure she was dressed appropriately for her digital visitors. She was. At least, from the front it looked as if she was. The webcam couldn't see the extra band of elastic she had fitted to the strap of her bra. The problem was that a bra that accentuated her not inconsequential bosom in the way that she wanted wouldn't do up at the back. Hence the elastic. Jessica used a small compact mirror to check her make-up and to ensure that she had just the right sheen of perspiration on her face. She knew that her customers liked that touch. The final check was to ensure that she had enough French Fancy Cakes in front of her, which she did. There was a further supply in her kitchen cupboard, just in case she had a successful evening on the webcam. Or got peckish later. Either way, the cupboard would probably be empty by the end of the evening come what may. With a trembling finger, she reached out to the touch screen to turn the webcam on, and was rewarded with the reassuring red glow of the light. She was live.

It was only a couple of minutes before her first potential customer arrived. Jessica could see from the admin screen of the website that she worked for how many people were watching. Waiting. Considering. Jessica didn't want to think about what else they might be doing in their private digital darkness. She didn't need to know, didn't want to know, and didn't care as long as they paid.

Jessica managed not to jump as a loud electronic 'ding' told her that wherever was watching her had just made a purchase. She glanced up at the screen, even though she knew that the customer had bought a French Fancy. After all, that was the only thing on her menu this evening. The only thing she was interested in was how much he had paid to watch her eat it.

'A tenner? Fuck me sideways,' Jessica whispered to herself. The normal going rate for a single French Fancy was only a quid. As she stared at the screen, an instant message popped up.

'A yellow one, please.'

Jessica grinned at the webcam and slowly waved her podgy fingers at the red light. In her head, she started to add up how many French Fancies she had, and how much they would earn her if her mysterious customer was willing to pay to watch her eat them all. Even if it was only the yellow ones, she was fairly sure that by the end of the evening she would be at least fifty quid up. And that was if no-one came in for any of the other colours. Sensing a very profitable evening ahead of her, Jessica reached forward and picked up one of the small square yellow cakes.

Looking at a French Fancy in a sensual manner wasn't a skill that Jessica had yet mastered. She'd watched a fair few videos on YouTube about how to look at food as if you wanted to fuck it, but none of them involved small square pieces of confectionary. One of the weirdest YouTube channels she had come across was called 'Crouching Woman Hidden Cucumber', but that hadn't really helped her much. It was interesting, if only in an anatomical sense, but not helpful for her area of expertise.

She narrowed her heavily made-up eyes at the yellow cake and licked her lips before taking a tentative nibble at the corner of the icing. There was a ding on the screen.

'Slow down,' the message said. For a tenner a cake, Jessica would happily take half an hour eating the bloody thing, but she was hungry. She made a valiant effort to caress the cake with her lips and tongue, but a moment later she crammed it into her mouth.

'Sorry,' she mouthed at the webcam through a mouthful of sponge and icing. 'I couldn't wait.' Jessica stared at the screen for what seemed like ages before it dinged again.

'Dirty girl.'

Jessica wiped her lips with a pre-moistened napkin that she'd prepared earlier.

'I can be dirtier,' she typed carefully while pouting at the screen. 'If you want?' There was another long wait before whoever was on the other end of the computer replied. The ding signalled another purchase. Twenty quid this time.

'A pink one, please,' the message popped up on the screen. 'And if you don't take your time eating it…'

Jessica waited for at least twenty seconds before replying. She had thought about turning the camera off and maybe cramming a couple of cakes into her mouth — the blue ones seemed particularly unpopular in her experience — but thought better of it if the price per cake was going up.

'What will happen?' she typed, taking her time to make sure that each finger only hit one key. There was another long wait for the reply.

'I will kill you.'

2

E mily Underwood pulled up in the pub car park, turned the engine off, and sighed. She looked through the windscreen at the pub that she had come to inspect. This would be her third food safety inspection that day, and hopefully, the final one. The previous two had gone okay, or at least in comparison to some of her other visits. She'd not been threatened, chased off the premises, or sexually assaulted in any way. In Emily's book, that made it a good day. Her first inspection was of a food stall selling fudge in Norwich's Castle Mall shopping centre. The Food Standards Agency was unreliable at the best of times, but sending her to inspect a fudge stall when the fudge itself was made in a completely different location was a new one. Although at some point someone would have to go and inspect the proprietor's kitchen — which was in a converted garage on a local council estate — the inspection of the stall itself had taken about ten seconds. Is it clean? Yes. Job done. Emily was planning on doing the inspection of his kitchen herself if she could swing it at the Food Standards Agency. The fudge was absolutely amazing, and the stall owner had given her several "samples" to sweeten her up. Emily's mouth started watering at the memory, and she thought with longing about the paper bag in the boot of her car. No matter how many calories were in it, she couldn't wait to get home.

The other inspection was a proper one, but dull as ditchwater. It was of a Burger Queen restaurant in Norwich's other shopping centre. Emily had never found so much as a napkin out of place in any Burger Queen restaurant she'd inspected, and this one was no different. No free samples, but she'd already been told off for docking a hygiene star or two off for that one by her boss.

The pub in front of her was potentially a completely different story. It was called "The Heartsease" after some bizarre pansy that only grew every other year in a small part of the Norfolk Broads, so Emily had heard. It was also the name of a large council estate nearby, which was a much more likely reason for the name. Targeted marketing. Looking at the shabby locals wandering aimlessly up and down what passed for a high street, Emily felt very over-dressed in her smart business suit. She would have looked posh in a shell suit.

The Heartsease was a fairly large building located right next to one of the most terrifying roundabouts in the whole of East Anglia — at least if you were a learner driver. There was nothing unusual about the roundabout, but for some reason, it was feared by anyone learning to drive and instructors alike. The generally accepted wisdom was that the best way to get over it was to shut your eyes and put your foot down. Every few months, a learner driver would end up accidentally parked in the middle of the roundabout itself but it didn't stop those bastards at the test facility down the road making everyone who took their test their going round it at least three times. Emily's flat mate had gone out with an invigilator for a while and apparently there was a sweepstake in their crew room for the most number of nervous breakdowns caused by the roundabout. If Emily remembered correctly, there was a scoring system with tears at the bottom and accidental soiling of the driver's seat at the top.

Emily got out of the car and walked as slowly as she could toward the door of the pub, shivering in the cold November air. According to her boss, the landlord had a soft spot for petite blondes. That being the reason why Emily had landed the job had been denied back at the Food Standards Agency, but if it was true, Emily planned on making the most of the fact that she was a petite blonde. Maybe not as petite as she would like to be — too much food over Christmas — but those few extra pounds would soon disappear if she could ever be arsed to get to the gym. Besides, her boyfriend Andy claimed to like the extra bouncy bits. Emily wasn't sure whether that was a compliment or not but seeing as he was hardly male model material himself, it didn't really matter.

To Emily's surprise, the pub looked open even though it wasn't supposed to be at that time in the morning. The door swung open as she knocked on it, so Emily walked inside, waiting on the doormat for a moment to let her eyes adjust to the gloom. When she stepped into the pub itself, her shoes almost got abandoned at the door. If the doormat was that sticky, Emily thought, God only knew what the rest of the pub would be like.

Emily glanced around the interior of the pub, taking in the yellowed walls that hadn't seen a lick of paint since well before the smoking ban, the rickety looking tables with an assortment of chairs balanced on top, and the small child perched behind the bar. She walked towards him, plastering a smile on her face, and stopped a few feet away. He wasn't who she'd been expecting to be behind the bar when she walked in. The boy was maybe nine or ten, floppy blonde hair, with an innocent face and dressed in Star Wars pyjamas. He wouldn't have looked out of place in the cathedral choir, apart from the pyjamas of course, and Emily could well imagine him in a cassock with a ruff doing a solo with a crowd of elderly ladies simpering over him.

The boy was concentrating on a peanut that was on the bar in front of him. When Emily realised that the he hadn't noticed her come in, she cleared her throat softly to avoid startling the young lad.

'Fuck off,' the boy said, not even looking up at her. 'We're closed.'

'Oh,' Emily replied, momentarily thrown. 'Er, I'm from the Food Standards Agency. Is your dad about?' She had no idea if this was the landlord's son or not, but it seemed like a fair call. He glanced at her for a second before staring back down at the peanut on the bar.

'Ssshh,' the boy replied, his index finger to his mouth. 'If you're not going to fuck off, at least shut your cake hole.' Emily bristled for a moment before replying.

'Is there a grown up here?' she asked. He didn't reply but just shushed her again.

'You need to be quiet, or he won't come out.'

'Who?' Emily's question was ignored. 'Your dad?'

'No. Mr Crisp.' The boy returned his attention to the peanut.

Emily took a deep breath and opened her briefcase. She pulled out the inspection paperwork and examined it to see what the landlord's last name was. A few seconds later, she found it — it wasn't Crisp.

'Who's Mr Crisp?' she asked. The boy raised his finger

to his lips. 'Who's Mr Crisp?' she repeated, this time in a whisper.

'Here he is.'

Emily followed the boy's gaze towards a small hole in the woodwork between the bar and the wall. The first thing she saw was a very small whiskered nose, followed by a mouse scampering across the bar. It dodged a suspicious looking stain on the bar before running over, grabbing the peanut in its mouth, and hurrying back through the hole. The boy looked at Emily and grinned, showing a mouth that must have cost the Tooth Fairy a fortune.

'That's Mr Crisp,' he said, triumphantly. 'He's a cheeky little bastard, isn't he?'

3

Jack Kennedy hated banks. He always had done, ever since he was a small boy. There wasn't any particular reason as far as he could remember. One of his earliest memories was sitting on his Dad's vestry floor helping him count up the coins in the collection from the old people at church. He and his father would sit there in a companionable silence while Jack counted up all the pennies and two pence pieces, and his Dad would count all the silver coins. By the time Jack was nine or ten, they had to swap over. There weren't any near as many silver coins in the collection by then.

So, it wasn't money that was the problem. It was just banks. It hadn't been his father who'd taken the money to the bank though. It had been his mother, and she always took Jack with her. If any of the carefully labelled bags didn't have exactly the right amount of money in them — and the bank had a special machine that counted the coins — then Jack knew he'd be in for a beating later. No matter what colour the coins inside the bag were. If they were wrong, then he was in for the slipper when they got back to the vicarage.

'Mr Kennedy?' A woman's voice interrupted his unpleasant memories. 'Mr Kennedy? The bank manager's ready for you now.' The receptionist smiled at Jack, and he ran his finger around the collar of his shirt as he got to his feet.

'Thanks,' he mumbled at the receptionist, whose smile broadened. He could feel her staring at him as he walked through the door and into the manager's office.

The interior of the office was pretty much how he expected it would look. It was a corner office, with large windows looking out over the market square in the middle of Norwich. Prime real estate, if it wasn't owned by a bank.

'Mr Kennedy,' the bald-headed man behind the large mahogany desk said. 'I'm Mr Parsons, the manager of Norwich Mutual.' He got to his feet, his ill-fitting suit hanging off him, and shook Jack's hand.

'Hi,' Jack replied, ignoring the temptation to crush the other man's hand in his own. Mr Parson's grip was so weak Jack didn't know whether to shake his hand or kiss it. The bank manager obviously did't get to the gym much.

'Please, have a seat.' Mr Parsons gestured towards the chair on the other side of the desk. Jack sat, and the chair creaked under his bulk. He put his hands in his lap, and flexed his shoulder muscles to try to relieve the tension in his neck. When he heard the material complaining, he relaxed his shoulders. It wouldn't do to burst out of his shirt like a pink version of the Incredible Hulk. 'We've reviewed your business loan application, and I've just got a few follow up questions for you.'

'Okay,' Jack said.

'Right then.' Mr Parsons wriggled in his own much more comfortable chair and leafed through the paperwork in front of him. 'So, you're a fitness instructor, right?'

'Yep.'

'Good. Now, according to your application, you've been doing that here in Norfolk for a year. But, you're what, twenty-seven. Can I ask where you were living before moving here?'

'Up north,' Jack said. He wasn't going to be anymore specific than that with this odd looking man.

'Ah, I see.' Mr Parsons looked back at the paperwork. 'And what were you doing up there?'

'I was a medical student,' Jack replied with a sigh. He knew what the next question would be.

'You didn't finish your medical degree?' Mr Parsons asked.

'Obviously not,' he said, trying to keep the irritation out of his voice. 'Or I wouldn't be a fitness instructor, would I?'

'Er, no.' Mr Parsons found something very interesting to stare at on the piece of paper in his hands. 'Right, now where was I. Oh, yes. Your financial history.' Mr Parsons smiled, revealing some expensive dentistry. 'Quite healthy, really. No mortgage, sole ownership of Hill Top Farm.' His smile slipped for a second. 'You do know about the history of that place, don't you?'

'You've seen the price I paid for it?' Jack nodded at the paperwork. 'It wouldn't have been that cheap without some sort of strings attached.'

'Yes, very true. Bizarre business. First that mad butcher, then the weird vegetarian lot.' Mr Parsons looked at Jack. 'Very strange place indeed.'

Jack sat for a second, wondering whether that was some sort of question.

'Well, it's mine now and I've got plans for it.'

'Yes, your plans.' Mr Parsons' attention returned to the paperwork. 'It's a very comprehensive business plan, Mr Kennedy.'

'Thank you.'

'You're welcome. May I ask, do you have anyone who could put forward some additional capital to support your venture? Your parents, perhaps?'

'No.'

'Oh,' Mr Parsons face fell. 'I see.'

'My father passed away a year ago,' Jack explained, even though it was none of Mr Parson's business. 'I used the inheritance to buy the farm, do up the farmhouse and one of the outbuildings. But I can't convert the original pig shed into a fitness suite without a loan.' He took a breath, aware that was the longest sentence he'd said since he walked into the manager's office. 'It's all in there,' he continued with a nod at the papers.

'Yes, so it is,' Mr Parsons replied. 'It's just that the bank isn't sure of the long-term economic viability of a fitness suite in that particular location.'

'Because of the farm's history?'

'No, more the location. It's not exactly central, is it?'

Jack sighed. He thought he'd explained all this in the business plan.

'It's a very niche customer base,' he said, 'who will be more than happy to travel to a rural location.'

'Rural? It's in the middle of bloody nowhere!' Mr Parsons started laughing, but cut it short when Jack gave him a fierce look.

'Look, Mr Parsnip or whatever your name is. Can I have the money or not?'

Mr Parsons put Jack's business plan down on his desk.

'Mr Kennedy, it's not a no,' the bank manager said, a slight tremble creeping into his voice. 'It's just a "not now". We can assign you a business mentor to help you develop your plans and then re-evaluate in, say, six months?' Jack glared at the bank manager, imagining for a second what would happen if he just leapt across the desk and started throttling him. 'If you speak to Lynne, my receptionist, she'll assign you a mentor,' Mr Parsons continued, almost in a warble. Jack looked at him, shook his head, and got to his feet without another word.

Outside Mr Parsons' office, the receptionist was nothing but sympathetic.

'The thing is, Jack,' she said, 'Mr Parsons hardly ever gives anyone any money first time round, so you shouldn't be too upset.' He looked at her, noticing for the first time that she was quite pretty. A bit on the mousy side perhaps, and she wouldn't look out of place working in a library, but Jack thought she was pretty enough. If she got herself a decent haircut to replace her pony tail, and put a bit of make-up on, she wouldn't be half bad at all.

'Thanks, er, Lynne was it?'

'Yes,' she smiled, a touch of colour rising to her cheeks. Jack stared at her for a few seconds, watching her cheeks getting redder as he did so. 'Short for Lynnette.'

'Really?' Jack said, managing not to laugh. 'That's a lovely name.'

'Aw, thank you,' Lynne replied, almost in a whisper. She touched her hand to her ear and fixed a stray couple of hairs. 'I read in your business plan that you're a fitness instructor? That must be fun.'

They chatted for a few moments about nothing in

particular. Jack noticed that she managed to drop into the conversation that she was single, but stopped short of asking him if he was. It turned out that Lynne was a very keen painter, and Jack almost asked her if she would like him to pose for her sometime, but he wasn't sure if he'd be able to ask and keep a straight face.

'So what sort of things do you do, when you're not making people all fit and buff?' Lynne asked, running her eyes over his upper body. She was, Jack thought, definitely interested.

'I like doing things with my hands,' he replied, flexing his fingers.

'What sort of things?'

'All sorts. I like making things.'

'Stop teasing,' Lynne said with a giggle. 'What sort of things do you make?' Jack looked at her. He arched one eyebrow, a trick his father had taught him to do years before, and replied.

'I make candlesticks.'

∾

The Candlestick Maker is available now..

Made in the USA
Monee, IL
15 August 2021